CAUGHT OFF GUARD!

Falconi eased through the door, ready for action — but not quite ready enough. A strong hand grabbed his wrist and pulled him the rest of the way in. The major was caught in the iron grip of a big blond kid. He looked like the type of football player whom colleges recruit from Pennsylvania coal-mining areas — and seemed twice as strong.

"Leggo that piece!" the kid snarled, swinging the army officer hard against the wall.

Falconi's vision turned to blinking lights for a second and he felt his hand go limp, the pistol clattering to the floor. But then the Falcon recovered and threw a right jab that smashed into Football Player's nose. Cartilage caved in and blood sprayed out, but the big guy threw a forearm smash that slammed into Falconi's jaw like a sledgehammer. The major hit the wall, then bounced off it in time to catch two lightning-quick left and right crosses that flipped his head from side to side so hard his neck vertebrae popped in protest.

Robert Falconi was in trouble. The kid was good . . . maybe too good!

THE BEST IN ADVENTURES FROM ZEBRA

To the paratroopers who served in Company L, 325th Airborne Infantry Regiment 82nd Airborne Division of the old "Brown Boot" army of the 1950s

Special acknowledgment to: Patrick Andrews and W. L. Fieldhouse

THE BLACK EAGLES ROLL OF HONOR

(Assigned or Attached Personnel Killed in Action)

1LT Blum, Marc — United States Air Force

SGT Boudreau, Marcel — United States Army

SGT Carter, Demond — United States Army

SSG Dayton, Marvin — United States Army

SFC Galchaser, Jack — United States Army

SGT Hodges, Trent — United States Army

MR. Hosteins, Bruno — Ex-French Foreign Legion

PO2 Jackson, Fred — United States Navy

CPO Jenkins, Claud — United States Navy

SGT Limo, Raymond — United States Army

PO3 Littleton, Michael — United States Navy

SFC Miskoski, Jan — United States Army

SSG Newcomb, Thomas — Australian Army

1LT Nguyen Van Dow — Army of the Republic of Vietnam

SFC Ormond, Norman — United States Army

SGT Park, Chun Ri — Republic of Korea Marines

SFC Rivera, Manuel — United States Army

MSG Snow, John — United States Army

LT Thompson, William — United States Navy

1LT Wakely, Richard — United States Army

ROSTER OF THE BLACK EAGLES
(*Operation Saigon Showdown*)

Major Robert Falconi
United States Army
Commanding Officer

Master Sergeant Duncan Gordon
United States Army
Detachment Operations Sergeant

Master Sergeant Chun Kim
Republic of Korea Marines
Detachment Light Weapons Leader

Sergeant First Class Calvin Culpepper
United States Army
Detachment Demolitions Sergeant

Sergeant First Class Malcomb McCorckel
United States Army
Detachment Medic

Staff Sergeant Archibald Dobbs
United States Army
Detachment Scout

Staff Sergeant Liam O'Quinn
United States Marine Corps
Detachment Supply Sergeant

PROLOGUE

The C-130 eased over onto the proper heading and slowly lost altitude. The pilot continued the gradual descent, finally easing back on the control column until the big aircraft settled down and its tires squealed in protest at the contact with the concrete runway of Tan Son Nhut Air Base.

The plane taxied down the runway, but instead of turning to the general disembarking area, it was steered in the opposite direction. Its destination was an area without a hangar where a small building surrounded by barbed wire stood.

Chuck Fagin, an American CIA case officer, and Lt. Andrea Thuy of the South Vietnamese Women's Army Corps, stood in front of the gate leading to the compound. The C-130 came to a stop in front of them. The two watched as a side door opened and the crew chief dropped the stepladder to facilitate the passengers' exit.

The first man off was Maj. Robert Falconi. Clad in battlegear and incredibly soiled and sweat-soaked camouflaged fatigues, his exhaustion was evident even from a distance. He turned to watch his first two men leave the airplane. The pair, burdened by a stretcher they carried, worked their way from the door and stepped gingerly down to the concrete. A corpse, covered by a G.I. poncho, rested on the litter.

Two more men followed and they also carried a stretcher burdened with a dead man.

A stranger, his hands bound behind his back, came off after them. A tall, husky master sergeant, with one hand tightly grasping the prisoner, pushed him along.

Fagin stepped forward as the group approached. He pointed to the dead men. "Who are they?" he asked.

"Sparks Jackson and Dinky Dow," Falconi answered. "They were the only bodies we could recover. Tommy Newcomb, Horny Galchaser and Popeye Jenkins are still out there. I've noted the locations of their graves—except for Horny—so they can be recovered and sent home."

"I take it you lost Galchaser's body," Fagin said.

"Right. It was policed up by the enemy," Falconi replied. "There was no way we could recover it."

"I'm sorry, Falcon," Fagin said. "About him—and the others."

"Yeah. Well, they got a little sloppy," Falconi said coldly. "Men have a tendency to do that. Especially if they're pushed to the limit—or beyond."

Andrea Thuy took Falconi's arm. Svelte and graceful, she displayed the beauty peculiar to Eurasian women. Her eyes were soft and caring. "Wait, Robert. Don't say anything yet. There are things you must find out."

Falconi's jaw tightened. "There are already *things* that I've found out."

Fagin's expression remained calm. "This is the prisoner, of course," he said as the master sergeant, a tough professional soldier named Top Gordon, shoved the man forward.

"Yeah," Falconi said. "His name is Rolf Stahler, a captain in the East German police."

Stahler's face was a mask of hate as he stared straight into

Fagin's face with a silent, but intent fury.

"I have some MPs to turn him over to," Fagin said. "They'll take care of him."

"Think we can make a good case in the UN from this bastard?" Falconi asked. "He's walking-talking proof that American troops didn't commit those war crimes up in the northern operational areas. We can testify firsthand about the East Germans pulling their dirty tricks in American army uniforms."

"It doesn't matter," Fagin said. "He won't be used for that anyhow. A quick exchange has been arranged for one of our people captured in Czechoslovakia."

"What?" Falconi asked angrily. "The only reason for our mission was to prove to the world that Reds were committing atrocities while disguised as U.S. troops."

"They'll never know now," Fagin said. "I guess the upper echelons figured the exchange of prisoners was more important."

"Shit!"

Fagin watched the rest of the detachment go inside the building. "I know how you feel."

"No you don't!" Falconi snapped. "And I'm going to tell you something here and now, Fagin! My boys are going on R&R, understand? This was their third time out into the cold without a break."

"They'll be staying here in Saigon," Fagin said.

"Good."

"But not on R&R," he added.

"What the hell are you talking about?"

"I'm not going to give it to you easy, Falconi," Fagin said. "I'm about to let you have it right between the eyes."

"I wish the hell you would," Falconi remarked.

"The Reds not only knew every move you made out there, but when and how you were going to do it."

"What the fuck are you talking about, Fagin?" Falconi demanded. "Who told 'em?"

11

"I did."

"*You did?*"

Fagin walked toward the gate leading to the interior of the compound. "Come on. Like Andrea said—there's a hell of a lot you've got to find out."

"Damn, Fagin. You can start cluing me in anytime."

"Let me begin with this cheerful bit of news," Fagin said. "At this very moment you and the Black Eagles are heading for a showdown in Saigon."

CHAPTER ONE

1964, an eventful year, had come to an end.

In the United States, during those twelve months, the Warren Commission made an investigation into the assassination of President John F. Kennedy which had happened a little more than a year previously. Those learned gentlemen reported that there was no conspiracy involved in the murder. A lone killer, Lee Harvey Oswald, was determined to have been acting alone.

On the political front Senator Barry M. Goldwater of Arizona made an unsuccessful bid for the presidency, losing out to the incumbent Lyndon B. Johnson.

Science had not been standing still that year either. The continued use of polio vaccine made terrific inroads into the terrible disease. This was proven by statistics that showed there had been only 100 cases of the crippler in 1964 while in 1953 more than 35,000 persons had suffered attacks of the dread sickness.

But the year had been one of a few disasters too. An earthquake in Alaska killed 114 people while doing $500,000,000 worth of damage. A couple of airline crashes wiped out a few people, and there was a riot at a soccer match in Lima, Peru in which 300 fans were killed.

But the news in sports wasn't all terrible. There was some glitter too. A brassy and mouthy young fighter named Cassius Clay won the world heavyweight title from Sonny Liston; the Australian team beat the Americans to win the Davis Cup in tennis; Jack Nicklaus was the big money winner in professional golf by garnering $113,000-plus in tournaments; and St. Louis defeated the Yankees to win baseball's World Series.

Another, even more popular, event was the explosion of "Beatlemania" across the United States. The British singing group, made up of four rather well-groomed young men sporting unusual hairstyles, produced an album entitled *Meet the Beatles* that sold two million copies in less than a month. Americans weren't left out altogether in the pop music industry. A trio of black women, calling themselves the *Supremes*, issued their own hit records such as *Stop in the Name of Love*, *Baby Love*, and *Come See About Me*.

In Southeast Asia, however, there had been more ominous events. North Vietnam PT boats attacked the American destroyer *Maddox* in the Gulf of Tonkin. The United States retaliated by bombing Red bases in North Vietnam. And congress, not to be outdone by the armed forces, passed a resolution giving President Johnson power to order retaliation for any attacks on U.S. forces.

The ball was starting to roll then. Not even the experts in various government "Think Tanks" would be able to accurately forecast the final results of this enigmatic Asian struggle.

The year 1965 was brand new when the seven very unique men were assigned billets at Special Operations Group headquarters located on Peterson Air Base in Saigon, South Vietnam. They were the remnants of twenty-seven individuals who had participated in four major operations against

14

the Communist forces in the north.

Being members of a unit which had suffered seventy-four percent casualties had left them numb and wrung out both emotionally and physically. Official documents listing the numbers of KIAs didn't include the angry grief the dead men's buddies felt. But, even then, it wouldn't have been quite so bad for them if they had been able to enjoy some R&R—Rest and Recreation—between missions, but an insidious encroachment into their security had all but compromised them, causing the unit to be held in isolation at a Special Forces B Camp out in the distant boonies.

These individuals belonged to Maj. Robert Falconi's Black Eagles Detachment. This small command, attached to Special Operations Group of MACV, was under the direct supervision of the Central Intelligence Agency through Chuck Fagin, a CIA case officer. His experience in clandestine warfare went back to working with Yugoslavian partisans in World War II, and he thought he had seen everything when it came to conducting secret missions that penetrated deep into enemy territory. But there in South Vietnam he found danger lurking back in the friendly areas too.

The Black Eagles' first operation had been several months earlier. Their efforts had been directed against a pleasure palace in North Vietnam. This bordello *par excellence* was used by Communist officials during their retreats from the trials and tribulations of administering authority and regulation over their slave populations. There were no excesses, perverted tastes, or unusual demands that went unsatisfied in this hidden fleshpot. Falconi and his wrecking crew sky-dived into the operational area in a HALO (High Altitude Low Opening) infiltration, and when the Black Eagles finished their raid on the whorehouse, there was hardly a soul left alive to continue the debauchery.

Their next foray into the enemy's hinterlands was an even more dangerous assignment with the difficulty factor multiplied by the special demands placed on them. The North

Vietnamese had set up a special prison camp in which they were perfecting their skills in the torture-interrogation of downed American pilots. With the conflict escalating in Southeast Asia, they rightly predicted they would soon have more than a few Yanks in their hands. A North Korean brain-washing expert had been assigned to them to teach the fine points of mental torment. The prisoners behind that barbed wire were few—but important. A U.S.A.F. pilot, an army Special Forces sergeant, and two high-ranking officers of the South Vietnamese forces were the unwilling tenants of the concentration camp.

Falconi and his men were not only tasked to rescue the POWs, but also had to bring along the prison's commandant and his North Korean tutor. Falconi pulled the job off, fighting his way south through the North Vietnamese army and air force to a bloody showdown on the Song Bo River. The situation deteriorated to the point that the Black Eagles' magazines had their final rounds in them as they waited for the NVA's final charge.

The next operation took them to Laos where they were pitted against the fanatical savages of Pathet Lao. If that wasn't bad enough, their method of entrance into the operational area was bizarre and dangerous. This type of transport into battle hadn't been used in active combat in more than twenty years. It had even been labeled obsolete by the military experts. But this didn't deter the Black Eagles from the idea. They used a glider to make a silent flight to a secret landing zone. After a hairy ride in the flimsy craft, they hit the ground to carry out a mission designed to destroy the construction site of a Soviet nuclear power plant the Reds wanted to install in the area. Everything went wrong from the start and the Black Eagles fought against a horde of insane zealots until their extraction to safety was completely dependent on the illegal and unauthorized efforts of a dedicated U.S.A.F. pilot—the same one they had rescued from the North Vietnam prison camp. The air force colonel was determined to help the same men who had saved him, but many times even the deadliest determination isn't enough.

Their final mission of 1964 had been doubly dangerous because of an impossibility to make firm operational plans. Unknown Caucasian personnel, posing as U.S. troops, had been committing atrocities against Vietnamese peasants. The situation had gotten far enough out of control that the effectiveness of American efforts in the area had been badly damaged. Once again Falconi and the Black Eagles were called upon to sort things out. They went in on a dark beach from a submarine and began a deadly reconnaissance until they finally made contact with their quarry. These enemy agents, wearing U.S. Army uniforms, were dedicated East German Communists prepared to fight to the death for their cause. The Black Eagles admired such unselfish dedication to the extent that they gave the Reds the opportunity to accomplish that end—give their lives for Communism. But this wasn't accomplished without the situation deteriorating to the point the Black Eagles had to endure human wave assaults from a North Vietnamese army battalion led by an infuriated general. This officer had been humiliated by Falconi on the Song Bo River several months previously. Another Black Eagle victory—but not before five more men had died.

Brought back to Saigon at last, the seven survivors had cleaned their weapons, drawn fresh, clean uniforms and prepared for a long awaited period of R&R.

It was not to be.

Chuck Fagin stood by the briefing room door waiting for Falconi and his men to appear. He glanced inside and saw Lt. Andrea Thuy tack the city map of Saigon on the large bulletin board mounted on the wall. When he turned back he saw Falconi, followed by his men, appear from the stairwell and walk toward him.

17

Fagin nodded a silent greeting to each Black Eagle as they filed by him. Maj. Robert Falconi, darkly handsome, standing six-feet, one inches tall, stared ominously through his sea-green eyes at Fagin. He went into the room without uttering a word, and sat down in a chair near Andrea.

The next man was MSgt. Duncan "Top" Gordon, the senior noncommissioned officer of the detachment. His job consisted of several tasks. Besides forming the operational plans for the missions, he was also responsible for maintaining discipline and efficiency in the unit. A husky man, his jet black hair was thinning perceptibly, looking even more sparse because of the strict GI haircut he wore. His entrance into the Black Eagles had been less than satisfactory. After seventeen years spent in the army's elite spit-and-polish airborne infantry units, he had brought in an attitude that did not fit well with the diverse individuals in Falconi's command. Gordon's zeal to follow Army Regulations to the letter had cost him a marriage, but he hadn't let up a bit. To make things worse, he had taken the place of a popular detachment sergeant who was killed in action on the Song Bo River. This noncom, called "Top" by the men, was an old Special Forces man who knew how to handle the type of soldier who volunteered for unconventional units. Gordon's first day in his new assignment brought him into quick conflict that soon got so far out of hand that Falconi began to entertain notions of relieving the master sergeant and transferring him back to a regular airborne unit.

But, during Operation Laos Nightmare, Gordon's bravery under fire earned him the grudging respect of the Black Eagles. Finally, when he fully realized the problems he had created for himself, he changed his methods of leadership. Gordon backed off doing things by the book and found he could still maintain good discipline and efficiency while getting rid of the chicken-shit aspects of army life. It was most apparent he had been accepted by the men when they bestowed the nickname "Top" to him. He had truly become the "top sergeant" then.

The third man to follow Falconi into the briefing was a short, stocky South Korean marine sergeant named Chun Kim. Kim, a light infantry weapons leader and expert in Tai Kwan Do karate, had been serving continuously in the military since 1948. His experience ran the gamut from the poorly trained and equipped South Korean armed forces that melted under the Communist onslaught from the north in June of 1950, to the later highly motivated and superbly disciplined elite marines created in the years after the cease-fire.

Kim suffered a bad attack of heatstroke on his first mission with the Black Eagles. Upon his arrival in South Vietnam he had immediately gone into active ops without time to become properly acclimated to the steamy weather. Despite the unfortunate incident not being his fault, Kim considered it a personal disgrace. In order to save face, he had fought with a dedicated fanaticism on the next operation proving his worth and courage to the others in the unit.

Kim was followed by SFC Calvin Culpepper. This tall, brawny, black man handled the explosives chores that popped up from time to time. Ten years of dedicated service in the United States Army had produced an excellent soldier. Resourceful and combat-wise, Calvin pulled his weight — and then a bit more — in the dangerous undertakings of the Black Eagles.

The team medic, SFC Malcomb "Malpractice" McCorckel, came in on Calvin's heels. An inch under six feet in height, Malpractice had been in the army for twelve years. He had a friendly face and spoke softly as he pursued his duties in seeing after the illnesses and hurts of his buddies. He nagged and needled in his efforts to keep them healthy. The men bitched back at him for his mother-hen attitude, but they appreciated his concern. They all knew that nothing devised by puny man could keep Malpractice from reaching a wounded Black Eagle and pull him to safety.

19

SSgt. Liam "Lightfingers" O'Quinn, a proud member of the United States Marine Corps, was responsible for the detachment's supplies. A scrounger and thief, he worked long and hard to see that the Black Eagles had everything they needed—plus a bit more—to do the jobs assigned to them. Short and husky, Lightfingers liked to eat. There was no doubt that if it wasn't for the hard physical demands of the lifestyle he had chosen, he would have been a veritable tub of lard.

Finally the last man of the unit strolled in. This was SSgt. Archie Dobbs, the point man and scout. Reputed to be the best compass man in the United States Army, his seven years of service were fraught with stints in the stockade and dozens of "busts" to lower rank. Fond of women, pot and booze, Archie's claim to fame—and object of genuine respect from the other men—was the fact that he had saved their asses on more than one occasion by guiding them safely through throngs of enemy troops while behind the lines.

Chuck Fagin waited until they had settled down in the various chairs scattered around the room. Then he closed the door and joined Andrea Thuy at the wall map. Fagin turned and faced the Black Eagles. "You see that rendition of the streets of Saigon behind me?" he asked. "Well, that's your next operational area."

Archie Dobbs lit a cigarette and scowled. "That don't sound like R&R to me."

"It isn't," Fagin said. "And I owe you guys a hell of a lot of explaining."

"Right," Top Gordon agreed. "We're busting with curiosity about what you said to the Falcon when we landed at Tan Son Nhut. It was some small offhand remark about telling the Reds every move we were going to make even before we made it during the last operation."

"I did exactly that," Fagin admitted.

"I'm thinkin' about shootin' your ass," Calvin Culpepper

said. "Unless you got a good excuse for doing it."

Andrea Thuy's eyes snapped with anger. "He does! And you should keep your threats and insults to yourselves until you hear what he has to say!"

"I got five reasons not to!" Malpractice McCorckel snarled. "Dinky Dow, Tommy Newcomb, Sparks Jackson, Popeye Jenkins and — most of all — Horny Galchaser."

"He risked his job for you!" Andrea cried. "I've been listening to you talk since you returned from Operation Asian Blitzkrieg, and you've done nothing but blame Chuck Fagin for all your troubles and — "

"We'll give him a chance, Andrea," Maj. Robert Falconi said calmly. "In fact, that's exactly what we're doing now." He motioned to Fagin. "Go ahead."

"Thanks," Fagin said. "When I get done, and you still think I made the wrong decisions then let me know. I'll step down and you can get a new case officer. Fair enough?"

"You'll do more than step down," Lightfingers O'Quinn said with a menacing tone in his voice. "There won't be none o' this *resigning from office* bullshit. The price is gonna be a helluva lot higher than that."

Fagin's eyes narrowed. "You're a bad ass — I'm a bad ass. Conflicts between bad asses always end up bloody."

"Let's knock it off," Top Gordon commanded. "Go to it like the Falcon said, Fagin. Tell us why you compromised the detachment."

Andrea Thuy glared at the Black Eagles. "He was ordered to — *ordered to* — by your own people in the CIA."

Fagin raised his hand in a calming gesture. "Just let me get on with it, Andrea. Although I do appreciate your backing." He crossed his arms and looked straight out at the angry faces that stared back at him. "While you were out in the cold we were approached by a high-ranking officer of the South Vietnamese Army intelligence. This man, named Col. Ngai Quang, gave me an official demand to keep him and his staff posted with up-to-date briefings on your activities and whereabouts. This started with Operation Laos Nightmare and went on with Operation Asian Blitzkrieg."

"Clayton Andrews made him do it," Andrea said. "Chuck was even forced to make a public apology to Ngai for refusing at first."

"I really have nothing on Ngai except a gut feeling of distrust," Fagin continued. "I did a bit of clandestine snooping through Col. Tran Hoc of the national police. We found out that Ngai is a compulsive gambler who frequents a mah jongg parlor owned by a refugee from Red China named Tsing Chai."

"Sounds like a classic set-up to bring Ngai under their control," Falconi said.

"Exactly," Fagin said. "Colonel Tran assigned an undercover man to penetrate Tsing's operation. Tsing, by the way, is supposedly a refugee from the Communist take-over of mainland China back in 1948. He, like thousands of others who were landowners, involved in racketeering, or followed other lifestyles not approved by the Reds, fled for their lives from Mao's brand of justice."

Falconi nodded. "He seems a bit unsavory at best. What happened to the guy sent in to check him out?"

"The man was killed," Fagin answered. "And this makes us think that there's a good chance Tsing's a Red agent. Ngai could have fed him the information that I gave him."

"Was *forced* to give him," Andrea interjected.

"No sweat," Archie Dobbs said. "Let's get on down to the gambling joint and grab the Chinaman. We can sweat the info we want out of him. And that Colonel Ngai too."

"Neither one of those ploys will work," Fagin said. "If Tsing is indeed a Red operative, we want to move in to take his contacts and agents with him — all of them. A sudden rush on his place would result in capturing him alone — if he is an agent — and alert the rest of the spy ring, allowing them to escape. And we certainly can't touch Ngai without good, solid evidence. The South Vietnamese government would raise holy hell about that. Especially if it turns out he is innocent."

"Somebody had to have had a lot of intel on us passed to them out there," Falconi surmised. "How could that NVA battalion know exactly where we would be while we were chasing those East Germans? We walked right into one big ambush. The bastards were waiting for us."

"This is frustratin'," Malpractice said. "What're we gonna do about all this?"

"Yeah!" Calvin echoed. "I don't wanna just sit around here jawin' about gittin' shit on."

"Listen, guys," Fagin said. "This situation here in Vietnam is a brand new one for your government and armed forces. There's beaucoup intrigue and backstabbing, not to mention out-and-out treason among our own allies. And there's a slow, but certain resentment and anti-war fervor building on the home front."

"Okay," Archie Dobbs conceded. "It's weird. So who gives a shit? All I want to know is where we go from here."

"The first thing is to convince the bad guys involved that the Black Eagles are virtually destroyed and have been pulled out of active ops," Fagin said.

"That ought to be easy," Falconi said. "Since it's true."

"We're to go a bit further than that. We'll also make it appear as if you've been placed on another detail," Fagin said. "We'll pull a few raids here in Saigon to ferret out some of our own turncoats and drug dealers. That'll make it seem as if you guys have been put on a combination counter-intelligence, anticrime operational status. You'll work hand-in-hand with the National Police through Colonel Tran's special men."

"Just what is this Colonel Tran's position?" Falconi asked.

"He is a hand-picked staff officer of the National Police who reports directly to Gen. Nguyen Ngoc Loan," Fagin answered. "A dedicated anticommunist, he is uncorruptible. And so is the liaison man he has assigned us."

"How do you know that?" Lightfingers asked.

"Because it was his brother that Tsing's men murdered and left on a garbage heap in a Cholon neighborhood," Fagin explained. "The young man, a sergeant named Chin Han, wants revenge." He nodded to Andrea. "Please ask Sergeant Chin to join us."

Andrea opened a side door to admit a husky, tough-looking young Oriental. Heavy shouldered and trim looking in his well-fitted civilian suit, Chin joined Fagin. He turned to face the Black Eagles and stood looking at them with a solemn, expressionless gaze.

Fagin smiled at the Black Eagles. "Sergeant Chin doesn't like to talk about himself, so I'll give you his background. He is a fourth-generation national policeman with five years service. His education includes not only the Vietnamese police academy, but he's had criminology courses in France conducted by the French *Surete*. He has attended the FBI school at Quantico, Virginia. Needless to say, he speaks fluent English and French. He has been decorated several times during counterinsurgency operations in various urban areas of this part of the world and has served two years with the South Vietnam rangers during campaigns in the highlands. He holds a third-degree black belt in Tai Kwan Do—" Fagin glanced at Chun Kim— "that should interest you, Sergeant."

Kim, speaking for the first time since the briefing started, bowed his head slightly toward Chin. "I would be most happy for chance to spar with you."

Chin's only reply was to nod toward the Korean.

"Chin is also an expert in handguns," Fagin continued. "And he has informed me that the .45 auto is about the best weapon to use in the type of operations you'll be participating in."

"Also sawed-off shotguns," Chin added. Then he cleared his throat. "I don't like to speak much. Perhaps that means

24

I am not an intellectual. I do not know. I do not care. Tsing Chai killed my older brother. I want to kill Tsing Chai. I want to kill all of Tsing Chai's friends. If his family were in Vietnam, I would rape his sisters and violate his mother and aunts. The road to revenge against this man has many tight curves. It is not a long trek, but it is a dangerous one."

"We feel the same way, Sergeant Chin," Falconi said. "You have lost one brother through his treachery — we've lost many. The Black Eagles are ready to start this trek you're talking about at any time."

Chin smiled coldly. "All journeys begin with the first step. Let us do that now."

CHAPTER TWO

Kaminatake was a big man. He stood six-feet, three inches tall and carried three hundred and fifty pounds on his large-boned frame. Although his body was covered with a generous layer of fat, there were slabs of rock-hard solid muscle beneath that soft flesh. His belly was more than ample, protruding enough to give him an immense girth. But, unlike most men with this physical adornment, Kaminatake's was not from careless overeating. He carried that gigantic stomach for a reason—it gave his body a low center of gravity. This was most important in his line of work.

Kaminatake was a *sumotori*—a professional sumo wrestler.

At this particular time he sat with other wrestlers in the dressing room of Tokyo's grandest arena. Clad in a *torimawashi*, the gigantic silken loincloth of the sport, he watched the closed-circuit TV which showed bouts going on at that very moment out in front of the packed audience. His own name would be called very soon and he would participate in the most important match of his career.

Kaminatake was ranked as a *makushita*, which put him but one step down from the coveted *sekitori* division. If he attained his next promotion, he would step up into the big leagues of sumo with all the fame, money-making opportunities, and prestige available in that exalted category. So far, in this particular tournament, he had wrestled fourteen matches and won them all. Ordinarily this would have meant a clear-cut victory in his division, but another *makushita* had also garnered fourteen victories. Both he and Kaminatake were scheduled to meet head on to decide the real winner of their division—and attain that all-important advancement up the sumo ladder.

Uchida, his trainer, walked up behind him and tapped him on the shoulder. "Kaminatake, it is time."

The big man stood up and bowed. "*Hai! Nado no genkei yoi shite!* I am ready!"

"Everyone in the stable is proud of you, Kaminatake," Uchida said. "We pray your *karma* is kind to you."

Kaminatake slammed his huge hands together. "This is my *karma*—*chikara*—my strength. I leave wishes for the gods' blessings to the weak."

"You must display more humility and respect for the gods, Kaminatake," Uchida urged him with a hint of disapproval in his voice. "That includes your honorable opponent too."

"*Bakana*!" Kaninatake exclaimed with a sneer. Haughty and already hating his opponent, he walked from the room and down through the crowd to the *dohyo*. This eighteen square feet of clay, standing two feet above the floor, was the ring where sumo warfare took place. A circle fifteen feet in diameter was marked off in straw atop it. This small area was considered so sacred that women were not allowed to even set one foot into it.

Kaminatake squatted down below the ring and waited for the preliminaries to begin. Suddenly a specially robed attendant clapped two blocks of wood together to announce the commencement of the match. Following that, the referee shrilled the names of the wrestlers. First the man called out the opponent, then Kaminatake's name.

The *sumotori* stepped into the ring and faced his opponent. Following sumo tradition, Kaminatake raised his left leg high and brought the foot crashing to the ground. He followed this with the right to complete the *shiko* exercise. The previous wrestler from his stable presented him with a ladle of water. After drinking it, Kaminatake wiped his mouth and body with a square of *chikaragami*—strength paper—before walking to a special box in the corner of the ring. He scooped up a handful of salt from the container, dabbed a bit on his tongue, then tossed the remainder to the *dohyo* to complete the purification ceremony.

Both wrestlers went to the edge of the ring and squatted down facing each other to begin the psychological part of the bout. Kaminatake rubbed his hands together, then brought them slowly upward with the palms up. Again standing, he performed another *shiko*, then sank back to squat on his heels and stared at his adversary.

"*Kamaete!*" the referee cried.

Kaminatake slowly lowered his fists to the ground and glared into his opponent's eyes. He felt hatred, pure and undeniable, as he looked at the man. He had a sincere desire to smash the other wrestler to the clay and stomp the life from him. This individual stood between him and the coveted *sekitori* class he had worked so hard these past six years for.

Then the referee turned his war fan and held it flat against his body.

Kaminatake's *tachiai*—initial charge—exploded and he threw himself toward his attacking opponent. The two, nearly seven hundred pounds of Japanese machismo, collided like a pair of steaming locomotives. Kaminatake's huge arms encircled the other wrestler and his hammy fists locked down tight on the man's *torimawashi*. The two human-mountains struggled against each other, pitting brute strength against brute strength as they fought, pushed and thrust.

Then Kaminatake's impelling desire to win paid off and he was able to perform a letter-perfect *tsuri-dashi*. His powerful arms and shoulders, the muscles hunched and coiled, lifted his opponent off his feet and, with a final explosive heave, threw him outside the straw rope. Kaminatake was the victor!

The match had taken one and a half seconds.

Now he bowed coolly to his defeated opponent and once again squatted down. The referee approached and handed him the envelope containing the *ken-sho*. This was a prize donated by a wealthy patron of the sport. After accepting his winnings, Kaminatake walked back through the throng displaying an expressionless countenance to the crowd. Only when he returned to the dressing room did he allow his emotions to run rampant. He whooped and grinned, waving the *ken-sho* above his head and announced the important win to the other wrestlers in his stable.

His sumo mates cheered his victory. They had seen the match on the closed circuit TV and already knew about his triumph. Although Kaminatake was not popular among them, his victory and coming promotion brought honor on the whole stable.

Uchida, the trainer, was also ecstatic. This great step up the sumo ladder reflected well on him too. For he was the one who had spotted Kaminatake and had taken him under his wing in the wild hopes that some day the young man would reach the highest rank of sumo — the grand champion — the *Yokozuna*!

Kaminatake had always been big.

Born in a fishing village of Samuimizu in northern Japan, his real name was Ryoshi Dosi. During those early years of his boyhood, Dosi had thought little of his size other than noting that he seemed to be physically surpassing his contemporaries in school until he was head and shoulders above them. The unpleasant aspect of this difference between himself and his schoolmates became apparent when the teasing started.

At first the names he was called were rather inoffensive. *Oushi* — Bull, *Kujira* — Whale, and *Yama* — Mountain, — among others, were bearable if a bit irritating. But when a few adjectives began to be added to the taunts, such as *Okii Bakana Kujira* — Big Stupid Whale, Dosi started to resent it.

His anger at first was silent and sullen. When walking to school and beset by several other boys shouting names at him, he would step up his pace and get far enough ahead of them so he could either no longer hear the teasers clearly or they would fall silent after becoming tired of the game. But one day the proverbial last straw was laid on the pile of taunts and Dosi turned on his tormentors.

It was to their credit that a couple stood up to him — though the act was not particularly complimentary to their intelligence — and they were badly thrashed. This same type of incident repeated itself several times before the local boys finally learned to connect teasing Dosi with getting their *shiris* kicked.

Dosi was not the most popular boy in school perhaps, but he sure as hell was the most respected.

It was in his fourteenth year that this respect increased tenfold. Uchida, acting as a scout from his Tokyo sumo stable, was out looking for available talent. During a trip north, he heard of a large, robust boy living in the fishing village of Samiumizu. He made a special trip up to the hamlet and visited Dosi's house.

The youth's father, Ryoshi-san, politely invited the important stranger to dine with him. As the two ate, the entire population of the little town was gathered outside to see what the outcome would be. After the meal was finished, Dosi was called into the room and bade sit down at the table.

His father indicated their guest. "This gentleman is from a famous sumo stable in Tokyo."

Dosi nodded. "*Hai*."

Uchida smiled at the boy. "Do you know about sumo?"

Again Dosi nodded. "*Hai*. I have seen their pictures in the magazines."

"What do you think of them, Dosi?" Uchida asked.

"They are very big men," Dosi answered. "And they must be strong too."

Uchida laughed. "Indeed they are! And I imagine that you are quite strong for a boy, are you?"

Dosi smiled modestly. "*Hai*. I am stronger than all the other boys in the village."

"Can you beat them fighting?"

"*Hai*," he answered affirmatively.

Ryoshi-san reached over and playfully ruffled his son's hair. "I told you he was a good *senshi*."

Uchida looked directly and seriously at Dosi. "Would you like to become a sumo wrestler?"

Dosi shrugged. "*Shiri-masen* — I don't know."

His father frowned. "Of course he knows. Tell the gentleman you wish to become a sumo wrestler, Dosi."

"I wish to become a sumo wrestler," Dosi intoned.

"It is a tough life," Uchida warned him. "Lots of hard work and training. The exercises are very painful."

Dosi started to say something else, but he felt his father's eyes glaring at him, so he simply blurted out another, "*Hai*."

"But if you're good, there are many rewards," Uchida continued. "You could become quite wealthy and famous."

"Yes," Ryoshi-san interjected. "And take good care of your poor parents in their old age."

"*Hai*."

"I can take you to Tokyo to my sumo stable," Uchida said. "You would become an apprentice. There older wrestlers would teach you the sport and its ways. If you meet the rigorous qualifications of *sumodo*, you will become one of us. If not—well, you may return to your village a wiser and better young fellow for the experience just the same."

"*Hai*."

"It's settled then!" Ryoshi-san exclaimed happily. He leaned toward the other room where his wife waited his bidding. "*Tsuma*! More *sake*!"

The two men sat up late that night consuming the rice wine and striking the deal allowing fourteen-year-old Dosi to travel south to Tokyo and the sumo profession.

Dosi's arrival at the wrestling stable was marked by three events. The first was learning much more about Uchida. This man was an *oyakata*—retired wrestler—who now supervised the instruction and conduct of the wrestlers. Going off the ponderous diet of an active sumo had reduced his fighting weight of two hundred and seventy-five pounds to around one-hundred and eighty. This made him a bit smaller than many of the trainees, but he more than made up for it during sparring in the practice ring with his superior knowledge of the sport.

The second occurrence for young Ryoshi Dosi was the assignment of his new name. Sumo wrestlers do not compete under their own. They go forth to do battle under colorful titles called *shikona*. These are designed to intimidate the enemy and build up the confidence and morale of their bearers. A wrestler may be called Osorishitora (Awful Tiger) or perhaps something simpler but just as meaningful as Unarubofu (Roaring Hurricane). When it came time to pick Dosi's *shikona*, Uchida sat him down in the middle of the practice *dohyo* and paced around him, carefully studying the boy.

"You look like you are brave," Uchida said. "Are you?"

"I try to be," Dosi answered with as much as modesty as sincerity.

"Mmmm, yes," Uchida said thoughtfully. "There is a sort of *shikona* that has not been used for hundreds of years."

"Why not, Uchida-san?" Dosi asked.

"Because the wrestlers who had it as part of their names suffered great losses and setbacks," Uchida explained. "But as I look at you I can tell you are an unusual boy—one with great promise."

"*Arigato*, Uchida-san."

"I really think you can change that cursed *shikona*," Uchida said. "And you would be even more famous for having done it." He continued his circular stroll about the kneeling boy for several more long moments before he finally made up his mind. "*Hai*! I will call you that—*take*—mountain peak. But it needs something to go with it—"

"There is much thunder in the mountains above my village," Dosi said.

"*Hai*! That's it! You will be *Kaminatake*—Thundering Mountain Peak."

Thus Ryoshi Dosi, son of a simple fisherman, ceased to exist while Kaminatake the sumo wrestler was born.

That same day he made his third discovery of his new environment. The world of the *maezumo*—apprentice wrestler—was one of hard work, humiliation and out-and-out drudgery.

The *maezumo* were not only required to clean the stable building and all the rooms in it, but also to cook the meals and act as valets, errand-boys, and punching bags for the older journeymen wrestlers. All this while participating in one of the most demanding sports in the world.

Kaminatake, like his fellow apprentices, arose at four a.m. and hurriedly dressed in the early morning chill to report to the training room. Here, under Uchida's stern supervision, they learned the basic techniques of *sumodo* in not only bruising contests between themselves and their mentor, but through rigorous, tortuous exercises.

There was the foot-stamping *shiko* that brought painful ankles, sore hips and hurting feet. But this was easy compared to the agony of the *matawari*. In this movement, the trainees sat on the ground and spread their legs as far as they could. If their efforts didn't satisfy Uchida he would grab the offending limb and push it out until the *maezumo* grimaced in pain. Then, to add to the discomfort, the novice wrestler would then be required to lean forward—farther—farther until his chest touched the ground. Again, Uchida offered his unsolicited aid to see that the exercise was carried out to its proper limit.

This was followed by a stiff session on the *teppo*. This was no more than a pillar mounted in the ground which Uchida demanded be ruthlessly attacked until the *maezumo* were bruised, scratched and bleeding.

Even after that the ordeal was not over. The final activity was called *butsukari-geiko* in which the apprentices took turns standing in the ring enduring charge after charge of their fellows until all were completely wrung out and exhausted.

By then it was eight a.m. and the journeymen sumo shuffled into the training room to begin their own workouts while the apprentices limped away to begin preparation of the first gigantic meal of the two that would be consumed by all members of the stable that day.

At least this was an advantage of sinking one's self into *sumodo*. There was more than enough to eat, and apprentices were required to literally gorge themselves to begin putting on the incredible weight they would need when they finally stepped onto the *dohyo* for the first time. Kaminatake shoved millions of grams of carbohydrates and calories into his growing body during those gargantuan meals.

The apprentice's afternoon session—which went on while the older wrestlers took their naps—consisted of studying sumo and samurai history, the treatment of injuries, calligraphy, and even the writing of poetry. It was here that the gentler aspects of the art were acquired. They learned the three key elements that make up *sumodo*.

Shin—mind, in which one's inner disciplines and drives originate.

Gi — art, the beauty and skills of their sport.

Tai — the body, which puts into action the two above.

The youngsters also learned of the etiquette of sumo wrestling where arrogance, boasting, or even the slightest discourtesy or disrespect had no place.

Then they spent the rest of the day cooking, cleaning, toting, and fetching until they fell into bed exhausted before getting up to begin the routine again.

Kaminatake sank himself into this feudal world and tried with all his heart to excel. He performed all chores cheerfully and willingly. He worked hard at his wrestling techniques, taking each whack of Uchida-san's bamboo pole across his buttocks as well-deserved punishments when he made mistakes. But there was something within his personal make-up that rejected the courtesies and gentler aspects of sumo. Kaminatake had a killing instinct and his fantasies of winning future matches consisted of mental pictures of smashing his opponents to the clay, leaving them bleeding, bruised hulks of devastated humanity. This became most evident during the *butsukari-geiko*, when he did more than toss his fellow *maezumo* from the ring. Many times Kaminatake would lose his head and go after them, beating and kicking the unfortunate losers until Uchida drove him off with heavy blows from his bamboo staff.

Despite this cruel streak, however, he was ready for his first tournament within a few months.

The apprentices, whose names are not even on the program, opened each sumo event. These preliminary matches started early in the morning and were sparsely attended. The crowd didn't build up until later when the higher ranked journeymen made their appearances.

Kaminatake's preliminary outing was a huge success. He won his first two matches and was awarded a white star. This allowed him to progress from the *maezumo* class to the *honchu* division.

That same day he again clashed in the *dohyo* and won

36

another white star. This advanced him into the *jonokuchi* division, the classification in which he would be allowed to compete in the next tournament. And it meant his name would be on the program for that event.

Uchida-san was very pleased with him. "I never expected any of our *maezumo* to progress in this first tournament," he said to his young charge. "And it looks like you will be the one to remove the hundreds of years of bad luck that has been the curse of the *take* name."

Kaminatake, reluctantly conceding to the lessons in modesty and courtesy, bowed low to his teacher. "*Arigato*, Uchida-san." He really wanted to say, "*Anata mirumasen mada* — you ain't seen nothing yet!"

This was the start of a long, hard road that lasted six trying years. It was also a period of poverty. Sumo wrestlers do not get paid for their efforts until they reach the *sekitori* division. Until then, the best they can hope for is money for expenses, an occasional bonus, or outright gifts of money or luxuries from devotees of the sport.

These are generally rich individuals or fan clubs who admire one particular wrestler. They shower him with presents, and he must be content with these in lieu of solid cash. This has been one of the reasons it is difficult to recruit apprentice *sumotori* in modern Japan. Why would a youngster go into the extremely demanding feudal world of *sumodo* when there are good jobs available at various automobile and electronic companies? The cruelest aspect of the system is that if one of the aspirants fails to make the grade, he is turned out of his stable. Generally without the education or skills to get himself profitable employment.

Kaminatake contented himself with fantasies of the life he would lead as a champion. There would be plenty of money from wrestling then. And that didn't include the millions of yen he could earn endorsing products on television commercials and in magazine advertisements.

The young man literally charged into his career. He suffered a few setbacks in the form of an occasional defeat, but managed to forge ahead as his skill and strength increased. Soon he was advancing rapidly up the sumo ladder: *Jono-kuchi* to *Jonidan* to *Sandanme* until arriving at the *Ma-kushita* Division just one step below the coveted *Juryo* which would make him a *Sekitori*, that coveted neighborhood where the highest ranking *Yokozuna*—the Grand Champions—trod in all their splendor.

Kaminatake awoke on his *futon* sleeping pad and heaved his great bulk to a sitting position. He was in a most wonderful mood. Not only had he won those fifteen matches in a row, but the *ken-sho* prize donated by the *tanimachi* patron turned out to be a brand new Honda sedan.

Banzai! his mind cried. And he would be a *sekitori* before the day was out too.

There was no sense in trying to sleep. He was too excited. He sprang to his feet and slipped into a beautiful silk *kimono* decorated with writhing golden dragons. This, too, had been a *ken-sho* from another admirer. Kaminatake could hear the apprentices sweeping their brooms in the hallway outside the journeymen's sleeping quarters. He slid the door to his room open and stepped out. Usually he had a scowl for the youngsters, but today he beamed at them. "*O-hayo, maezumo!*"

Normally they feared this man and his sharp temper. But that day they sensed his good mood and the youngsters happily replied to his greeting. "*O-hayo gozai-masu*, Kamina-take-san!" they called out. "Congratulations on your great victory last night. *Iwai!*"

"Is Uchida-san in his room?" Kaminatake asked.

"*Hai!*"

Kaminatake went down the highly polished hardwood floor to the end of the hallway and rapped lightly on the door. "Uchida-san? Uchida-san? Are you in?"

"*Hai*," came the answer from within. "*O-hairi*."

He stepped into his trainer's room expecting to be greeted with a wide smile. But Uchida was not only not grinning, he was weeping.

"Uchida-san! What's wrong?"

Uchida, sitting on the floor at his small writing table, picked up a letter and held it out. "You are not to be advanced to *sekitori*!"

"What? This can't be. I won fifteen matches in a row!" Kaminatake protested. He took the letter and read it slowly and carefully. His voice was weak as he spoke. "This is preposterous!"

Uchida shook his head. "No, Kaminatake. The association is within its rights. I have long feared this because of your attitude. Thus, the elders have refused to advance you because you have the spirit of demons looking out through your eyes. Perhaps it is all my fault for not concentrating enough on your *shin*."

"What does that matter? This cannot be," Kaminatake protested. "I even won a car."

"That and your bonus," Uchida reminded him.

"Bonus!" Kaminatake said angrily. "A few thousand yen was all. That was only a little over a hundred and eighty American dollars. And I owe all that out."

"At least you have a car."

"A car! What do I care about a *jidosha*? I can't even put gasoline in it."

Uchida looked with disapproval at the angry young wrestler. "You may display disappointment and grief. But never ire. Remember your place, Kaminatake! You, as a lowly *makushita*, have no right to criticize or even question the Sumo Association. You must write them and thank the elders for their kind criticism and promise you will cast the evil from your soul."

"I have been working hard for six years," Kaminatake snarled. "I received no pay other than paltry bonuses, yet the stable and the sumo big-shots have made plenty of money off my efforts. And they won't even advance me to a higher rank as I deserve."

"Lower your voice!" Uchida commanded. "Do you want the *maezumo* to hear you?"

"They should hear me," Kaminatake said. "Maybe they'll know what they really are. A bunch of *manuke*—chumps!"

Uchida's face was sincerely sad. "Even now you are not conducting yourself in accordance with *sumodo*."

"To *jikogu* with *sumodo*!" Kaminatake yelled. He whirled his ponderous body and strode out of the room and turned down the hall. As he passed the apprentices he cuffed one, sending the boy crashing through the paper wall of a journeyman's bedroom.

The other youngsters cowered back from the huge, maddened man who glared at them. "Get back to work, *bakamono*! What are you staring at?" After treating them to one more furious glance, he turned and continued on his way.

When he arrived back at his own quarters, Kaminatake quickly dressed and left the stable. That night, he vowed to himself, Tokyo was going to be treated to one of the wildest drunks in the history of the city.

And a few citizens were going to get their faces bashed in too!

CHAPTER THREE

The dawning sun was pink and wan over Saigon's notorious Cholon District as the three sedans eased slowly down the narrow unmarked street. They came to a rolling stop a few meters from an intersection of crowded dilapidated buildings. Fifteen men climbed out of the autos as quietly as they could. Among that number was CIA case officer Chuck Fagin, Sgt. Chin Han of the National Police, a half-dozen of his men, and Maj. Robert Falconi accompanied by the other six Black Eagles.

Although the Vietnamese police were attired in their regular uniforms, Falconi and his men wore nondescript civilian clothing. Their shirts, though different in color, were similar in shape: a bit baggy to afford more concealment to the cumbersome GI shoulder holsters they used to hold their .45 automatic pistols.

They converged on the front car and gathered around Chin. "The target is down that street," he said indicating the direction by pointing. "Remember we will be moving in on a group of buildings that afford lots of cover for the bad guys. And they're going to resist to the bitter end."

Archie Dobbs pulled the Colt .45 auto from his waistband. "Good. I'm in the mood to off a coupla dopers."

"What's the matter, Arch?" Calvin Culpepper asked. "That bunch overcharge you on your last buy of pot?"

"Yeah," Archie answered matter-of-factly. "A quarter of the shit they sold me was ground tea leaves."

Calvin chuckled. "Christ! You musta been stoned to fall for that one."

"I was," Archie admitted. "And it was a little over a year ago too. But I'm still mad as hell about it."

Falconi looked at Archie with a frown. "You remember what I told you about pot. I don't give a damn what you do on R&R, but if I so much as catch you with a roach on ops, I'll can you. Got it?"

"Sure, Skipper," Archie acknowledged agreeably. "I've always known where you stand on that issue."

Falconi nodded, then turned to Top Gordon. "It won't hurt for another quick run-down on this mission."

"Right, Falcon," the detachment operations sergeant said. "We're moving in on a gang headquarters that's deeply involved in narcotics. These are real bad-asses and there are a few Americans involved in the operation too. They're mostly G.I. deserters and will take a real hard fall if they're policed up. They and their Vietnamese partners-in-crime have ever'thing to lose and nothing to gain from this raid. They'll act accordingly. Remember your assignments, cover each other and be ready for the worst."

"Don't sound much worse'n what we usually go through," Archie Dobbs remarked.

Top grinned at his sardonic humor. "Now here's the lay-out of the place. It's located behind a high fence. The building is two-stories high and shaped like a 'U'. And you can make book that there are escape hatches to the roof. So be alert to that possibility."

"Right," Falconi said. He winked at Chin. "Let's do it to it."

"Yes, sir," Chin said. He spoke some quick orders to his

men in Vietnamese. The task force, after leaving security on the sedans, moved down the street and around the corner.

The gang's safehouse was out of sight behind a high wooden fence. The barrier had been constructed specifically to obscure any view of the buildings behind it. The owners had operated for months without interference and, under normal circumstances, would not have been raided. Hence there were no guards or watchmen posted by the criminals to keep an eye on the street.

It was their tough luck that they happened to fall into the plans designed to move the Black Eagles closer to their real quarry — Tsing Chai and his organization.

The raiders positioned themselves on each side of the door. Falconi looked back down the street and waved a signal. Seconds later, one of the automobiles slowly turned the corner and traveled at a quiet snail's pace toward them. When the driver drew up even with the door in the fence, he cranked the wheel and stomped down on the accelerator. The car slammed through the wooden barrier sending broken slabs of board whirling through the air.

Falconi and the rest of the men charged through the opening, splitting up into small groups of two or three men to attack their respective objectives. The major sprinted toward the center building in the complex of ramshackle dwellings. He caught a movement in the corner of his eye and looked up to see a husky, buck-naked American step through a second floor door. The man held a revolver in his hand and was aiming down into the crowd of intruders. Falconi whipped his own weapon into action, holding the pistol with both hands and crouching down in a combat firing position. The Colt barked twice.

The first round hit the doper in the chest just below the throat, picking him up and throwing him back into the same room from which he had just emerged. The second bullet, which would have been a perfect headshot, whizzed through empty air and lodged in the upper doorjamb.

Calvin Culpepper waved at the Falcon. "Nice shot!"

At the same time, down on the lower floor to the left, Chun Kim charged up to a door and cut loose with a flying *choh-do* kick. The door flew inward, breaking off its hinges and hanging there as the South Korean marine, followed closely by Malpractice McCorckel, charged into the room. Their barking pistols spit .45 slugs. An Oriental man, lying on a mattress with a woman of the same race, had only managed to get up on his elbow in time to have a round crash into his teeth and explode out the back of his skull. His girlfriend screamed her horror at the crap that splattered on the wall behind the crude bed.

Kim, not slowing, ran to the bed and quickly grabbed her by one arm. He jerked the shapely woman from under the covers to her feet and slung her, naked and yelling, across the room. A quick search of the sparse room produced only one weapon. No doubt it was the property of the dead man whose blood now flowed profusely from his mangled cranium and soaked into the mattress. Kim and Malpractice quickly left for their next target. The terrified girl sank to the floor, staring in shocked fascination at the cadaver of her lover.

Meanwhile Falconi, with pistol in hand and Archie Dobbs on his heels, raced up a flight of stairs to a long balcony that gave access to several rooms on the second floor. The major stopped at the first room and aimed at the door knob. The .45 bucked as it was fired. The slug smashed into the flimsy portal and splintered it. Falconi kicked it open. "Let's go! Outside!"

"Oh, man!" an American voice inside groaned. "I caught the round in my belly."

Falconi, tensed, spoke again. "Then crawl out, goddamnit!"

"I can't, man—oh—you musta killed me."

The major eased through the door, ready for action—but not quite ready enough. A strong hand grabbed his wrist and pulled him the rest of the way in. Falconi was caught in the iron grip of a big blond kid. He looked like the type of football player whom colleges recruit from Pennsylvania coal-mining areas — and seemed twice as strong.

"Leggo that piece!" he snarled swinging the army officer hard against the wall.

Falconi's vision turned to blinking lights for a second and he felt his hand go limp, the pistol clattering to the floor. He instinctively kicked out and caught his attacker who had dived for the weapon. The man yowled and flipped over on his back. He made another grab for the Colt but only succeeded in sending it skidding across the room to the opposite side.

Falconi, now a bit more recovered, kicked again. He was a trifle slow and Football Player took a stinging graze across the ribs. The attack served to make him that much angrier. He rolled to his feet and charged.

The Falcon threw a right jab that smashed into Football Player's nose. Cartilage caved in and blood sprayed out, but the big guy threw a forearm smash that slammed into Falconi's jaw like a sledgehammer. The major hit the wall, then bounced off it in time to catch two lightning-quick left and right crosses that flipped his head from side to side so hard his neck vertebrae popped in protest.

"How'd you like that, shithead?" Football Player asked. He whipped a right uppercut, but Falconi stepped back against the wall allowing his opponent's large fist to fly upward into empty space.

Falconi drove the heel of his hand into Football Player's damaged snotbox in three rapid punches. His eyes watering, the narcotics peddler momentarily lost his vision. Falconi, not wasting the opportunity, spun on his heel and drove a tremendous elbow smash into the guy's solar plexus. Football Player swooshed out an instinctive expulsion of breath and fell to his knees. His face tilted forward at the exact second that Falconi's knee had risen to meet it.

Football Player tipped over to the floor, and made one attempt to rise before collapsing into unconsciousness.

Falconi finally regained his equilibrium and full senses in time to note Archie Dobbs finishing up his own bit of argument by slapping his pistol against another American criminal's face with vicious blows that had already gashed one cheek so badly it was possible to see the guy's teeth through the cut. Falconi hurried up behind the man and slammed a heavy fist between the shoulder blades to end the fight.

Archie Dobbs, panting, stepped back. "Damn — I don't know — what was — holdin' that — bastard up."

"Pure determination, my boy," Falconi said walking over and retrieving his pistol. "Let's get on and join the rest of the boys."

"Right, Skipper."

Lightfingers O'Quinn, the USMC's donation to the Black Eagles, was in another part of the building. He and Calvin Culpepper had rushed into an empty room that had three closed doors offering exits from the place. The marine impetuously opened one. A Vietnamese, waiting on the other side, cut loose with one round from a .357 Magnum. The concussion brought blood from Lightfinger's ears and the right side of his face took a powder burn. But his hand, holding a Colt, had flinched out of reflex and squeezed the trigger of the weapon. The round zipped into the Vietnamese's midsection and continued into his body to split the man's spine before turning upward and exiting out just under the right shoulder blade. He made another attempt to shoot the marine, but his legs — no longer receiving messages from the brain — turned to rubber and he sat down. He tried to raise the heavy pistol, but Lightfingers simply grabbed the barrel and pulled it from his grasp. Then the American stuck his own G.I. weapon into the shoulder-holster under his shirt. Now the possessor of the .357, he pointed it at the Vietnamese criminal's head and blew it off.

Calvin, going past him to continue down the hall, grimaced at the sight. He shook his head ruefully at the marine. "Damn, Lightfingers! You sure do make a mess!"

Top Gordon, doing his own bit, was downstairs across from where Kim and Malpractice were operating. The detachment sergeant, older and more cautious than the other Black Eagles, had been carefully investigating several rooms. After methodically checking under beds and behind furniture, he had moved on in each instance finding nothing. This had happened in three of the small chambers he'd searched.

The fourth was not empty.

A tall, thin, and gangly blond American had been stuffing money into a suitcase when Top broke in on him. The guy spun to face the Black Eagle while at the same time displaying a *nanchaku*. He grimaced at the master sergeant and positioned the deadly weapon. He flipped it around his head and caught it, then passed it from hand-to-hand in a *hi-muchi* movement. Next, snarling viciously, he performed several rapid figure-eights then held them in the *kokutsu dachi* position. He took the first step toward Top. "Whattaya think o' this shit, asshole?" he asked.

Wordlessly, the master sergeant raised his pistol and shot the *nanchaku* expert through the throat. The martial artist, his eyes opened wide in indignation at such disrespect toward his skills, stepped backward and fell to the floor. Top took a furtive look at the chained weapon sprawled across the cadaver, then went on his way to the next room.

Chuck Fagin, a bit overweight and out of shape, was game despite the physical deterioration the long months at a desk had brought him. It took a lot of effort, but he managed to keep up with Chin Han as the police sergeant smashed through room after room in pursuit of several fleeing suspects.

"Damn—they gotta—reach a—dead end—soon," Fagin gasped as he dogged his younger companion's heels.

"Lots of rooms in this complex," Chin said. He paused at

a door and blew it apart with the last four rounds in his pistol. After quickly shoving a fresh magazine into the grip, he kicked what was left of the wreckage away and charged through.

This, indeed, was the final room in the fugitives' rush to freedom. A ladder, built into the wall, led to a trapdoor in the ceiling. Chin started to ascend the rungs, but Fagin grabbed him.

"How about letting—me lead the way—for a change?"

Chin smiled. "Certainly, Mister Fagin. Help yourself."

Fagin waited a couple of beats to settle his breath down, then began a careful climb. When he neared the top he stopped and listened intently.

"Hear anything?" Chin asked in a whisper.

Fagin shook his head. He eased up some more, then slowly brought his head high enough to let his eyes peer over the top.

The wood exploded in front of his face and he lost his grip, falling down into the room. He landed on Chin and both hit the floor. They didn't spend much time in that undignified position, however.

The grenade that fell in from above hissed angrily at them.

The two men managed to dive to safety in the other room as the device exploded, sending a cloud of dust rolling out the door. Chin quickly eased back to the entrance to the room and waited.

Sure enough, a head dropped down through the opening for a look around to check the damage his grenade had done. The slug from Chin's .45 hit the doper's forehead and mushroomed out the top of the skull, flipping the dope seller's scalp over to cover his face.

Down on the other side of the building, Falconi and Archie Dobbs had managed to work their way to the roof. Their trail through the large, rambling two-story shack was marked with no less than four corpses as well as Football

Player and his buddy whom they'd left handcuffed in that first room.

Falconi had scrambled through an opening to the roof at about the same moment Chin had shot the man peering down to check the damage of the grenade. The grenadier had two other friends with him. Chin's shot into the head of their curious buddy had taken their attention just long enough for the major to take a quick snap shot from the prone position.

That bullet missed, but the second punched into one baddie's lower belly and set him down. His companion was quick however, and returned fire.

Falconi shot back twice more and gritted his teeth when the slide of his pistol stayed back rather than slam forward in battery. His magazine was empty.

Archie Dobbs, who had ducked back in when the doper had cut loose on Falcon, popped back out again. He took a quick shot, the slug hitting the man in the left thigh and turning him around to face the opposite direction. Archie put the next bullet into the guy's right shoulder and whirled him back to face the Americans once more. The third, and final round hit the criminal in mid-chest and flipped him over on his dead buddy.

Another head appeared at the opening where the bad guys had been gathered around. Archie almost squeezed off another shot, but recognized Chin just as the police sergeant ducked back.

Falconi grinned and yelled. "Hey! The roof is secured. C'mon out."

Within moments a cautious Chin, followed by Fagin, climbed out on the roof and walked toward them. Fagin looked down into the compound below them and noted the rest of the Black Eagles and their Vietnamese police allies ushering several prisoners out into the open. "Looks like things are in hand down there too," he said.

Falconi shoved the fresh magazine into the grip of his pistol. "I don't like running around with this thing empty," he said reholstering it. He walked to the edge of the roof and yelled down at Top Gordon. "We got any casualties?"

"Everybody down here is okay," Top hollered back. "What about Fagin and Archie?"

"They're up here with me," Falconi said. He noted that the South Vietnamese policemen had already begun to drag the corpses of the dead narcotics peddlers outside. He turned to Fagin. "I guess it won't be long until the word is out about this raid."

"Sure won't. I hope Tsing Chai is convinced enough by the news to believe the Black Eagles are really out of active ops in enemy territory."

"If he's not," Falconi mused. "Moving in on his place will make this exercise look like a Sunday school picnic."

The guard limped down the row of cells in the Tokyo *chusin no* jail. One of his eyes was badly discolored and swollen completely shut. A heavy strip of tape lay across his broken nose, and his damaged ribs were tightly bandaged with several yards of surgical elastic wrap. He reached the final cell and peered in at the huge prisoner sitting sullenly on the hard floor. That one man had been the cause of all the injuries.

Kaminatake glanced up at the policeman and glared with such hatred, the officer blanched. Then the *sumotori* turned his head and went back to his angry staring at the confining walls.

His drunken binge the night before had truly been one of momentous destruction and havoc. It had all started when he stormed out of the wrestling stable after Uchida had informed him of the Sumo Association's refusal to promote him up into the *sekitori* ranks. Before leaving he had traded the paperwork on the Honda auto he had won in the tournament for cash worth only half the value of the car. But

50

Kaminatake didn't give a damn. He wanted some quick money to shove in the pockets of his specially tailored Hong Kong suit (another *ken-sho* from a wealthy patron of sumo wrestling).

His first stop was the nearest bar. Kaminatake downed a couple of angry bottles of *sake* there, which did little to affect him other than keep the fires of anger in his soul alight.

From that point he progressed closer and closer to the Ginza district pouring more alcohol into his enormous gut until it finally began to build up enough in his bloodstream to affect him. By the time he staggered into the one bar filled with American sailors, he was roaring drunk and looking for trouble.

Within a scant two minutes of his entrance, he was the only patron being served by the thoroughly frightened bartender. The representatives of the U.S. Navy were in a groaning pile outside, the more conscious trying to figure out exactly what had roared in on them.

Kaminatake finally grew bored of drinking alone and announced his farewell by heaving an empty Scotch bottle into a mirror before departing the premises. On the way out he took only enough time to growl at the American servicemen who were helping each other to their feet. Then the *sumotori* staggered down the street like a runaway bull elephant.

His next stop was a whorehouse. Here he was a bit calmer as he finally spent his sexual drives on three young prostitutes he left sore and exhausted. They would be unable to work until at least a three-day recuperative period. Before leaving, he gave the bordello's bouncer a quick study. Deciding the man was a pretentious ass, Kaminatake picked him up and hurled him through a wall to land on a shocked customer who had just reached the final, delicious stages of his sexual union with his pillow-lady. The climax was the man's most intense, if not the most memorable.

From that point on his journey into drunken madness deteriorated in his memory to a foggish swirl of fighting, drinking, bellowing, and stomping until the squad of Tokyo riot police broke in on him and cornered him in a small, completely wrecked nightclub on the far side of the Ginza.

It had taken no less than a dozen tough cops to finally bring him down for the cuffs and shackles to be applied. It also took every one of them to lug his ponderous carcass out to the paddy wagon and hurl him, cursing and threatening, into the back.

It had truly been a memorable evening.

Now Kaminatake looked up from his cell as the guard returned. The policeman, a bit cautious, slipped a large key into the door and swung it open. "You're free," was all he said.

The *sumotori* slowly got to his feet. "How is that? I have no money."

"Everything has been taken care of," the guard said. "The damages, your fines — everything."

Kaminatake shuffled out of the confinement of the bars and brushed his rumpled suit. No doubt either the stable or the Sumo Association had taken care of everything. That would be customary in a case like this. Because he was from the sumo world, they would feel responsible to take care of the situation. Then he'd receive a one-way ticket back to the little fishing village of Samuimizu and that would be that. The end — *haji*.

He followed the policeman from the cell block, down a long steel corridor to a small door at the other end. The officer opened the heavy metal portal and motioned him to pass through. Kaminatake stepped into the next room fully expecting to see Uchida-san, a look of disapproving anger on his face, standing there with his ticket home.

Instead a rather small man in a chauffeur's uniform greeted him with a bow and a polite, "*Konnichi wa*, Kaminatake-san."

Puzzled, Kaminatake returned the bow. "*Konnichi wa*."

"I represent Mister Matsuno. He has taken care of your—ah, difficulties—and invites you to his home."

"Matsuno? Is he not a *tanimachi*?"

"*Hai*," the chauffeur answered. "He is a great patron of sumo wrestling. In fact, it was he who donated the *ken-sho* of the automobile to you after your magnificent victory in the last tournament." The man gestured with an outstretched arm. "Please step this way."

Kaminatake trailed him out of the building to a Cadillac limousine parked by the curb. He slipped in through the door held open for him, and settled down.

The ride was a long one. The driver, experienced and skillful, wheeled his large vehicle through the congested streets with ease. They finally reached the outskirts of the great, sprawling city and continued on through lighter traffic. Even this dropped off after awhile and they turned off the main road to follow a narrow, winding thoroughfare that came to a dead-end at a huge gate mounted in a high, thick stone wall.

A tough-looking young man in a business suit stepped from a small door in the imposing barrier and walked up to the car. After wordlessly perusing the limousine's occupants, he turned and nodded toward the gate. It slowly swung open, and the chauffeur drove through it up a continuation of the road until coming to a stop in front of a huge mansion built in a pagoda style of architecture.

A pretty young woman in a kimono was waiting for them. She opened the door for Kaminatake. "*Dozo. Tsuzukumasu.*"

Kaminatake did as she bid and followed her up the walk into the house. After stopping at the raised entrance long enough for him to remove his shoes and slip into some soft slippers, they entered the domicile and went down a lacquered hallway to the bath house.

The woman turned and bowed to him. "Matsuno-san thought you might wish to bathe. I am Kaika—at your service."

Kaminatake nodded. "*Arigato*."

He allowed himself to be undressed and taken through the bath ritual. After pouring hot water over him, the young woman set to work soaping down the wrestler. As she worked, she wondered if one bar would be enough to lather the huge bulk of muscle and fat she had to wash down.

Kaminatake sat silently as Kaika's small hands spread the sweet smelling suds over him, then once again poured water to rid his body of the soap. Then he went to spend almost half an hour soaking in the near boiling water of a large tub.

Finally, his hangover and fatigue forgotten, he climbed out and stood naked as Kaika finished toweling him dry. Following that, she dressed him in a fresh, clean kimono and once again bowed to the huge *sumotori*.

"*Dozo*. I will take you to Matsuno-san now."

They left the bath house and walked through the huge mansion, crossing a small rock garden located in an open square situated in the middle of the huge, sprawling building. They found Mister Matsuno in his office. He was seated on the floor in front of a low desk. Dressed in a traditional kimono, the patron of the sport was signing papers being handed to him by a man who was obviously a secretary or administrative clerk of some sort.

Matsuno was an extremely short, very thin, middle-aged gentleman. He peered at the world through thick, hornrimmed glasses perched on his pug nose. His moustache, thin and gray, was well-trimmed and tidy.

When Kaminatake entered the room with Kaika, Matsuno dismissed his scribe. "*Konnichi wa*," he said displaying a buck-toothed grin to the *sumotori*.

Kaminatake bowed. "*Konnichi wa*, Matsuno-san. *Arigato*. Thank you for your kindness."

"I am pleased to have offered some small assistance to such a skillful *sumotori*."

Kaika pulled a sitting cushion from a panel in the wall.

She set it down for the huge man. After bowing politely, she quickly withdrew.

Kaminatake settled his expansive body down. "I fear I am no longer a member of the sumo world, Matsuno-san."

Matsuno nodded. "*Hai*. I have been made aware of your predicament. The refusal to advance you to *sekitori* was inexcusable. I was most upset."

"*Arigato*."

"My secretary made an inquiry into your case at the Sumo Association. I fear they have, indeed, decided to expel you from *sumodo*. Therefore, I have taken the liberty of inviting you to visit me in order to offer you employment," Mister Matsuno said. "Would you be interested?"

"*Hai*." Kaminatake hid the flood of grateful emotion behind the blankness of his huge, expressionless face.

"I am a businessman," Mister Matsuno went on. "An investments speculator, if you wish. I deal in great amounts of money and there are times I need protection and bodyguards. You would fit in quite well in that category."

"*Hai*."

"However, my offer of a job is not that of a low-ranking member of my staff. I wish you to be in charge of a special group I have formed," Mister Matsuno explained. "Would you be interested?"

"*Hai. Arigato*."

"Excellent," his new employer said. "I sometimes find myself involved in certain commercial enterprises which are—well, Kaminatake-san,—they are against the law. I am not a member of the *yakuza* and do not enjoy their protection from the police or other authorities. And, with my sudden and quite substantial interest in gambling, the pillow-world, and narcotics in Southeast Asia, I fear I have developed the need for a private army of sorts."

"Forgive my ignorance, Matsuno-san," Kaminatake said humbly. "But I am from the country and my entire experience in the city has been in my wrestling stable. I do not understand the term *yakuza*."

"It is an organization of gangs," Matsuno explained kindly. "Very much like the Mafia in America. Except that our people are more sophisticated and have much more tradition behind them. In fact, the *yakuza* live by *samurai* codes."

"Ah so!" Kaminatake said. "*Arigato*, Matsuno-san."

Then Kaminatake listened quietly as Mister Matsuno went on to explain about the growing presence of American troops in South Vietnam and the certain expanding markets created by such an influx of young, robust soldiers who would be seeking diversions and forms of recreation which offered the investor a fantastic return on his money.

"What I shall require of you, Kaminatake-san," Mister Matsuno explained in conclusion, "is to infuse my new staff with the spirit of *sumodo* and train them in the philosophy of that martial art. You, too, shall acquire new skills. There are various handfighting styles that will supplement your own magnificent experience. Also there is the use of firearms for you to learn. Does that interest you?"

"*Hai*," Kaminatake answered enthusiastically.

"And there is one more advantage to the job — travel," Mister Matsuno said. "Especially with opportunities to visit South Vietnam on business trips to my colleagues there."

Kaminatake bowed his head in agreement. He smiled at his *koyosha*. "*Hai*. I shall look forward to serving you. And also to bringing misfortune to those who would oppose your endeavors and enterprises."

CHAPTER FOUR

Robert Michailovich Falconi was born an "army brat" at Fort Meade, Maryland in the year 1934.

His father, 2nd Lt. Michael Falconi, was the son of Italian immigrants. The parents, Salvatore and Luciana Falconi, had wasted no time in instilling an appreciation of America and the opportunity offered by the nation into their youngest son as they had their other seven children. Mister Falconi even went as far to name his son Michael rather than the Italian Michele. The boy had been born an American, was going to live as an American, so —*per Dio e tutti i santi*— he was going to be named as an American!

Young Michael was certainly no disappointment to his parents or older brothers and sisters. He studied hard in school and excelled. He worked in the family's small shoe repair shop in New York City's Little Italy in the evenings, doing his homework late at night. When he graduated from high school Michael was eligible for several scholarships to continue his education in college, but even with this help, it would have entailed great sacrifice on the part of his parents. Two older brothers, both working as lawyers, could have helped out a bit, but Michael didn't want to be any more of a burden on his family than was absolutely necessary.

He knew of an alternative to having to pay to attend a university. The nation's service academies, West Point and Annapolis, offered free education to qualified young men. Michael, through the local ward boss, received a congressional appointment to take the examinations to attend the United States Military Academy.

He was successful in this endeavor and was appointed to the Corps of Cadets. West Point didn't give a damn about his humble origins. The Academy didn't care whether his parents were poor immigrants or not. The fact that his father was a struggling cobbler meant absolutely nothing. All that institution was concerned about was whether Michael Falconi could cut it or not. It was this measuring of a man by no other standards than his own abilities and talents that caused the young man to develop a sincere, lifelong love for the United States Army. He finished his career at the school in the upper third of his class, sporting the three chevrons and rockers of a brigade adjutant on his sleeves upon graduation.

Second Lieutenant Falconi was assigned to the 3rd Infantry Regiment at Fort Meade, Maryland. This unit was a ceremonial outfit that provided details for military funerals at Arlington National Cemetery, the guard for the Tomb of the Unknown Soldier and other official functions in the Washington, D.C. area.

The young shavetail enjoyed the bachelor's life in the nation's capital, and his duties as protocol officer were not too demanding but interesting. He was required to be present during social occasions that were official affairs of state. He coordinated the affairs and saw to it that all the political bigwigs and other brass attending them had a good time. He was doing exactly those duties at such a function when he met a young Russian Jewish refugee named Miriam Ananova Silberman.

She was a pretty brunette of twenty years of age, who had the most striking eyes Michael Falconi had ever seen. He would always say all through his life that it was her eyes that captured his heart. When he met her, she was a member of the League of Jewish Refugees attending a congressional dinner. She and her father, Josef Silberman, had recently fled Josef Stalin's antisemitic terrorism in the Soviet Union. Her organization had been lobbying congress to enact legislation that would permit the American government to take action in saving European and Asian Jewry not only from the savagery of the Communists but also from the Nazis who had only begun their own program of intimidation and harassment of Germany's Jewish population.

When the lieutenant met the refugee beauty, he fell hopelessly in love. He spent that entire evening as close to her as he could possibly be, while ignoring his other duties. He was absolutely determined he would get to know this beautiful Russian girl better. He begged her to dance with him at every opportunity, was solicitous about seeing to her refreshments and engaged her in conversation, doing his best to be witty and interesting.

He was successful.

Miriam Silberman was fascinated by this tall, dark, and most handsome young officer. She was so swept off her feet that she failed to play any coquettish little games or try to appear hard-to-get. His infectious smile and happy charm completely captivated the young woman.

The next day Michael began a serious courtship, determined to win her heart and marry the girl.

Josef Silberman was a cantankerous elderly widower. He opposed the match from the beginning. As a Talmud scholar, he wanted his only daughter to marry a nice Jewish boy. But Miriam took pains to point out to him that this was America — a country which existed in direct opposition to any homogeneous customs. The mixing of nationalities and religions was not that unusual in this part of the world. Josef argued, stormed, forbade, and demanded — but all for naught. In the end, so he would not lose the affection of his daughter, he gave his blessing. The couple was married in the post chapel at Fort Meade.

A year later their only child, a son, was born. He was named Robert Mikhailovich.

The boy spent his youth on various army posts. The only time he lived in a town or civilian neighborhood was during the three years his father, by then a colonel, served overseas in the European Theater of Operations in the first Infantry Division — the Big Red One. A family joke developed out of the colonel's service in that particular outfit. Robert would ask his dad, "How come you're serving in the First Division?"

The colonel always answered, "Because I figured if I was going to be one, I might as well be a Big Red One."

It was one of those private jokes that didn't go over too well outside the house.

The boy had a happy childhood. The only problem was his dislike of school. Too many genes of ancient Hebrew warriors and Roman legionnaires had been passed down to him. Robert was a kid who liked action, adventure and plenty of it. The only serious studying he ever did was in the karate classes he took when the family was stationed in Japan. He was accepted in one of that island nation's most prestigious martial arts academies where he excelled while evolving into a serious and skillful *karateka*.

His use of this fighting technique caused one of the ironies in his life. In the early 1950s, his father had been posted as commandant of high school ROTC in San Diego, California. Robert, an indifferent student in that city's Hoover High School, had a run-in with some young Mexican-Americans. One of the Chicanos had never seen such devastation as that which Bobby Falconi dealt out with his hands. But he stuck in there, took his lumps and finally went down from several lightning quick *shuto* chops that slapped consciousness from his enraged mind. A dozen years later, this young gang member — named Manuel Rivera — once again met Robert Falconi. The former was a Special Forces sergeant first class and the latter a captain in the same elite outfit.

SFC Rivera, a Black Eagle, was killed in action during the raid on the prison camp in North Vietnam in 1964.

When Falconi graduated from high school in 1952, he immediately enlisted in the army. Although his father had wanted him to opt for West Point, the young man couldn't stand the thought of being stuck in any more classrooms. In fact, he didn't even want to be an officer. During his early days on army posts he had developed several friendships among career noncommissioned officers. He liked the attitudes of these rough-and-tumble professional soldiers who drank, brawled, and fornicated with wild abandon during their off-duty time. The sergeants' devil-may-care attitude seemed much more attractive to young Robert than the heavy responsibilities that seemed to make commissioned officers and their lives so serious and, at times, tedious.

After basic and advanced infantry training, he was shipped straight into the middle of the Korean War where he was assigned to the tough 2nd Infantry Division.

He participated in two campaigns there. These were officially designated by the United States army as: *Third Korean Winter* and *Korea Summer-Fall 1953*. Robert Falconi fought and froze in those turbulent months. His combat experience ranged from holding a hill during massive attacks by crazed Chinese Communist Forces, to the deadly cat-and-mouse activities of night patrols in enemy territory.

He returned stateside with a sergeancy, the Combat Infantryman's Badge, the Purple Heart, the Silver Star, and the undeniable knowledge that he had been born and bred for just one life—that of a soldier.

His martial ambitions also had expanded. He now desired a commission but didn't want to sink himself into the curriculum of the United States Military Academy. His attitude toward schoolbooks remained the same—to hell with 'em!

At the end of his hitch in 1955, he reenlisted and applied for Infantry Officers Candidate School at Fort Benning, Georgia.

Falconi's time in OCS registered another success in his life. He excelled in all phases of the rigorous course. He recognized the need for brain work in the classrooms and soaked up the lessons through long hours of study while burning the proverbial midnight oil in quarters. The field exercises were a piece of cake for this combat veteran, but he was surprised to find out that, even there, the instructors had plenty to teach him.

His only setback occurred during "Fuck-Your-Buddy-Week." That was a phase of the curriculum in which the candidates learned responsibility. Each man's conduct—or misconduct—was passed on to an individual designated as his "buddy." If a cadet screwed up he wasn't punished. His buddy was. Thus, for the first time in many of these young men's lives, their personal conduct could bring joy or sorrow to others. Falconi's "buddy" was late to reveille one morning and he drew the demerit.

But this was the only setback in an otherwise spotless six months spent at OCS. He came out number one in his class and was offered a regular army commission. The brand new second lieutenant happily accepted the honor and set out to begin this new phase of his career in an army he had learned to love as much as his father did.

His graduation didn't result in an immediate assignment to an active duty unit. Falconi found himself once more in school—but these were not filled with hours over books. He attended jump school and earned the silver parachutist badge; next was ranger school where he won the coveted orange-and-black tab; then he was shipped down to Panama for jungle warfare school where he garnered yet one more insignia.

Following that he suffered another disappointment. Again, his desire to sink himself into a regular unit was thwarted. Because he held a regular army commission rather than a reserve one like his other classmates, Falconi was returned to Fort Benning to attend the infantry school. The courses he took were designed to give him some thorough instruction in staff procedures. He came out on top here as well, but there was another thing that happened to him.

His intellectual side finally blossomed.

The theory of military science, rather than complete practical application, began to fascinate him. During his time in combat — and the later army schooling — he had begun to develop certain theories. With the exposure to infantry school, he decided to do something about these ideas of his. He wrote several articles for the *Infantry Journal* about these thoughts — particularly on his personal analysis of the proper conduct of jungle and mountain operations involving insurgency and counterinsurgency forces.

The army was more than a little impressed with this first lieutenant (he had been promoted) and sent him back to Panama to serve on a special committee that would develop and publish official U.S. Army policy on small unit combat in tropical conditions. He honed his skills and tactical expertise during this time.

From there he volunteered for Special Forces — The Green Berets — and was accepted. After completing the officers course at Fort Bragg, North Carolina, Falconi finally was assigned to a unit. This was the 5th Special Forces Group in the growing conflict in South Vietnam.

Now a captain, he worked closely with ARVN units and even helped to organize village militias to protect hamlets against the Viet Cong and North Vietnamese. Gradually, his duties expanded until he organized and led several dangerous missions that involved deep penetration into territory controlled by the Communist guerrillas.

This activity brought him to the attention of a Central Intelligence Agency case officer named Clayton Andrews. Andrews had been doing his own bit of clandestine fighting which involved more than harassment in VC areas. His main job was the conduct of missions into North Vietnam itself. He arranged an interview with Capt. Robert Falconi to see if the officer would fit into his own sphere of activity. He found Falconi exactly the man he had been looking for. Pulling all the strings he had, Andrews saw to it that the Special Forces man was transferred to his own branch of SOG — the Special Operations Group — to begin work on a brand new project.

Capt. Robert Mikhailovich Falconi was tasked with organizing a new fighting unit to be known as the Black Eagles. This group's basic policy was to be primitive and simple: *Kill Or Be Killed*!

Their mission was to penetrate deep into the heartland of the Communist enemy to disrupt, destroyed, maim, and slay. The men who would belong to the Black Eagles would be volunteers from every branch of the armed forces. And that was to include all nationalities involved in the struggle against the Red invasion of South Vietnam.

Each man was to be an absolute expert in his particular brand of military mayhem. He had to be an expert in not only his own nation's firearms, but also those of other friendly and enemy countries. But the required knowledge in weaponry didn't stop at the modern ones. This also included knives, bludgeons, garrotes, and even crossbows when the need to deal silent death arose.

There was also a requirement for the more sophisticated and peaceful skills too. Foreign languages, land navigation, communications, medical, and even mountaineering and scuba diving were to be within the realm of knowledge of the Black Eagles.

They became the enforcement arm of SOG, drawing the missions which were the most dangerous and sensitive. In essence they were hit men, closely coordinated and completely dedicated, held together and directed through the forceful personality of their leader, Maj. Robert Falconi.

As unit integrity and morale built up, the detachment decided they wanted an insignia all their own. This wasn't at all unusual for units in Vietnam. Local manufacturers, acting on designs submitted to them by the troops involved, produced these emblems that were worn by the outfits while "in country." These adornments were strictly nonregulation and unauthorized for display outside of Vietnam.

Falconi's men came up with a unique beret badge manufactured as a cloth insignia. A larger version was used as a shoulder patch. The design consisted of a black eagle — naturally — with spread wings. Looking to its right, the big bird clutched a sword in one claw and a bolt of lightning in the other. Mounted on a khaki shield that was trimmed in black, the device was an accurate portrayal of its wearers: somber and deadly.

They even had an unofficial motto, though it wasn't part of their insignia. The statement, in Latin, was simple and quite to the point:

CALCITRA CLUNIS

It translated as "Kick Ass."

Col. Ngai Quang, a senior intelligence officer of the South Vietnamese Army, turned to his American MP escort and thanked him before stepping into Andrea Thuy's office. He smiled pleasantly at the pretty young Eurasian woman. "*Chao co*," he greeted her.

Andrea stood up behind her desk. "*Chao ong, Dai Ta Ngai*," she said. "*Ong manh gioi cho?*"

"I am fine, thank you. Is Mister Fagin in?"

"Yes, sir," Andrea said. "He is expecting you." She flipped the button on the intercom situated on her desk. "Mister Fagin, Colonel Ngai is here."

"Send him in, please," came back Fagin's voice.

Ngai waited for Andrea to open the door for him, then he walked into Fagin's inner sanctum. "Good day, Mister Fagin."

"How are you, Colonel?" Fagin said coming around his desk and offering his hand. "Nice to have you drop by again."

"I was most pleased to receive your kind invitation to do so," Ngai replied taking a chair indicated to him. "And I am most gratified by your continued friendship after our rather strained relationship in the past."

Fagin smiled. "A slight misunderstanding and a bad arrangement of priorities on my part. I really meant that apology I gave you."

"I accepted it with the same sincerity, Mister Fagin."

Andrea appeared with a tray of cups and a pitcher of hot coffee. She served the two men, then took a seat off to one side of the room.

Ngai had watched her appreciatively. "You are looking well, Lieutenant Thuy."

"*Cam on ong*," she replied.

Ngai chuckled. "Any time you grow tired of working for our illustrious and honored allies and desire to return to duty with the Vietnamese army, I hope you will consider applying for a position on my staff, Lieutenant."

"I certainly shall," Andrea said.

"Until then I shall guard her jealously," Fagin said good naturedly.

"I don't blame you a bit," Ngai remarked. He sipped his coffee waiting for Fagin to get on with the serious side of the conversation.

"We have taken your government's request to keep you informed of the activities of our special detachment, the Black Eagles, most seriously," Fagin said. "And I fully intend to follow the orders given me by my superiors involving the situation."

"We are appreciative of being kept up to date," Ngai said. "The South Vietnamese Army did not wish to be difficult, Mister Fagin. It is only that we desire to know everything — *everything* — that is going on in our country. Even those operations and missions being conducted by our good friends and allies, the Americans."

"Perfectly understandable."

"It is not only because of national pride, Mister Fagin," Ngai continued, "but we, too, have various projects we are conducting. It would be a terrible thing if we found ourselves working at cross-purposes or duplicating each other's efforts because of a silly or unnecessary lack of communication between our forces."

Fagin nodded his agreement. "And that is exactly my purpose in having you here today, Colonel. I wish to communicate to you the latest program in which our Black Eagle group is participating."

Ngai displayed his toothy grin. "Thank you."

"Major Falconi and his men, because of the horrendous casualties they have sustained during the four operations they conducted in enemy territory, have been removed from further similar missions. We feel they are a bit ineffective at the moment in that line of endeavor.

Therefore, we have assigned those seven surviving men the less arduous task of participating in a recently planned effort of ridding Saigon of certain criminal elements in which Americans have become involved."

Ngai continued to smile, but there was a hint of suspicion in his eyes. "I see."

"Of course this isn't an independent action on our part," Fagin said. "We are doing this in cooperation with your national police. As a matter of fact, we completely wiped out a drug peddling headquarters the other day."

"An early success in your endeavor, hey?" Ngai said.

"Yes. Of course we would have submitted a full report on the effort, but Colonel Tran—excuse me, do you know him?"

"Yes," Ngai answered coldly. "He is on Gen. Nguyen Ngoc Loan's staff."

"Correct, Colonel. At any rate, any information you desire will be given you through his office," Fagin said.

"But our arrangements were for *you* to keep us informed," Ngai insisted.

Fagin smiled. "Sorry. You'll have to take that up with Colonel Tran. This was at his insistence."

Ngai set his coffee cup down and stood up. His face showed some strain. "Thank you for this information. I'm afraid this is a very busy day for me. Good day, Mister Fagin." He turned to Andrea. "*Chao co, Trung Uy* Thuy."

Andrea lowered her eyes in the proper feminine manner. "*Chao ong, Dai Ta* Ngai."

The Vietnamese officer made a hurried exit leaving the two sitting there. Fagin chuckled and slapped his hands together. "That ought to be a bee in that son of a bitch's bonnet."

Andrea was not as cheerful. "Be careful, Chuck. He is a dangerous man and will be most suspicious at this point."

"Well, his suspicions just might end up being the death of him," Fagin said.

"Or Robert Falconi and the Black Eagles," Andrea warned him. She picked up the pot. "Care for more coffee?"

It was early evening, with the sun beginning to set, as Matsuno's chauffeur sat in the car he had parked by the curb a scant twenty minutes previously. The man, named Kaji, was not driving the Cadillac limousine as he usually did. Instead he had taken a rather inobtrusive Volkswagen Bug that was kept in a small garage on the Matsuno estate. Kaminatake, the ex-*sumotori,* sat in the back, his huge body filling out the entire rear seat.

Kaminatake rubbed his hand across his new, short haircut. The topknot of the sumo had been snipped away by Matsuno's personal barber. Now the big man wore his hair in a short style similar to the American "flat-top."

"There they are now," Kaji whispered, pointing to an alleyway located fifty meters away. "The three scum are making their appearance for their evening customers."

Kaminatake peered through the gloom, making out the figures of the men. "Those are the peddlers who have cheated Matsuno-san?" he asked.

"Yes. I know them well."

"Then I shall tend to my duties." Nimble and graceful despite his great size, Kaminatake eased quickly out of the small car and gently closed the door. Then he strolled leisurely toward the three men.

The trio caught sight of him coming and watched with curiosity as the human hulk approached them. The taller, a skinny, bug-eyed type, bowed slightly. "*Konnichi wa.*"

Kaminatake smiled back. "*Komban wa.* I wish to conduct business with you."

The three eagerly closed in on him. They looked up and

down the street to make sure no one was watching. The tall, skinny one did the talking. "You wish to buy some of our wares? Hashish or opium, perhaps?"

"Oh, no," Kaminatake said. Suddenly his huge right hand shot out and grabbed the man by the face. "I am here to collect money that you owe Matsuno-san."

"*He!* Let me go!" Skinny said with some difficulty.

One of his friends immediately launched an attack, but Kaminatake threw an arm into his face with such force that a spray of blood speckled scarlet drops over all four men in the alleyway. The narcotics peddler collapsed to the pavement.

The third man, believing fervently in avoiding violence with men who stood a foot taller than he and outweighed him by two hundred pounds, streaked away into the darkness.

Kaminatake caught Skinny's movement in time to reach out and grab the man's right wrist. He snapped it over and broke it, the knife clattering to the pavement. "I'll take the money now," he said.

"*Atchi ni itte kudasai!*" Skinny implored.

"Certainly. I shall go away as soon as you give me Matsuno-san's money." Kaminatake said.

"I — I haven't — got — it!" Skinny said through his pinched face. "*O-kane o wasure-mashita.*"

"Forgot your money, eh?" Kaminatake snarled. He tightened his big ham of a fist over the other man's face. Tighter — tighter — tighter — then pop!

The jaw snapped loose at the hinge and hung in place by cartilage and muscle.

Skinny wanted to scream out his agony, but it was impossible with the huge hand smothering him.

"You will get the money to Matsuno-san before this time tomorrow evening," Kaminatake announced. He eased up the pressure somewhat. "Or I shall return to visit you again."

"*Hai!*" Skinny hissed through his tortured mouth.

Kaminatake dropped him to the alley, then turned and trod lightly back to the Volkswagen. He slipped almost daintily into the vehicle. "He will have the money to Matsuno-san within twenty-four hours."

Kaji grinned and nodded. "*Hai. Watashi motsu-masen utagi.* I have no doubt!"

Then he started the engine and pulled away from the curb for the long drive back to Matsuno's mansion.

CHAPTER FIVE

Andrea Thuy stood in front of Chuck Fagin's desk, impatiently tapping her foot on the floor. "Well?"

"I'm thinking — I'm thinking!" he exclaimed in irritation.

"There's already been enough time for that," Andrea told him. "And the situation has changed. You must admit that."

"I'm not sure it has," Fagin said. "And that's what's bothering me."

"I should be working with them," Andrea said. "Now there's no reason for me not to."

"Oh, yes there is, young lady!" Fagin insisted. "And you know exactly why."

"Falconi and I haven't been lovers for months," Andrea said. "So the affair's over and done with."

"I'm not convinced of that at all." Fagin was not particularly happy to have been suddenly caught in an argument that had been going on between them for the previous several months.

"When the Central Intelligence Agency had me taken to Langley for all that training, they certainly didn't mean for me to come back here and be your secretary," Andrea said.

"You're much more than that and you know it, for Chris-

' sake," Fagin said. "Your official title isn't bullshit. You're the coordinating and operations officer for the Black Eagle activities of SOG. And that is exactly what you do."

"But that hardly reflects on my past performances," Andrea said. "I've assassinated three officers of the North Vietnamese Army, a Russian propaganda official, and two Reds in Laos and Cambodia. And let's not forget my participation in combat with the Black Eagles on their first mission."

"I know, Andrea," Fagin said. "But your usefulness faded the minute you hopped into the sack with Robert Falconi. It would be ludicrous for any sane and logical case officer to have you two working together after that."

"Damn it!" Andrea said under her breath. She knew that falling in love with the Black Eagles' commander had not been a smart thing to do. But a woman—even one who is a dedicated agent against Communism—is forever fighting with her emotions. Her romance with Falconi had been the result of losing just such a battle with her heart.

She would never forget that one and only time she'd let her defenses down and had become a woman in love.

It had started out as a simple date for dinner and some dancing. It seemed like a normal thing to do. After all, they had been working closely together in the formulation and preparation for Operation Hanoi Hellground. She'd accepted Falconi's request to go on the town with him out of a desire to know him better and, she had to admit, because of a growing sexual attraction for the American officer.

They'd headed for their evening of diversion dressed as civilians with the expressed desire to forget the war for awhile and simply enjoy themselves. The date evolved through a quiet dinner to some dancing and finally—a small room in a backstreet hotel where she'd succumbed happily to his lovemaking.

Their *liaison d'amour* was interrupted by a phone call. Falconi had cursed the order to always let MACV-SOG be aware of his exact location. The lovers had to hurriedly dress to return to Peterson Field to go into the isolation phase of what was to become the Black Eagles' first mission.

They had managed to keep their coupling to themselves until their return from the mission. But their solicitous caring and affection for each other became apparent to everyone concerned.

Clayton Andrews, when he was promoted upward from the Black Eagles' CIA case officer and replaced by Chuck Fagin, had informed the new man of the relationship between the detachment commander and the beautiful Andrea Thuy.

Fagin had made a quick and logical decision. A love affair involving operatives was the absolute worst thing that could happen between them. He'd immediately pulled Andrea off active ops and put her into a paperwork position in his own office.

Now Andrea wanted her old status back. She seethed for action. Fagin's first reaction was to refuse her request. But the situation was a bit different now. The Black Eagles were operating right under his nose here in Saigon.

Fagin looked up at Andrea. "I'll give it some real serious thought and get back to you, okay?"

"Okay," Andrea answered sullenly. Then she went back to her desk.

Andrea Thuy, a first lieutenant in the South Vietnamese Army, was a beautiful Eurasian woman in her mid-twenties. Five feet, six-inches tall, she was svelte and trim, yet had large breasts and shapely hips and thighs that rounded out even her uniforms with a provocative shape.

Andrea was born in a village west of Hanoi in the late 1940s. Her father, Doctor Gaston Roget, was a lay missionary physician of the Catholic church. Deeply devoted to his native patients, the man served a large area of northern French Indochina in a dedicated, unselfish manner. The man did not stint a bit in the giving of himself and his professional talents.

He had met Andrea's mother just after the young woman had completed her nurse's training in Hanoi. Despite the difference in the ages—the doctor by then was 48 years old—the two fell in love and were married. This blending of East and West produced a most beautiful child, young Andrea Roget.

Andrea's life was one of happiness. The village where she lived was devoted to *Bac-si* Gaston, as they called her father, and this respect was passed on to the man's wife and child. When the first hint of a Communist uprising brushed across the land, the good people of this hamlet rejected it out of hand. The propaganda the Reds vomited out did not fit when applied to the case of the gentle French doctor who devoted his time to looking after them.

This repudiation of their ideals could not be ignored by the fanatic Communist movement, so the local Red guerrilla unit made a call on the people who would not follow the line of political philosophy they taught. To make the matter even more insidious, these agents of Soviet imperialism had hidden the true aims of their organization within the wrappings of a so-called nationalization movement. Many freedom-loving Indochinese fervently wanted the French out of their country so they could enjoy independence. They were among the first to fall for the trickery of the Communist revolution.

When the Red Viet Minh came to the village, they had no intention of devoting the visit to pacification or even of winning the hearts and minds of the populace. They had come to make examples of areas of the population who rejected them—they had come to kill and destroy.

Little Andrea Roget was only three years old at the time, but she would remember the rapine and slaughter the Red soldiers inflicted on the innocent people. Disturbing dreams and nightmares would bring back the horrible incident even into her adulthood and the girl would recall the day with horror and revulsion.

The first people to die were *Docteur* and *Madame* Roget. Shot down before their infant daughter's eyes, the little girl could barely comprehend what had happened to her parents. Then the slaughter was turned on the village men. Shot down in groups, the piles of dead grew around the huts.

Then it was the women's turn for their specific lesson in Communist mercy and justice.

Hours of rape and torment went on before the females were herded together in one large group. The Soviet burp guns chattered like squawking birds of death as swarms of steel-jacketed 7.63 millimeter slugs slammed into living flesh.

Then the village was burned while the wounded who had survived the first fusillades were flung screaming into the flames. When they tried to climb out of the inferno, they met the bayonets of the "liberators."

Finally, after this last outrage, the Communist soldiery marched off singing the songs of their revolution.

It was several hours after the carnage that the French paratroopers showed up. They had received word of the crime from a young man who lived in a nearby village. He had come to see Doctor Roget regarding treatment for an ulcerated leg. After the youth had heard the shooting while approaching the hamlet, he'd sneaked up for a quick look. When the young Indochinese perceived the horror, he had limped painfully on his bad leg the fifty kilometers to the nearest military post.

The paratroopers, when they arrived, were shocked. These combat veterans had seen atrocities before. They had endured having their own people taken hostage to be executed by the Gestapo. But even the savagery of the massacre of this inconsequential little village was of such magnitude they could scarcely believe their eyes.

The commanding officer looked around at the devastation and shook his head. *"Le SS peut prendre une lecon des cettes bêtes*—the SS could take a lesson from these beasts!"

The French *paras* searched through the smoking ruins, pulling the charred corpses out for a decent burial. One grizzled trooper, his face covered with three days' growth of beard, stumbled across a little girl who had miraculously been overlooked during the murderous binge of the Viet Minh. He knelt down beside her, his tenderest feelings brought to the surface from the sight of the pathetic, beautiful child. He stroked her cheek gently, then took her in his brawny arms and stood up.

"Oh, *pauvre enfante*," he cooed to her. "We will take you away from all this *horreur*." The paratrooper carried the little girl through the ravaged village to the road where a convoy of secondhand U.S. Army trucks waited. These vehicles, barely useable, were kept running through the desperate inventiveness of mechanics who had only the barest essentials in the way of tools and parts. But, for the French who fought this thankless war, that was only par for the course.

Little Andrea sat in the lap of the commanding officer during the tedious trip into Hanoi. The column had to halt periodically to check the road ahead for mines. There was also an ambush by the Viet Minh in which the child was protected by being laid in a ditch while the short but fierce battle was fought until the attackers broke off the fight and turned away.

Upon arriving in Hanoi, the *paras* followed the usual procedure for war orphans and turned the girl over to a Catholic orphanage. This institution, run by the *Soeurs de la Charite*—the Sisters of Charity—did their best to check out Andrea's background. But all records in the home village had been destroyed, and the child could say only her first name. She hadn't quite learned her last name, so all that could be garnered from her baby-talk was the name "Andrea." She had inherited most of her looks from her mother, hence she had a decidedly Oriental appearance. The nuns did not perceive the girl had French blood. Thus Andrea Roget was given a Vietnamese name and became listed officially as Andrea Thuy.

Her remaining childhood at the orphanage was happy. She pushed the horrible memories of the Viet Minh raid back into her subconscious, concentrating on her new life. Andrea grew tall and beautiful, getting an excellent education and also learning responsibility and leadership. Parentless children were constantly showing up at the orphanage and Andrea, when she reached her teens, did her part in taking care of them. This important task was expanded from the normal care and feeding of the children to teaching school. Andrea was a brilliant student and plans were made to send her to France where she would undoubtedly be able to earn a university degree.

But Dien Bien Phu fell in 1954.

Once again, the war had touched her life with insidious cruelty. The orphanage in Hanoi had to be closed when that city became part of Communist North Vietnam. The gentle *Soeurs de la Charite* took their charges and moved south to organize a new orphanage in Attopeu, Laos.

Despite this disruption in her education, Andrea did not stop growing physically and spiritually. She was a happy young girl, approaching womanhood, being loved and loving in return as she performed her tasks with the unfortunate waifs at the orphanage.

Then the Pathet Lao came.

These zealots made the Viet Minh look like Sunday school teachers. Wild, fanatical, and uncivilized, these devotees of Marxism knew no limits in their warmaking. Capable of unspeakable cruelty and displaying incredible savagery and stupidity, they were so terrible that they won not one convert in any of the areas they conquered.

Andrea was fifteen years old when the orphanage was raided. This time there was no chance for her to be overlooked or considered too inconsequential for torment. She, like all the older girls and the nuns, were ravished countless times in the screaming orgy. When the rapine finally ended, the Pathet Lao set the mission's buildings on fire. But this wasn't the end of their "fun."

The nuns, because they were Europeans, were murdered. Naked, raped and shamed, the pitiable women were flung alive into the flames. This same outrage, as committed by the Viet Minh, awakened the memory of the terrible event for Andrea. She went into shock as the murder of the nuns continued.

Some screamed, but most prayed, as they endured their horrible deaths. Andrea, whose Oriental features still overshadowed her French ancestry, was thought to be just another native orphan.

She endured one more round of raping with the other girls, then the Pathet Lao, having scored another victory for Communism, gathered up their gear and loot to march away to the next site in their campaign of Marxist expansionism.

Andrea gathered the surviving children around her. With the nuns now gone, she was the leader of their pathetic group. Instinct told her to move south. To the north were the Red marauders and their homeland. Whatever lay in the opposite direction had to be better. She could barely remember the gruff kindness of the French paratroopers, but she did recall they went south. Andrea didn't know if these same men would be there or not, but it was worth the effort.

The journey she took the other children on was long and arduous. Short of food, the little column moved south through the jungle eating wild fruit and roots. For two weeks Andrea tended her flock, sometimes carrying a little one until her arms ached with the effort. She comforted them and soothed their fears as best she could. She kept up their hope by telling them of the kind people who awaited them at the end of the long trail.

Two weeks after leaving the orphanage, Andrea sighted a patrol of soldiers. Her first reaction was of fear and alarm, but the situation of the children was so desperate that she had to take a chance and contact the troops. After making sure the children had concealed themselves in the dense foliage, Andrea approached the soldiers. If they were going to rape her, she figured, they would have their fun but never know the orphans were concealed nearby. Timidly, the young girl moved out onto the trail in front of them. With her lips trembling, she bowed and spoke softly.

"*Chao ong.*"

The lead soldier, startled by her unexpected appearance, had almost shot her. He relaxed a bit as he directed his friends to watch the surrounding jungle in case this was part of an insidious Viet Cong trick. He smiled back at the girl. "*Chao co*. What can I do for you?"

Andrea swallowed nervously, but felt better when she noted there was no red star insignia on his uniform. Then she launched into a spiel about the nuns, the orphanage — everything. When the other soldiers approached and, quite obviously meant her no harm, she breathed a quiet prayer of thanks under her breath.

She and the children were safe at last.

These troops, who were from the South Vietnamese Army, took the little refugees back to their detachment commander. This young lieutenant followed standard practice for such situations and made arrangements to transport Andrea and her charges farther back to higher headquarters for interrogation and eventual relocation in a safe area.

Andrea was given a thorough interview with a South Vietnamese intelligence officer. He was pleased to learn that the girl was not only well acquainted with areas now under occupation by Communist troops, but was also fluent in the

Vietnamese, Laotian and French languages. He passed this information on to other members of his headquarters staff for discussion as to Andrea's potential as an agent. After a lengthy conversation among themselves, it was agreed to keep her in the garrison after sending the other orphans to Saigon.

Andrea waited there while a thorough background investigation was conducted on her past life. They delved so deeply into the information available on her that each item of intelligence seemed to lead to another until they discovered the truth that even she didn't know. She was a Eurasian, and her father was a Frenchman—*Monsieur le Docteur* Gaston Roget.

This led to the girl being taken to an even higher ranking officer for her final phase of questioning. He was a kindly appearing colonel who saw to it that the girl was given her favorite cold drink—an iced Coca-Cola—before he began speaking with her.

"You have seen much of Communism, Andrea," he said. "Tell me, *ma chere*, what is your opinion of the Viet Minh, Viet Cong, and Pathet Lao?"

Andrea took a sip of her drink then pointed at the man's pistol in the holster on his hip. "Let me have your gun, *Monsieur*, and I will kill every one of them!'

"I'm afraid that would be impossible," the colonel said. "Even a big soldier could not kill all of them by himself. But there is another way you can fight them."

Andrea, eager, leaned forward. "How, *monsieur*?"

"You have some very unusual talents and bits of knowledge, Andrea," the colonel said. "Those things, when combined with others that we could teach you, would make you a most effective fighter against the Communists."

"What could you teach me, *monsieur*?" Andrea asked.

"Well, for example, you know three languages. Would you like to learn more? Thai, Japanese, possibly English?"

"If that would help me kill Pathet Lao and Viet Cong,"

Andrea said, "then I want to learn. But I don't understand how that would do anything to destroy those Red devils."

"There would be skills you could learn—along with others—that would enable you to go into their midst and do mischief and harm to them," the colonel said. "But learning these things would be difficult and unpleasant at times."

"What could be more difficult and more unpleasant than what I've already been through?" Andrea asked.

"A good point," the colonel said. He recognized the maturity in the young girl and decided to speak to her as an adult. "When would you like to begin this new phase of your education, *mademoiselle*?"

"Now! Today!" Andrea cried, getting to her feet.

"I am sorry, *mademoiselle*," the colonel said with a smile. "You will have to wait until tomorrow morning."

The next day's training was the first of two solid years of intensified schooling. Because of being able to mask her true identity, South Vietnamese intelligence decided to have her retain the name Thuy—as the *Soeurs de la Charite* had named her.

Andrea acquired more languages along with unusual skills necessary in the dangerous profession she had chosen for herself. Besides disguises and a practice at mimicking various accents and dialects, the fast-maturing girl picked up various methods of killing people. These included poisons and drugs, easily concealable weapons, and the less subtle methods of blowing an adversary to bits with plastic explosive. After each long day of training, Andrea concluded her schedule by poring over books of mug shots showing the faces and identities of Communist leaders and officials up in the north.

Finally, with her deadly education completed, seventeen-year-old Andrea Thuy *nee* Roget, went out into the cold.

During two years of operations, she assassinated four top Red bigwigs. Her devotion to their destruction was to the extent that she was even willing to use her body if it would lower their guard and aid her in gaining their confidence. Once that was done, Andrea displayed absolutely no reluctance in administering the *coup de grace* to put an end to their efforts at spreading world socialism.

When the American involvement in South Vietnam stepped up, a Central Intelligence Agency case officer named Clayton Andrews learned of this unusual young woman and her deadly talents. Andrews had been tasked with creating an elite killer/raider outfit. After learning of Andrea, he knew he wanted her to be a part of this crack team. Using his influence and talents of persuasion, he saw to it that the beautiful female operative was sent to Langley Air Force Base in Virginia to the special CIA school located there.

When the Americans finished honing her fangs at Langley, she returned to South Vietnam and was put into another job category. Commissioned a lieutenant in the ARVN, she was appointed a temporary major and assigned to Special Operations Group's Black Eagles Detachment which was under the command of Robert Falconi.

Andrea accompanied the Black Eagles on their first mission. This operation, named Hanoi Hellground, was a direct action type against a Red whorehouse and pleasure palace deep within North Vietnam. Andrea participated in the deadly combat which resulted, carrying her own weight and then some, in the fire fights that erupted in the green hell of the jungle. There was not a Black Eagle who would deny she had been superlative in the performance of her duties.

But she soon fell out of grace.

Not because of cowardice, sloppy work, or inefficiency, but as the result of that one thing that seems to be able to disarm any woman—love. She went head-over-heels into it with Robert Falconi.

Clayton Andrews was promoted upstairs and his place was taken by another CIA case officer. This one, named

Chuck Fagin, found he had inherited a damned good outfit except that its commander and one of the operatives were involved in a red-hot romance. An emotional entanglement like that spells disaster with a capital "D" in the espionage and intelligence business.

Fagin had no choice but to pull Andrea out of active ops. He had her put in his office as the administrative director. Andrea knew that the decision was the right one. She would have done the same thing. She or Falconi might have lost their heads and pulled something emotional or thoughtless if either one had suddenly been placed into a dangerous situation. That sort of illogical condition could have led not only to their own deaths, but to the demise of other Black Eagles as well.

But now, with Maj. Robert Falconi and his men back in Saigon, it looked as if things had evolved to the point Andrea would be able to once again take an active part in their operations.

And this was an opportunity she wasn't going to let pass — even if it killed her.

Col. Ngai Quang, a senior intelligence officer in the South Vietnamese general staff, wore civilian clothes as he sat in Tsing Chai's smoky mah jongg parlor. Despite the fact he was very angry after his visit with the American CIA man Chuck Fagin, he gave his full concentration to the gambling he was involved in.

He studied his opponents across the table from him. To his left was a fat Vietnamese. The man sweated profusely with each roll of the dice, playing his tiles as if each movement caused him physical agony.

To Ngai's right was a Pakistani. His incredibly dark face was in stark contrast to the brilliant white of his shirt. The only show of emotion he allowed himself was a slight twitch of his heavy, black moustache. Ngai wondered how the game, a favorite of Orientals, had attracted this foreigner.

Directly across from the colonel was a skinny little Chinese man of indeterminate age. Bald, with a wispy moustache, the oldster kept the same silly smile on his face whether he won or lost. At this point in the game he was East Wind which meant if he won, the other players had to pay him double. On the other hand, if another player mah jongged, the Chinese gentleman would be required to pay *him* double. Either way didn't seem to bother the oldster a bit.

Ngai carefully planned his strategy as he surveyed the tiles in front of him. Unable to draw the right combination to make his sets, he felt frustrated. Especially in a high-stakes game like this one. He discarded a two-of-bamboo.

"Ah!" The old Chinese gentleman hissed the exclamation and immediately claimed the tile. Then he flipped his over to display a complete hand—four sets and a pair.

The Vietnamese groaned softly and the Pakistani bared his teeth. Ngai, showing no emotion, pulled out his wallet and forked over a hundred and fifty thousand piasters.

Then, wordlessly, the quartet of players shoved all the tiles to the center of the table and began shuffling them for the next game. Now the Pakistani was the East Wind.

Ngai began stacking his hand when a figure walked up behind him. The man was one of the parlor's bouncers. "Excuse me, please, Colonel Ngai. Master Tsing is in his office now."

Ngai hated to leave the game. He was almost a quarter of a million behind at that point. But he had no choice. He stood up and bowed slightly to the others. "I regret I must leave you now," he said. "Pressing business."

He no sooner made his exit than a spectator, eager to get in on the play, slid into his chair.

Ngai followed the bouncer off the gaming floor, through a curtained exit that led down a corridor. They stopped in front of a door. The houseman knocked lightly. "Colonel

Ngai is here," he announced through a small opening.

The heavy portal swung open to reveal another husky Vietnamese man. He bowed to Ngai and motioned him to enter.

Ngai stepped into the room. Tsing Chai was seated at his desk. His wide, moon face was lit with a delighted smile. He wore a silk kimono, a pillbox Chinese hat perched on his head. He greeted Ngai by standing up and holding his hands out in a welcoming gesture.

"So good to see you, *Dai Ta* Ngai."

"*Cam on ong,*" Ngai said. "*Ong manh gioi cho?*"

"Fine, thank you," Tsing replied. He motioned to a chair in front of his desk. "Please sit down. Would you care for some tea?"

"*Cam on ong,*" Ngai said.

Tea was served to the two men, then they were left alone. Tsing took a delicate sip from the small cup he held in his pudgy hand. Then he set it down. "Your message said you had most important information."

"Yes," Ngai said. "Important and surprising."

"It involves, of course, our nemesis, the Black Eagles."

"Yes," Ngai said. "They have been pulled from active operations."

Tsing shrugged. "While there may be some importance applied to that, it is not surprising. The capitalist swine have been through much."

"You are assuming they are on a period of rest," Ngai said. "But that isn't the case."

"If they are not involved in raids into the Workers' and Peasants' Paradise, what else would they be doing?" Tsing asked.

"I have been informed that they are operating against criminal organizations here in Saigon in which Americans are involved," Ngai answered.

Tsing laughed. "Most interesting. But I see no problem there." He paused and looked closely at Ngai. "But on second thought — will you still be kept up-to-date on their activities?"

"Alas, no," Ngai said. "They are working directly under Colonel Tran of the National Police."

"Tran?"

"Yes. And it was your men who killed one of his sergeants only a few weeks previously," Ngai reminded him. "A most unwise move—"

"Never mind your comments!" Tsing snapped. "I deal with my own men and take care of their discipline as I see fit."

Ngai's voice was cold. "This problem is undeniably your fault, Master Tsing."

"How were we to know the man had been infiltrated into my organization by Tran?" Tsing demanded. "If you had kept on top of the situation, we would have been aware of this."

"I kept track of the Black Eagles as I was instructed," Ngai said. "There is no way I can compel the Central Intelligence Agency to reveal their plans with the National Police to me."

"It doesn't matter," Tsing said. "What has happened cannot be changed. But we must know if the Black Eagles are truly operating against local crime or are using this as a ploy to move in closer on me and my organization."

"The Black Eagles CIA man has taken advantage of this new activity. Now he is no longer under obligation to make periodical reports to me involving Falconi and his men," Ngai said. "Particularly in light of working hand-in-hand with our police. Unfortunately there is no way to know their true motives."

Tsing smiled. "You are not to worry, Colonel. The Communist espionage system is quite capable of dealing with Major Falconi and the Black Eagles. In fact, I hope he *is* using this as a ploy to move in on us. It will be that much easier to destroy them once and for all."

"But how?" Ngai demanded.

"Pardon me for repeating myself," Tsing said now smiling again, "but do not worry yourself. I will set the wheels of destruction into motion immediately."

Ngain stood up. "I am relieved. I hope I can be of service. I have much at stake here too."

Tsing was suddenly more sympathetic. "Of course you do, my dear *Dai Ta* Ngai. But you aren't the one who is going to die — it is Maj. Robert Falconi who is now close to his death."

CHAPTER SIX

Once again the dawning sun cast long shadows over the convoy of civilian autos that traveled slowly down a Saigon side street.

Maj. Robert Falconi and Sgt. Chin Han occupied the first car. Their men were divided up among the other three that followed. Again attired in civilian clothing, the Falcon was beginning to get used to that particular mode of dress. He also liked the idea of a hot shower every night, three square meals a day, and a bare minimum of eight hours of sleep—ten if he wanted it. Rested, well-fed and alert, he felt eager and a bit aggressive.

The difference between this particular raid they were about to commence, and the former, was that they carried M16 rifles besides the .45 autos they packed.

"Only one American involved in this set-up we're hitting, hey?" Falcon remarked to Chin.

The National Police sergeant nodded. "Right, Major. It's a Chinese organization—I should say Hong Kong—and their contact and bag man is an American sailor. Our surveillance crews say he's here at the Saigon headquarters. We nab the baddies from the Crown Colony and you get the

Yank."

"Or whatever is left of him," Falconi said. "These guys of mine seem to be in a mood to play rough."

"All well and good," Chin said. "That's exactly what it's going to take to handle this situation. The Hong Kong thugs are—as you Americans would say—real bad asses."

"And we're ready for 'em."

"Good," Chin said. "Because they're probably ready for you."

The sergeant slowed the car and eased it over to the curb before braking to a stop. He and the Falcon got out and waited for the rest of the raiding crew to join them.

The prospect for action ahead of them would not be so contained as before. Although their quarry occupied only a single one-storied building, it was a huge affair and offered access to countless alleys and side streets. Thus, the operation required a lot of coordination and prior planning.

Several squads of national policemen had already moved into position to block off any escape routes out of the neighborhood. Sergeant Chin had described that as a distinct advantage.

Archie Dobbs wasn't so sure. "It's about as advantageous as cornering a grizzly bear in a dark cave," he remarked.

"And about as much fun," Calvin Culpepper added with an ominous ring in his voice.

But, no matter the risk, the Black Eagles Detachment was a hundred per cent strong as they took their positions and waited for Chin to give the signal to begin their urban attack.

The group silently gathered into their two-man teams, rifles ready, peering back and forth from the target area to the Vietnamese police sergeant. Finally Chin nodded and motioned them to move forward.

The Falcon and Archie dogged Chin's heels as he rushed across the street to the tin-roofed building. When Chin reached the front entrance of the building, he raised his rifle and pulled the trigger. With the selector on full automatic, the slugs crashed into the door, blowing it wide open. Archie excited as always, leaped forward and beat the other two into the interior.

He rushed down a long corridor and stopped at the first room. One heavy crash of the rifle butt against the door was enough to knock it open.

The Chinese gangster behind it hadn't been caught asleep.

A shuriken fighting star whirled through the air. Archie barely managed to raise his weapon up in front of his throat in time for the killing instrument to bury itself in the rifle's stock.

Falconi was quick enough to prevent a second assault by snap shooting three quick times. The gangster hit the floor with a shuriken still clutched in his dying hand. Although torn up badly, he made a weak effort to heave it. The star only bounced to the floor.

Archie picked it up. "Might come in handy," he remarked.

"Yeah," Falconi said. "Let's go."

The two went back into the hallway and joined the attack. Now gunfire had broken out up ahead of them and they hurried to join the fight.

Malpractice McCorckel and Lightfingers O'Quinn were at the apex of the attack. Both were more used to the type of fighting encountered in dense jungle, but they unconsciously adapted quickly to this environment within wooden walls.

Lightfingers caught a movement from a room. "Drop!" he yelled.

Malpractice, being well accustomed to taking such imperatives seriously from his friends, went instantly to the floor without so much as a questioning glance. Lightfingers pumped the trigger of the M16, the slugs flying into two half-dressed Chinese punks. Both spun and crashed together under the bullets' impact and fell to the floor in a bloody heap.

Malpractice made sure the situation was under control by firing a couple of more rounds into each of them. "Glad you seen them guys," he yelled over the din of shooting.

"Yeah," Lightfingers agreed. "They was gonna wait 'til we passed by then jump outta the room and let us have it in the back."

Master Sergeant Gordon and Calvin Culpepper were assigned to cover the outside of the building in the back. When the others charged into the interior, they rushed around the side to cover the windows.

The pair had no sooner settled down when glass flew out followed by the chair that had been heaved through the pane. A split second later, a lanky Caucasian dove through the opening he'd made for himself. He hit the alley dirt and rolled to his feet.

"Hold it!" Top yelled.

The guy stopped and looked at him. Then he grinned. "Goddamn! Americans! Boy, am I glad to see you guys."

"Just take it easy," Calvin said. "Ease on over here and keep your hands up."

"Hey, guys, those bastards had me locked up in there," the American said. "They grabbed me for turning in a doper to my ship's officers. He was dealing for these assholes. Lighten up, huh? I been through a lot of shit lately."

"We're real sorry about that," Top said. "But until everything gets sorted out, you'll forgive our lack of trust, won't you?"

The man laughed. "Sure. I'm just glad —" His hand flew behind him and instantly reappeared with a Smith & Wesson .38 revolver. "Motherfuckers!" He fired quickly — too quickly, and missed.

Calvin, his M16 at waist level, cut loose on automatic. Before he eased back off the trigger some eight rounds had flown from the muzzle. Five of them zipped into the American and slapped him into a couple of pieces.

The two piles of meat and red goop collapsed to the alley.

"Oooh, shit!" Calvin said in horror. "I wasn't expectin' that!"

"Calvin," Top said calmly. "I don't think that sonofabitch was either." He looked down at the man's face, the features blanched by the sudden draining of blood from the torso and head. "This must be the American involved with the gang."

Archie Dobbs' face suddenly appeared in the broken window. "Hey!" he yelled at them. "A guy just jumped through here. Did you—" He saw the mangled cadaver in the alley. "Ugh! Who the hell did that?"

Calvin swallowed weakly. "I did."

"Man," Archie said in wonderment. "You sure do play rough."

Then his face disappeared back into the building.

Not far from where Falconi and Archie now searched for hidden gangsters, Chun Kim was going through doors in his own style.

This consisted of first hitting the door knob with a *deet-bal-dem-chi* kick. If the door were unlocked it simply flew off its hinges and bounced into the room. If it were locked, it didn't go quite so far.

The South Korean marine's next course of action was to fire a fusillade of shots, then go in and see if there were many survivors.

There never were.

Kim's visit to four rooms left nine dead Chinese criminals sprawled across the bloody floors. He truly believed in the Black Eagles motto—"Kick ass!"

Falconi and Archie once again worked their way to the vanguard of the attack through the large building. Archie, panting beside his commander, started to complain.

"How come these sumbitches don't hole up in smaller places, Skipper?"

"It's all a plot, Archie," Falconi explained. "The entire underworld in the Southeast Asia has been designed to be a personal pain in the ass to you."

Archie cradled the M16 and pulled his .45 auto. He aimed the pistol toward the next door on their schedule and pulled the trigger. The metal knob spun off in the thundering report with a shower of sparks.

Falconi rushed past Archie, hitting the door in midstride. The wood gave way as it crashed into a man on the other side. This unfortunate went down under the splintered portal with the Falcon standing on top.

Another Chinese, however, was better prepared.

He leaped toward the American with a *jeh-teh* kick which Falconi recognized as Choy-lay-fut Kung Fu, a Chinese martial art. The leader of the Black Eagles threw up a forearm and took the bruising contact. Luckily, muscle absorbed most of the blow, but it hurt like hell.

The Chinese wasn't standing still at this time though. He threw a *ming-chuan* punch which caused Falconi to duck off to the side. The gangster followed through the attack by spinning completely around and confronting Archie as he stepped into the room.

An elbow *go-dar* blow hit the Black Eagle and he went down, his face displaying a silly grin and rolling eyeballs.

Falconi, noting that Archie would be of absolutely no help to him in his present unconscious state, went on the attack. He faked a groin kick, pulled it back and closed in for what seemed an obvious forearm smash to the face.

Instead, the Falcon drove his knee up to catch the Chinese's open crotch. But the man had danced lightly out of the way.

Then he charged again.

Falconi met the attack and was sent flying across the room to crash into the wall. It made him mad. He grimaced at the waiting Oriental. "Goddamnit! Every time I come on one of these raids, some asshole slams me around the room."

The gangster slowly and deliberately assumed a graceful *gung-bo* position, then launched himself through the open space. But Falconi wasn't there anymore. This time it was the Chinese who became violently acquainted with the wall. He hit it hard, but spun and, though dazed, prepared to continue the fight.

Archie, recovering slightly, got to his feet but was so dizzy he staggered forward. Unfortunately he did this at the exact time Falconi made his next attack. Caught between his commanding officer and the Chinese criminal, Archie took the best both could dish out.

He wheezed once and hit the floor like a sack of sand.

Falconi didn't waste a beat. He threw a *shuto* that slipped in deftly under the gangster's chin and mashed his adam's apple like a squashed peach.

Unable to breathe, and drowning in his own blood now, the man grasped his injured neck and sank to his knees in agony. He looked up once at the Falcon, his hate as vivid as ever—then he died, collapsing in dignity after the final fight of his life.

Falconi walked over and helped Archie to his feet. He supported him as they walked outside. Archie's head rang like a bell for a full five minutes before he finally regained his senses. When he came to, Archie wiped at his watering eyes.

"Oooh, God. Is it over, Skipper?"

Falconi looked around. "Seems to be."

Archie shook his head gently until his vision cleared some more. He glanced at the other Black Eagles and Vietnamese police dragging the cadavers of the Chinese gang outside to lay them in a neat row.

"Y'know, Skipper," Archie said gazing at the dead men, "We oughta try to *arrest* some o' those jokers from time to time."

The dry cleaning truck, its horn honking, eased through the pedestrians and pedicabs, then pulled up in front of Tsing Chai's mah jongg parlor.

The driver, a short, thin Vietnamese, got out and scurried around to the back doors. The sign on the vehicle proclaimed it as being from the dry cleaning plant at Tan Son Nhut Air Base. This establishment, much superior to even downtown Saigon cleaners, had a large list of clientele in the wealthier segments of the native population.

Grabbing hangers bearing business suits and a couple of Chinese kimonos, the driver hurried up to the door. He bowed to the burly bouncer stationed there. "*Chao ong. Chao ong*," he said.

The doorman growled at him. "Move along, *bo-cau*," he said contemptuously.

"*Co! Co!*," the driver said. "*Toi tiec.*"

He rushed inside the gambling establishment and, being careful with the clothing, threaded his way through the crowd. Every time he even as much as lightly brushed against any of the players, he was instantly apologetic. "*Xin loi ong! Toi tiec! Xin loi ong!*"

Finally he reached the curtained entrance leading to Tsing Chai's office. Again he bowed to the attendant there and was ushered through with a curt push. He hurried down to the door and knocked.

"Master Tsing! Master Tsing! Your dry cleaning is here, please! Master Tsing!"

"*Moi ong vao*," came Tsing's voice from inside.

The driver stepped into the office, then turned and carefully closed the door. Then he tossed the clothing to a nearby chair and strode over to Tsing's desk. "What's this information you say is so important?" he demanded.

Tsing stood and bowed deeply to him. "It concerns the Black Eagles, *Theiu-Ta* Xong, and requires your immediate attention."

"I'll decide that," Xong said. "But first, mix me a drink—
Mau len!"

"Of course, Comrade Major Xong," Tsing said. He hurried to the wet bar in the corner of the room and mixed a
screwdriver—Xong's favorite drink.

Xong took a sip and settled back in the chair. He had
come to South Vietnam right after the truce in 1954. Even
that early the Communists were planning their takeover.
He, as an intelligence officer with the rank of major, had
been chosen to play the role of a refugee. Arriving in Saigon, he firmly established himself with his phony papers to
the extent of even getting arrested on a misdemeanor in order to create more paperwork on himself.

After that he spent several years simply living a normal
life. He worked mostly at demeaning jobs where he would
come into contact with South Vietnam's social elite as they
came into close proximity of foreigners—particularly
Americans. Eventually he landed a most desirable job by
local standards—that of delivery driver for the Tan Son
Nhut Air Base dry cleaners.

That became his cover, and the sight of Xong driving his
delivery truck all over Saigon was a familiar one and drew
no particular attention from authorities.

After another long, slow drink, Xong looked pointedly at
Tsing. "Now I'll have that information."

"The Black Eagles are off their normal operations,"
Tsing began immediately, not wanting to mince words.
"They are currently operating in an anticrime campaign in
conjunction with the national police."

"Here in Saigon?" Xong asked.

"Yes, comrade."

Xong shrugged. "I see no problem as long as that idiot
Ngai keeps us informed of their activities."

Tsing was almost apologetic. "I am sorry, Comrade
Major Xong, but that is no longer possible. The national

' police have sealed them off from us."

"By what means?" Xong demanded.

"All reports on Black Eagle operations that go to the South Vietnamese government are now sent through Colonel Tran's office," Tsing said. "I regret that very much."

"As should we all!" Xong exclaimed. "Tran is one tough bastard."

"I think the whole thing is a ploy," Tsing ventured timidly. "Aimed at closing in on me while clouding their intentions with inconsequential police business."

Xong nodded his agreement. "You could be right. Bring me a pencil and paper, *mau len!*"

Tsing quickly complied, then stood back respectfully as Xong scribbled out a message.

"Send this to Comrade Krashchenko immediately," Xong ordered. "He will give us explicit instructions on how to handle this unusual situation."

"Yes, comrade," Tsing said. He hurried to the side door that led to the commo room. "Shall I contact you when he returns the message?"

"Of course, fool!" Xong snapped. "I will be available in the usual manner." He set his glass down and walked to the exit. "Don't waste a second."

"Yes, comrade!"

Xong left the office and, once more turning himself into a coolie, scurried past the bouncer to his truck waiting for him outside.

"Sagerumasu!"

Kaminatake's voice sounded extraordinarily loud as it bounced off the walls of the *dojo*.

Before him, doing their best to assume the painful *mata-wari* position, were a dozen husky young men. They sat with their legs spread out as far as possible while attempting to bend forward far enough to touch their chests to the

100

floor.

Kaminatake was contemptuous of their efforts. Any apprentice *sumori* could have done better than these people, and they, being Matsuno-san's corps of personal bodyguards, were all black belts in karate.

"You are not trying!" he implored them. "Do not be afraid of a little pain!"

The men, highly trained and with a maximum degree of spiritual discipline, still could not properly assume the position no matter how hard they worked at it.

Kaminatake walked among them, leaning down and pushing various individuals in an attempt to wrestle them into the *matawari*.

While his students wore their regular karate uniforms, Kaminatake walked about in the traditional sumo *torimawashi* loincloth. He looked a bit different, however, than before. His three hundred and fifty pounds had shrunk to a bit less than three hundred and he was losing even more. No longer required to maintain the enormous diet in order to keep his *sumodo* figure, the fat was melting off. And the hardening of his body showed there had been plenty of muscle underneath the blubber.

Finally, with his class straining and sweating freely, he announced, "*Jubun* — enough!" He waited while they struggled out of the difficult physical contortion to their more familiar seated position. Kaminatake was not happy.

"Matsuno-san has charged me with teaching you certain aspects of *sumodo*," he snarled. "He told me you were all disciplined *karatekas* and had more than ample background in mental and physical discipline. Yet you cannot get your bodies into the *matawari*. Men, and even boys, with enormous bellies are able to achieve this. I cannot understand why you pencil-waists cannot."

This was not the first time that Kaminatake had made disparaging remarks about the art of karate and its practitioners in a comparative sense with sumo wrestling.

The senior bodyguard, a seasoned fighter in his late thirties, had controlled his temper out of respect for his employer, but he decided it was time to speak back to the ponderous giant who drilled them so unmercifully in *sumodo*. He stood up and bowed, but he made no attempt to control the angry expression on his face.

"The sumo wrestlers spend years working on these gymnastics," he said. "We, on the other hand, have devoted our precious time to perfecting actual fighting skills and the exercises and *katas* necessary to hone them to absolute sharpness. Frankly, I see no advantage in this—this *matawari*."

Kaminatake sneered at him. "You are tough, *he*?"

The chief bodyguard shrugged. "I am a *karateka*."

"And I am a *sumotori*."

The other man smiled. "You say that as if it were a challenge."

"It is."

The karate man closed his eyes for a moment, letting his body seemingly go slack as his *ki* vibrated silently and invisibly throughout his soul.

Then he exploded into motion.

The horizontal *shuto* crashed into Kaminatake's left pectoral muscle—and bounced off. The *sokuto-geri* kick was blocked by the sumo wrestler's massive forearm.

Then Kaminatake charged.

Blinding speed and lightning reflexes marked the attack as the *sumotori* closed the short distance between them in a flashing millisecond. His huge hands grasped the bodyguard around the waist knocking the wind from him. Kaminatake picked up the man—who had already fainted from the sudden loss of oxygen—and held him over his head. Then he slammed him to the *dojo* floor so hard that several boards broke.

The *karateka* bounced two feet up before falling back.

The other members of the bodyguard group stood transfixed, looking at their chief lying motionless on the damaged floorboards. Finally one ventured forward and knelt beside the man. He looked up, his eyes open wide. "*Shinda*—he is dead!"

Kaminatake grabbed the cadaver by the loose folds of his uniform jacket and carried him to the door. He tossed the corpse into the garden outside the *dojo*. The *uekiya* working there with his rake, stopped his toiling and stared in dread fascination at what had just happened.

"Have this carrion removed!" Kaminatake snapped at him. Then he went back inside to face his class.

The other karate men were clearly nervous, shuffling around as they stared at the sumo man.

"What are you waiting for?" Kaminatake yelled. "*Matawari!*"

Maj. Truong Van sipped his tea and stared over the mug at the man seated at the desk on the other side of the office.

Truong smiled to himself. As a senior intelligence officer in the North Vietnamese Army, he had plenty of responsibility. An order of battle specialist, it had been his main job to keep track of the new American units and their commanders who were beginning to show up in the south. Then he'd been abruptly pulled off his regular duties and assigned to work with the Russian who now shared his office.

Lt. Col. Gregori Krashchenko was from the Soviet KGB. He had begun his military career in the Russian army serving as a young paratrooper officer in several of their more elite units. At first it had seemed his career would be normal for an eager junior lieutenant, but he quickly caught the attention of his regimental commissar.

Not only did Krashchenko display a great amount of attentiveness in the political classes, he even wrote several treatises expounding the philosophies taught in them. The commissar sent papers to higher headquarters extolling the eager shavetail's qualities of loyalty with a recommendation that he be switched from the role of line officer to the political branch of the Soviet army.

But Krashchenko did an even more "commendable" thing by turning in a fellow officer who had been making "unpatriotic" remarks regarding the institutions of Communism and particularly of the current Russian government. This normally would have cinched the political officer's job, but Krashchenko was able to do even better than that—and for a very good reason.

The man he turned in was his cousin.

Thus, Krashchenko came to the attention of the KGB. He was just their type of guy. In a political system which could not survive without snitching finks, the lieutenant was a natural.

After graduation from the KGB academy, Krashchenko was tested by being put into a counterinsurgency campaign in the Ukraine. He proved to be deadly efficient, even bringing in East German Police to combine the massacre of local peasants with on-the-job training for the visiting Krauts.

Krashchenko's career continued to soar. When news came out of North Vietnam of a special detachment of raiders led by an American officer, he was sent to gather intelligence on the group and begin the campaign to bring about their destruction.

The KGB agent used indigenous operatives in the south in combination with the North Vietnamese Army's G-2, to first identify the group. This was when Maj. Truong Van was assigned to him as an assistant and interpreter.

Within a few months, utilizing Major Xong—the dry cleaning truck driver—and his Saigon organization, they had blackmailed a South Vietnamese colonel named Ngai Quang into ferreting information on this group out of the Americans' Special Operations Group. Thus, Krashchenko knew all about Maj. Robert Falconi and his Black Eagles.

What excited the Russian colonel most was to learn that

Falconi's mother was a Jewish refugee who had illegally fled the Soviet Union in the early 1930s. By Russian law she was still a citizen, and that meant her son Robert Mikhailovich also belonged to the Workers and Peasants Paradise — whether he wanted to or not.

Thus, if Falconi could be captured, it would be lawfully proper (under the Communist system) to take him back to Russia to be tried as a traitor and a war criminal. Then he could be shot or used as a propaganda ploy to embarrass the West.

Major Truong admired Krashchenko's efforts and results, but he thought the man too eager. He was constantly adding to the files on the Black Eagles, duplicating his work through a triple system of rosters while displaying such gross inefficiency that Truong knew the same amount of work could have been accomplished in a third of the time the bureaucratically inclined Krashchenko had taken.

Yet, as the saying went, one cannot argue with success.

Now, dressed in a plain khaki uniform bearing the shoulder boards of an infantry lieutenant colonel, Krashchenko shuffled the papers on his desk. He glanced with open irritation at the lounging Truong sipping tea, but said nothing.

A knock on the door interrupted his thoughts.

A young woman from the communications center stepped into the room. "A message from Bua."

Krashchenko recognized Major Xong's code name. "Ah! Some more intelligence on Falconi and his devils no doubt."

The missive, in Vietnamese, was handed to Truong. He quickly read it, then announced its contents. "The Black Eagles are now operating against criminals in Saigon. Bua thinks it is a feint to allow them to draw closer to Tsing Chai without arousing suspicion."

Krashchenko was silent in thought for several moments.

Truong picked up his tea again. "What do you think, Comrade?"

"I believe that Bua is correct. There is no doubt that the

CIA man Fagin does not trust Ngai. Obviously they have checked into the idiot's background and know of his addiction to gambling. Since he does it all in Chai's mah jongg parlor, they now rightly suspect our Chinese comrade of being in on the anti-Black Eagle plot."

"I see no problem in eliminating or capturing Falconi in Saigon," Truong said. "It would be easier there than out in the jungle in combat conditions."

"Yes — yes." Krashchenko was again silent for several minutes before he spoke again. "But I don't want to use any of the regular Viet Cong urban organizations. If any of them have been compromised without our knowledge, they would be unable to accomplish the mission. At any rate, they must be saved for operations in Saigon in the future."

"But, Comrade," Truong protested in hesitation. "Who else can we use who would not run such a risk?"

"I suppose we could bring in some people from another city," Krashchenko mused. "Or perhaps send some people down from Hanoi. You have such organizations under your direct command, do you not?"

"Of course, Comrade," Truong said. "But it would take time to successfully infiltrate them. By then, Falconi and his Black Eagles might well have taken Chai into custody."

Suddenly Krashchenko smiled. "I know of someone better! There is an organization which works hand-in-hand with Comrade Chai in the narcotics trade. They have their own men who could go to Saigon quickly and easily. Their arrival would cause no particular stir and they could move about the city easily and openly until ready to make the final move to bring Falconi into our grasp."

Truong was puzzled. "I'm not sure who you are speaking of, Comrade."

"It should be easy for you to figure out," Krashchenko said. "I am referring, of course, to our Japanese colleague — Mister Matsuno!"

CHAPTER SEVEN

Robert Falconi sat in the back seat of the taxi and relaxed, letting the driver sweat and strain as he drove through Saigon's heavy early evening traffic.

The officer felt strangely at ease and content.

Dressed in a lightweight white suit he had purchased in Hong Kong a year previously, he gingerly held onto the bottle of wine in his lap. Falconi had the illusion that all was well with the world. He could almost forget that there was a very real possibility that some fanatic Viet Cong might be hidden in an alley nearby. Holding a grenade, he would be waiting for a cab or other vehicle bearing an American to come by. That would be the right time to make his move. A quick pull of the pin, then a rush forward to drop the explosive in the interior of the car.

It would have been easy to avoid such an incident by simply rolling up the windows. But, without air conditioning in the one hundred plus degrees, that could have been nearly as deadly as a grenade attack.

The Falcon would rely on his quick eyes and the .45 auto in his shoulder holster to avoid any such assaults on his person. As the taxi rolled along, he made visual checks on possible ambush points.

"Just a few more blocks, sir," the driver said in heavily accented English.

Falconi nodded. The local cabbies seemed to think it necessary to call out the distance from the destination every few minutes or so. Maybe it was something that went back to the French occupation, Falconi mused.

Every time the vehicle slowed enough, several street urchins would surge up to it offering trinkets and other junk for sale. Falconi always tensed at these moments, knowing full well that the Viet Cong were not above sending children on suicide missions. One of the playful little tykes might grin delightedly, then point a small caliber pistol at him and pump away at the trigger. At that short range, it would be hard to miss the big American.

"Here we are, sir," the driver announced. "We have, at this very moment, arrived at your destination."

Falconi grinned and wondered what phrase book the cabbie had garnered that one from. "*Cam on ong*," he said. He peeled off a few piasters from the roll he carried and handed them over.

The driver grinned and nodded his thanks. As soon as Falconi stepped out, he gunned the motor and disappeared back into the swarm of traffic.

The major stood at the entrance into one of Saigon's most unusual neighborhoods. Small, its buildings forming a barrier against the rest of the city, this area was called the *Quartier des Colons*.

The old edifices, though whitewashed, had a dingy, gray air about them. Their shutters had peeling paint and many were sagging on their hinges, looking as if they were about to fall to the street. The gutters were full of bits of trash, and the whole area looked like it needed a high-pressure waterhose turned on it to wash away the accumulated grime and litter.

The people who lived there were mostly French. Having once been a governing part of their nation's former empire, they were veterans of the military, civil service and other branches of the complicated bureaucratic machinery that administered French Indochina. When Dien Bien Phu fell in 1954, the Far East part of France's glory faded into North and South Vietnam. The Communists took the upper part, and the more democratically inclined inherited the lower.

The French who had lived there—called *colons*—packed up their belongings and returned home. But they soon discovered they no longer belonged in *La Belle Republique*. Years and years of selfimposed exile in the tropics had thinned their blood, and made them horribly susceptible to long bouts of colds and flu. Also the decades spent in a life where they'd been the big shots, complete with large houses, servants and the sensual luxury of being able to dawdle away long tropical evenings with small exotic mistresses, hardly made the cold reality of modern France attractive to them.

They had returned to South Vietnam to try to relive those great days of the past. But the time of colonial grandeur and authority were over. No longer rulers of this hot, humid land, they gradually congregated together to exist on their miserable pensions in this neighborhood that was soon dubbed *Quartier des Colons*—the Colonials' Quarter.

It was also a good place for clandestine meetings between certain agents and operatives of the Caucasian race. Here white men didn't attract much attention, and could sit in the bars and at the tables of one of the down-at-the-heels restaurants without causing anyone to look twice at them.

This was where Andrea Thuy Roget lived. She had managed to get a quite nice corner apartment up and away from the cluttered streets. The long hours she worked gave her little chance to make friends among the faded *colons*, but when she had the chance, she liked to sit at one of the small sidewalk cafes and sip *vin ordinaire* while conversing in

French with other patrons.

Falconi strode through the neighborhood toward Andrea's apartment house. He nodded politely to the big nosed Gallics who silently greeted him with polite nods and stares of open curiosity. Though none had ever seen him before, they rightly surmised whom he was going to visit. This caused a flurry of gossip to break out in heated whispers as the romantically inclined French discussed the possibility of a red-hot love affair between this man who was obviously American, and the lovely, mysterious, Eurasian woman who lived in the corner apartment house.

Falconi entered the building and ascended the rickety stairs to the second floor. He knocked on the door.

"Oui? Qui est-la?"

Falconi tried to remember the smattering of French he had at his command. *"C'est moi. Robert."* He pronounced his name in the French fashion — Ro-bair.

Andrea laughed and came to the door, opening it with a flourish. *"Entrez, monsieur,"* she said standing there.

He stared at her for one incredulous moment. She was dressed in a light blue, sleeveless dress with matching shoes. With only a bit of makeup, she looked wholesome and beautiful. A crucifix around her neck made up her entire selection of jewelry. This stark contrast between her usual uniform and that night's attire caused Falconi to stand there and stare at her.

"I said, *entrez*," Andrea remarked. "That means for you to come in."

"Gracias," he said entering the apartment.

She laughed again. "That's Spanish."

"When I run out of French, I always turn to Spanish." Falconi said. He handed her the wine. "Flower of the grape for the flower of my heart."

"You're so gallant, Robert."

"I always am when I'm invited to dinner."

"It's been such a long time since I've cooked anything,"

110

Andrea said. "I hope you like it."

Falconi sniffed the air. "It sure smells good."

"Something the nuns taught me to make." Andrea said. "*Pommes frites et omelette.* That's fried potatoes and omelet. I'm afraid we didn't eat too fancy at the orphanage. I've never had the opportunity to learn my country's more exotic cuisine."

"I love eggs and potatoes," Falconi said. "But I smelled fresh bread too, right?"

"I purchased it less than a half-hour ago at the neighborhood *boulangerie*," Andrea said. "There's nothing like French bread as it's baked by a French baker." She took him by the arm and led him into the apartment.

Andrea's living quarters reflected her lifestyle. With only the barest of furniture, the place was clean — although the word "antiseptic" would have described it better. Any casual observer would be able to tell that the inhabitant of the flat didn't spend a lot of time in it. And the lack of any unnecessary decorative objects would have caused some confusion as to the sex of the occupant as well.

As Falconi was taken over to the table, he glanced into the bedroom. He noticed a small, iron cot and a wooden, unpainted table bearing a lamp. These made up the only furniture in her sleeping quarters. There was no closet. Andrea's sets of various uniforms and three sets of civilian dresses, were hung in a simple frame of slats.

"Where's your corkscrew?" he asked.

"Oh, Robert! I don't have one," Andrea said from the kitchen. "But I can run down — "

"No, don't go anywhere," Falconi said. He pulled a red pocket knife from his pocket. "Swiss army type — has a small corkscrew along with sawblade, fingernail file, knife blade, scissors, etcetera, etcetera, and etcetera."

"Three etceteras, eh?" Andrea remarked with a smile. "That must have made it real expensive."

"Sure did," Falconi said. He began pulling the cork.

"You didn't say what we were going to have, so I bought a red wine, okay?"

Andrea came out with an expertly prepared omelet. "I've never read a gourmet cookbook, but I doubt if there's a section in it about the proper wine for eggs and potatoes." She took a spatula and removed about three quarters of the omelet, dropping it into Falconi's plate. After serving herself the remainder, she returned to the kitchen for the fried potatoes.

Andrea was being very modest about her omelet. Containing mushrooms, onions and tomatoes, it was actually a very delicious meal that she had prepared.

Within a couple of minutes the couple was seated consuming the meal. Andrea smiled self-consciously. "This is awful."

"What?"

"I invite you for dinner in my apartment and the only thing I know how to cook for you is . . . well, this."

"It's delicious," Falconi remarked, meaning what he said. "Hot, tasty, and nutritious too. I really like it."

"I should have fried some fish," Andrea said. "I'm pretty good at that."

"Sounds like something else you had in the orphanage," Falconi said.

"Yes. That and lots of rice," Andrea said. "I should have had a nice fish and rice dinner . . ." She stopped talking and laughed. "Here I've served the food and am already futilely changing the menu. We should have gone out to a restaurant for something good."

"I prefer to be here."

"Anyway, fish and rice would be better than this," she insisted.

Falconi took a healthy sip of the wine. "We'll have that next time, okay?"

"I promise."

"But I insist on one stipulation," Falconi said.

"Just name it."

"That I be allowed to take you out between now and then. Okay?"

Andrea nodded. "It's been quite some time, hasn't it?"

"Since we've gone out? Yeah. It sure has."

"Or made love," Andrea said.

There was an awkward silence.

"Yeah," Falconi finally said.

"I think we've reached a point that we're going to have an open and honest discussion about our relationship, Robert," Andrea remarked.

Falconi finished up the food on his plate. "Okay. Is that the reason for the dinner tonight?"

"Of course. You've made no attempt to be alone with me since you and the others returned from Operation Asian Blitzkrieg, Robert. Before that you wouldn't come over here or even take me out because you said that as long as the rest of the Black Eagles were stuck out in that Special Forces camp, you wouldn't do one thing they couldn't do," Andrea said.

"That's right."

"You said if they weren't getting any pussy, then you weren't either. Rather crude, but to the point."

"Sorry." Falconi poured them more wine. "We've been pretty busy on current ops here in Saigon. Working with the national police requires a lot of planning and coordinating."

"I am very much aware of the situation."

"Then we have to rehearse the raids," he continued.

"Never mind all that." Andrea raised her glass. "Now I want a declaration from you, Maj. Robert Falconi."

"I know where this conversation is heading," Falconi said. "And I want to know why."

"That should be obvious," Andrea told him. "I'm unhappy at the job I've been stuck in. As usual, in affairs of the heart, it's the woman that pays the price. We're responsible for the birth control, we catch the disapproval while our lovers get leering grins of congratulations from their men friends, we women are the ones that get pregnant and give birth, and—as in my case—I was the one taken off operations when it was discovered we were having an affair."

"I guess you're right," Falconi conceded. "But I didn't design nature or people's attitudes."

"I'm not holding you responsible," Andrea said. "I went to bed with you because I *wanted* to, not because I *had* to. I'll accept the rap for that. But I'm going to push a bit of final decision making back on you."

"I'm losing the drift of this conversation," Falconi remarked.

"You'll understand what I'm getting at in just a moment, Robert. I have a chance to get back into the swing of things in future operations," Andrea said.

"I wasn't aware of that."

"Well, it's true. As the administrative and operations officer I find out these things right after Fagin does," Andrea told him. "And my potential participation involves a prostitution ring."

"Doesn't sound right. Our cover is that we move in on narcotics scams that involve American servicemen."

"Fagin will explain the details, but let me assure you, the Black Eagles are going to come into contact with a bordello—and not as customers," Andrea said.

"I take it you would be undercover on it."

"Right, Robert. And it means I could be having sex with other men," Andrea said. "I've done that before in the line of duty, so I'm not pretending I'm a blushing young maiden about to sacrifice my virginity in the line of duty. But I am hesitating a bit."

Falconi forced himself to assume a cold attitude. "Why?"

"Because, Robert, darling, I am in love with you," Andrea said. "And my attitude toward other men fucking me has changed considerably. Can you understand that?"

"Sure."

"I haven't committed myself yet," Andrea continued. "And whether I do or not depends on what you say in the next five minutes or so."

"I'm still not following this drift of conversation."

"I love you, like I said, Robert. But I won't make a needless sacrifice of staying out of ops if that love isn't returned. I'm quite willing to continue my role as Fagin's administrative assistant and be faithful to you in body and spirit if — well, if it's worth it."

"And what'll make it worth it, Andrea?"

"A declaration of your love for me," she answered.

Falconi was silent.

Andrea looked into his eyes. "It'll only take those three words, Robert. You Americans even have a song called *Three Little Words*. You say them and I'll base my decision on that. If you don't, well . . . that's that. It was —" Her voice quavered a bit, but she got in control of herself. "It was nice, but not meant to be."

Falconi dawdled with his wine glass. "Laying it on thick and quick, aren't you?"

"I certainly am. But I have no choice. The orders for this operation came down today."

"You're asking for an all-out commitment from me, aren't you?" Falconi asked.

She looked directly into his face. "Yes, Robert. It's all the way or nothing."

Falconi sighed. "Sorry."

The only sign of emotion that Andrea allowed herself was to tighten her lips. Then she relaxed and stood up. "That's that then. I don't believe in prolonging things — particularly the inevitable."

"I agree," Falconi said.

Andrea walked to the door and opened it. She looked back at him. "Goodbye, Robert."

Falconi got to his feet and walked toward her. "Goodbye,

115

Andrea."

He continued on out the door.

Kaminatake waited on Matsuno-san's private shooting range for Kaji the chauffeur to show up. Dressed in a western sweatsuit and with Japanese *sandaru* sandals on his feet, he passed the time by doing *shiko* footstamping exercises.

This movement, as done at the commencement of sumo matches, was performed by alternately raising each leg high to the side, then bringing the foot crashing to the ground. Originally done to intimidate opponents, it also served to strengthen the lower limbs and keep the hips limber. Although always agile during his days of competition, Kaminatake noticed an increase in his ability to move about since losing so much weight. He had gotten down to two hundred and fifty pounds now and seemed to be staying at that size. His speed and agility had increased without loss of physical strength. Kaminatake felt very good and strong.

"O-hayo-gozai-masu!"

The ex-sumo turned at the sound of the voice and saw Kaji standing behind him. He nodded politely to the smaller man. *"O-hayo."*

"Are you ready for your pistol instruction, Kaminatake-san?" Kaji asked producing an automatic from his uniform jacket.

"Hai." Then he gave the other man a scrutinizing look. "I am beginning to realize that you are more than a chauffeur for Matsuno-san."

"Very true, Kaminatake-san," Kaji replied. "We used that as a bit of subterfuge in order for me to get closer to you and gain your confidence."

"I see," Kaminatake said.

"Shall we get on with this shooting now?"

"Hai."

"Good. First let me introduce you to the weapon." He

116

handed the pistol over. "Do not worry. It is unloaded. Have you ever fired one before?"

"No. In fact, this is the first time I've even held one," Kaminatake answered.

"Well, this is a Japanese model called the Nambu," Kaji explained. "It was designed by one of our nation's original firearms inventors in the early part of this century. His name was Nambu Kijiro."

Kaminatake hefted the weapon in his huge hands.

"It is of eight-millimeter caliber and the magazine holds eight bullets," Kaji continued. "Here I will show you how to load it, Kaminatake-san."

The chauffeur took the pistol. He pulled a magazine from his pocket and slammed it into the grip. "Now the bullets are in the pistol, but it is not yet ready to fire until we transfer one up into the barrel—*kakute*!" He pulled back on the charging knob at the end of the receiver and let it fly shut. "Now it is ready to fire."

"Must one do that each time one wishes to shoot?" Kaminatake asked, taking it back.

"Oh, no, Kaminatake-san. That is why the pistol is called an automatic. As long as there are bullets in the magazine, the pistol will fire with each pull of the trigger. *Ryokai-ka?*"

"Yes, I understand."

"Actually, the Nambu is not considered the best representative of the family of automatic pistols," Kaji said.

"Then why did Matsuno-san choose it for his organization?"

Kaji smiled. "Because our illustrious employer desired all things Japanese. So he went to the trouble of having his pistols machined and corrected so that each is a custom job, made individually by expert craftsmen. Thus, his pistols are not ordinary Nambus."

Kaminatake already appreciated the worth of the weapon he held. "Then this beauty was not mass-manufactured in a factory, eh?"

"No, Kaminatake-san. It was individually crafted by a master *teppokaji*. A beauty, is it not?"

"*Hai!* I cannot wait to learn to use it."

"Then aim it at the target downrange and pull the trigger, please."

Kaminatake did as he was told—rather awkwardly. He raised his arm and pointed the muzzle at the man-shaped silhouette target. The pistol fired, the recoil barely affecting his brawny arm. The impact of the bullet kicked up dirt high on the mound of earth behind the cardboard device.

Kaji smiled. "Do not worry, Kaminatake-san. Let me show you a better position." He took the weapon back and assumed the standard combat pistol firing attitude. Bent slightly at the knees, he held the weapon out straight in both hands. "See how much more steady I am. This is much better than simply sticking an arm out and letting it waver about." He rapidly pumped off the remaining seven rounds, the effort sending each bullet into the target. "If that had been a man he would be dead."

"*Hai!*" Kaminatake agreed.

Kaji loaded a fresh magazine and returned the pistol to the bigger man. "Now try again."

Kaminatake needed a bit of help in properly assuming the position. Once he was into it he fired eight times. Most of the rounds missed the target, but at least three hit it.

"You must learn to keep the sights aligned, Kaminatake-san," Kaji urged him. "The front and rear must be at the same level. Concentrate on that rather than speed."

Kaminatake followed the instructions to the letter. Within a matter of an hour he was sending slugs through the cardboard on a regular basis.

"*Soreina!* You show a great talent for this!" Kaji exclaimed sincerely. "You will be an expert shot before the week is out."

Kaminatake continued to practice for another two hours. His skill increased as he learned to load the empty magazines prior to sliding them into the pistol grip. His physical strength made his body a steady firing platform while the combination of excellent eyesight and faultless coordination evolved him into an efficient killing machine with the hand weapon.

The session was interrupted by the appearance of the girl servant Kaika. She had received an extra-curricular assignment in seeing to Kaminatake's sexual pleasure. The first month or so had been agony for the small woman as she submitted to the gigantic man who mounted her. No one had been happier about his steady loss of weight than Kaika.

She bowed deeply to both men. "*Dozo*. Matsuno-san *ketsubo-matsu miru ryoho shinshi chokesetsuni*."

"Tell him we shall be right there," Kaji said. "Is he in his office?"

"*Hai.*"

They quickly fired off the remaining bullets before leaving the range to walk through the grounds back to the main house. Once there, they left their shoes at the entrance and donned cloth slippers to pad down the highly polished floor of the long hallway that led to Matsuno's office.

Their chief waited for them. After the complimentary greetings, he wasted little time. "I have received a communication from a colleague of mine in Saigon. He requests aid from me. It seems that a most determined group of local police and American soldiers are slowly and steadily closing in on his organization. He desires some of our best men to fight these insidious enemies for him. I have chosen the two of you to go on a special mission there. Since Kaji is more experienced in these affairs, I have chosen him to be leader. Later on Kaminatake can take on such responsibility." He looked at the ex-*sumotori*. "Do you have any objections to this?"

"Of course not, Matsuno-san."

"I am happy to hear that." He turned his gaze to Kaji.

"Kindly pick a half dozen of our best *karateka* to accompany you. I must emphasize there will be a great deal of fighting involved. How did the *pisutoru* session go? Is the shooting program progressing well?"

"Quite well, Matsuno-san," Kaji answered. "I am happy to report that Kaminatake is already an excellent shot. With a few more hours of shooting, he will be an expert."

"*Odoroku!* He will soon make a practical application of his shooting abilities. And Kaminatake will also have a chance to further perfect his skills in Saigon. My friend there also has a pistol range—his is indoors." Matsuno reached into his desk and produced a fat envelope. "Here is cash and the plane tickets for you and your men. You will depart for Saigon this very afternoon."

"*Hai!* And who do we contact there?" Kaminatake asked.

"My associate's name is Tsing Chai," Matsuno answered.

Chuck Fagin stepped from his hotel apartment door and found Robert Falconi waiting for him. "What brings you around here?"

"I was with Andrea last night," Falconi said. "She asked me to make a decision. It was—"

"I know all about it," Fagin said. "C'mon. We can talk on the way to the office."

They went downstairs and into the hotel garage. Neither said anything until they got into the car. "Are you planning on sending her into a whorehouse?"

Fagin started the engine and backed out of his parking stall. "Depends on what she tells me this morning." He slipped the car into forward and eased out onto the street. "I take it whatever happened last night between you two settled the matter once and for all."

"She wanted to know if I loved her," Falconi said. "I told her no."

Fagin looked over at him. "Did you mean it?"

"I don't want a wife or even a steady girlfriend right now," Falconi said. "Especially with all this going on with the Black Eagles. Maybe if the troubles here got wrapped up and I ended up back in the States in a conventional unit and — hell!" He was silent for several moments. "I'm going to be in Special Forces for the rest of my career."

"And probably the CIA afterward," Fagin added.

"Yeah," Falconi agreed. "I'm really torn up about her, Fagin. I want her shipped out of the Black Eagles."

"Nope."

"She's getting to me," Falconi admitted. "I don't like the thought of her getting screwed by somebody else."

"You're possessive, but you're not in love," Fagin said. "I realize that now by the way you're taking the break-up between you two. I knew the confrontation between you two would bring the truth out. You're a typical male, Falcon. You want your sexual cake and eat it too — forgive any puns or Freudian slips there — but you can't have it."

"Fagin —"

"Let me finish, okay? Your attitude now proves one thing quite clearly to me. You'd never let your feelings interfere with a mission. So she's on ops now."

"What about *her* feelings for *me*? In her emotional state she might just make a fatal blunder."

"I've got to take the risk, Falconi."

"It seems Andrea's the one sticking her neck out," Falconi said.

"Yeah. You're right. And if she muddles up because of you, she'll die." He turned into the gate of Peterson Field. "Want some coffee before we go up to the office?"

CHAPTER EIGHT

Kaminatake gasped involuntarily when he stepped out of the JAL airliner onto the passenger ramp. The hot, wet blast of air seemed to envelop him in an invisible cloak of steam.

Kaji, behind him, tapped his massive shoulders. "Better get used to it, Kaminatake-san. This is the tropics."

"Uh! I would hate to wrestle in this place. An honest Japanese *sumotori* would melt in the heat."

Kaji grinned in agreement. "*Hai!*"

The two followed the other passengers over to Saigon's Tan Son Nhut Airport's customs division. They each put their single suitcase on the counter and waited for a customs official to check them out. They had no contraband with them — other than their personal Nambu pistols and ammunition — all of which was hidden in the false bottoms of their luggage.

A South Vietnamese officer took their passports. "Will you be in the country long?"

"No," Kaji answered. "Only a few weeks at the most."

"Are you here on business or pleasure?"

"Business, sir. We represent Matsuno Industries."

ɪne officer nodded. *"Cam on ong—arigato,"* he said in both Vietnamese and Japanese. "You may depart."

The two reclosed their bags and went through the customs area and out into the main terminal. Kaminatake looked around at the crowd. "There seem to be a great number of American soldiers here."

"Hai," Kaji said. "They are experiencing a big build-up in South Vietnam."

Kaminatake smiled in a sinister manner. "We will reduce that number somewhat."

"Masaka—indeed!"

They continued through the waiting area until they were once again outside. Kaji glanced up and down the walkway. Finally he spotted a man he recognized. "Come. There is our ride."

A tall, husky individual leaning against the fender of a late model Chrysler Imperial caught sight of them. He waved and opened the door. When they came up, he bowed. *"Chao ong, Ong* Kaji."

"Chao ong," the Japanese replied.

"Master Tsing awaits you. Please get in the car."

"Cam on ong." Kaji turned and motioned to his companion. "This is *Ong* Kaminatake."

The greeter looked with subtle alarm at the gigantic Kaminatake. "I am pleased to meet you. My name is Kahn."

The ex-sumo made no comment as he stepped inside the automobile. Kahn shut the door and hurried over to the driver's side.

"Ah! Air conditioning!" Kaji exclaimed as the motor was started. "It will take us a while to get used to the weather here."

Kahn pulled away from the curb. "Not at all like Japan, eh, *Ong* Kaji?"

"I'm afraid not." He settled back for the ride. "I am looking forward to seeing Master Tsing again. It's been a bit more than a year."

124

"Things have been going very well in the organization except for the situation you are aware of," Kahn said.

"I think we can have that straightened out before long."

Kaminatake remained silent during the drive to Tsing's mah jongg parlor. He found the sights and smells of Saigon's streets a heady new experience. Japan was crowded and literally teemed with its multitudes, but somehow it seemed more orderly and organized than this chaotic jumble outside the car windows.

When they reached the Cholon district, Kahn deftly wheeled and turned down various alleyways and side streets he knew would get them to their destination quicker than following a short, but more crowded route.

He pulled up behind the gambling establishment. The Chrysler had no sooner rolled to a stop than two bodyguards stepped from the building and opened the door.

"*Chao ong,*" one greeted crisply as Kaji stepped out. When the gigantic Kaminatake emerged, the man involuntarily stepped back from him. He swallowed and smiled weakly, nodding his head respectfully. "*Chao ong.*"

"*Konnichi wa,*" Kaminatake said in his husky voice.

The two were quickly ushered inside and taken directly to Tsing Chai's office. The Chinese, beaming and smiling, bowed to them as they entered his domain.

Kaminatake scowled unconsciously at Tsing. He had developed a slight dislike of the Chinese people during his boyhood. This was from listening to army veterans who had participated in the war against them in the 1930s and 40s. Most were contemptuous of these Oriental brothers. Kaminatake, noting Tsing's soft fleshiness, thought the man effeminate.

The Chinese gambling boss sensed the undercurrent of animosity, but he ignored it. Instead he widened his smile and said, "Ah, Kaji-san! So delightful to see you again."

"I am pleased to see you as well," Kaji said. He indicated Kaminatake. "This is Kaminatake-san. He holds a very spe-

125

cial place on Matsuno-san's staff."

"I do not doubt that," Tsing said sizing up the big man. "Are you a *sumotori*?"

"I was," Kaminatake replied.

"I am most familiar with your sport. I always attempt to time my trips to Japan during the tournaments. What stable did you wrestle with?"

"Mon No Taiyo," Kaminatake replied.

"A most illustrious one," Tsing said. "I believe the manager there is Uchida-san, no?"

"*Hai*."

Tsing knew better than to inquire more into Kaminatake's career as a *sumotori*. Whatever had taken the man from the sumo world was probably left better unexplored, so he changed the subject. "I believe there are more men due from Matsuno-san's organization."

"Yes, Master Tsing," Kaji said. "They will be arriving in twos and threes during the coming week. Matsuno-san thought it best to bring us into Vietnam in that manner."

"As usual, my illustrious colleague and friend is acting in an intelligent and clever manner," Tsing said. "We will have no suspicions aroused by the sudden arrival of a group of young Japanese men."

"Particularly if they cannot justify so many on a business trip," Kaji said.

"And also especially if they are all athletic and husky in appearance," Tsing added. "Of course we could tell the authorities they are here for an athletic event. But they would want free tickets, wouldn't they?"

"Indeed," Kaji agreed. "The Vietnamese government doesn't display the tenets of honesty to any great extent."

"So true," Tsing said. "Now, may I offer you gentlemen some refreshments? You must certainly need some after your trip and the drive through this unpleasant city."

"*Cam on ong*," Kaji said.

Once again the Japanese duo found themselves being

126

taken from one place to another. This time they walked through the gambling section of the parlor. "Do either of you play mah jongg?"

"I am rather fond of the game," Kaji said.

"Then please accept my hospitality and allow me to furnish you with some playing money," Tsing said. He looked at Kaminatake. "What about you, sir?"

"I only play *go*," Kaminatake said.

"A most excellent Japanese game," Tsing said.

"We played it a lot when I was in the sumo stable," Kaminatake said. "It passed the time."

"A lively recreation and mental challenge," Tsing said pleasantly.

"I would have rather spent more time in the training room," Kaminatake said in a flat tone.

Tsing gave him a careful look. "I dare say you would."

When they arrived at the designated place, they found a small table full of refreshments, and two pretty young Vietnamese girls waiting for them. The women paled somewhat at the sight of the gigantic sumo. But they walked forward and bowed to the visitors anyhow.

"Everything here is for your pleasure," Tsing said. "Do not be reluctant to indulge yourselves."

"You're very kind, *cam on ong*," Kaji said.

"*Arigato*," Kaminatake said, already lusting for the petite women who seemed even smaller and more delicate than the Japanese.

"I will have more food brought in," Tsing said giving Kaminatake an unconscious scrutiny. "And another woman too."

Andrea Thuy stepped from the taxicab after paying off the driver. He continued to watch her as she strode rapidly from the vehicle up to the building directly by the curb where he had parked. He was not the only ogler. Other men

127

in the street turned to watch the strikingly beautiful young lady during the short second it took her to walk across the sidewalk.

Andrea was not in her uniform — at least not the military one. She wore a bright red dress that reached just a bit above the knee. A long slit went up the side from the hem to her waist. Each step she took revealed flashes of smooth, firm thigh. The top of the blouse was cut low, almost to the nipples of the fleshy globes of her large breasts. A flashy hairdo and makeup, a bit heavily laid on, made up the rest of the picture. No one acquainted with Andrea would have recognized her without close scrutiny.

First Lt. Andrea Thuy Roget looked like a high-class Vietnamese whore — and that was the exact effect she had strived for when she'd gotten herself ready for this trip downtown.

And this wasn't the only preparatory activity she'd been involved in.

She'd moved from her apartment in the *Quartier des Colons* to one closer to downtown Saigon. The new domicile had been carefully searched out for her by Chuck Fagin. It was all part of a carefully constructed cover.

Her new neighborhood was made up of newly affluent vice merchants and the women they employed. Most had been barely struggling to make a living before, but the growing influx of American military men was making it possible for them to enter into all sorts of lucrative businesses involving bars, women, narcotics, and even pornography. Andrea had moved into that sub-culture lock, stock, and pretty new dresses.

By adopting this role and becoming a "call-girl" rather than a "bar-girl," a woman as beautiful as Andrea would eventually come into contact with the higher class, monied customers of the world's oldest profession. This, undoubtedly, would include Tsing Chai's mah jongg parlor.

She went inside the small foyer of the building. A clerk,

reading a newspaper at a counter, looked up at her arrival. *"Co?"* Unlike the men on the street outside, he didn't seem particularly impressed by her appearance. Beautiful, sexy women paraded past him on a regular basis.

"I am here to see *Ong* Nguyen," Andrea said.

The man picked up a telephone. *"Quy-danh la gi?"*

"Loc Andrea," she answered giving her cover name.

The fact she was using a European first name didn't faze him either. Most of the young women passing through did so. He spoke for a few short seconds in the phone, then hung up. *"Ong* Nguyen says for you to come straight up." He pointed at the door. "Through there, then take the stairs to the second floor. Go left down the hall to the last room."

"Cam on ong," Andrea said.

She followed the directions exactly, coming to a heavy mahogany portal. A bell was mounted in the wall beside it. She pressed the button and could hear chimes sounding out the first few notes of Tchaikovsky's Piano Concerto No. 1.

The door was opened by a small, elderly gentleman wearing a white houseboy's coat. *"Moi co vao,"* he said.

"Thank you." She stepped into the room and was almost stunned by the opulence of the place. Heavy European tapestries, easily identifiable as antiques, hung from the walls; expensive furniture, so old it was obviously handcrafted, was tastefully arranged around the area; and there were Chinese vases, heavy and formidable in appearance, yet possessing a certain amount of delicateness.

"Come with me, *co*," the old man said.

Andrea followed the ancient servant's doddering steps through a curtained exit. She realized that what she'd seen was only the entrance hall to the place. A large living room done in Louis XV style, complete with ancient oil paintings and miniature sculptures, stretched out before her.

Her escort stopped and indicated a settee. *"Moi co ngoi."*

"Cam on ong," she said sitting down.

Left alone, she stared around the room in wonder. Al-

129

though not completely schooled in fine antiques, she had seen some in her life, and could recognize a quality collection — or, as was obvious in this case, *part* of a quality selection.

She had to wait for a quarter of an hour before her thoughts were interrupted by the appearance of yet another individual. A short, fat Vietnamese man appearing to be in his late forties or early fifties, came into the room. He only nodded a curt greeting as he sat down on a sofa opposite her.

"You are Loc Andrea?"

"*Co*," she answered affirmatively.

"And how did you hear of me?"

"From a friend of mine — Ban Lulu," Andrea said. "She worked for you some time ago."

"Yes. I remember her well. Too bad about her illness and the effect the sickness had on her looks."

"A sad thing," Andrea agreed, thinking of the former prostitute. Ban Lulu had come down with a crippling muscular disease that had reduced her to a limping skeleton of her former voluptuous self. She'd been forced to beg on the streets until a local intelligence officer had recognized her. He realized her potential for information on high-class vice in Saigon and had given her a chance to earn some extra money by giving some hot tidbits on the sex habits of more than just a few bigwigs in the government.

Later the woman had been recruited by the CIA operative Clayton Andrews when he'd found out about the investigation into Saigon's high-class vice and sexual activities.

Since Lulu was now a bona fide agent, it was safe to use her name, and if Nguyen did any double-checking, she would back Andrea up as per previous arrangements.

"You have experience as a prostitute?"

Andrea managed to blush a bit as she lowered her eyes. "Yes." Normally the questioning would not be so blunt.

"Where have you been working?"

"Several bars downtown," Andrea said. "Lulu finally recommended that I contact you for work. She said it would be much better and pay more than the jobs I was doing."

"Of course. And it will be infinitely more pleasant, Miss Loc. You see, we only deal with the highest class of clientele," Nguyen said. "That is why I choose only the most beautiful of women." He lit a cigarette. "Do you understand how my organization works?"

"Not really," Andrea answered.

"I do not have a bordello *per se*," Nguyen explained to her. "All of my business is arranged over the telephone. When I receive a request for, ah—services—I contact the appropriate girl who is available and have her taken to the correct place for the rendezvous. This is generally in one of the city's better hotels, though sometimes certain officers clubs have proper facilities."

"*Xin loi ong*," Andrea said. "How much will I be paid for each call?"

"Forgive my lack of modesty, but I am a generous man," Nguyen said. "You will receive ten thousand piasters."

"Oh, sir!" Andrea exclaimed. "You are indeed generous!"

"You will find yourself servicing the elite of our nation and allies," Nguyen told her. "High ranking politicians, bureaucrats, general officers and so on. Rich business men too, of course."

"I certainly hope you will hire me," Andrea implored.

"If Ban Lulu recommended you—and I must check on that—then you must be what we require," Nguyen said. "Lulu would not waste my time, I am sure."

"Of course not, sir."

"Stand up and walk about the room for me, *xin co*."

Andrea did as she was told. She went from one end of the luxurious chamber to the other.

"Raise your skirt."

Andrea did so.

"Nice legs. Now kindly remove all your clothing."

Andrea plied her trade well here. She slowly and sensually removed each item until she stood absolutely naked in front of the man.

"Kindly walk about again."

Andrea complied.

"Is there anything you won't do with a man?" he asked.

"I don't like to be beaten—"

Nguyen frowned at her.

"—unless the money is worth it," she added.

He relaxed. "Will you perform in the French fashion?"

"Yes."

"Do you find the Greek way distasteful?"

"No."

Nguyen nodded. Then he turned toward the door he'd come from. "Dai, come here!"

A young Vietnamese man appeared. From his muscular build, Andrea deduced he was part of Nguyen's security. The man, however, paid no attention to her, only looking at his employer.

"This is Dai. Dai, this is Andrea."

"*Han-hanh gap ong*," Andrea said.

"Likewise," Dai replied.

"You two have sex," Nguyen commanded.

Dai nodded his obedience with about the same enthusiasm he would display if ordered to vacuum the carpet. He did not disrobe, contenting himself with merely dropping his trousers.

Andrea settled on the sofa and closed her eyes as the young man mounted her. She feigned great enjoyment, even going through a pseudo orgasm at the end.

"Wonderful, Andrea!" Nguyen said. "Consider yourself hired. Leave your address, and we will contact you about your first assignments. Do you have a phone?"

"Oh, Mister Nguyen. I am sorry I don't," Andrea said. "It's impossible—"

"Don't worry, my dear," Nguyen said. "We'll see that you

132

are supplied with one." He stood up. "Goodbye."

The two men left her alone.

Andrea dressed. Now she was very impressed with Nguyen. Getting a telephone installed required bribes and long waits. The fact that he could get one put into her apartment immediately showed just how extensive his contacts were.

After making a final adjustment of her clothing, Andrea went back through the curtained exit. The old servant was waiting for her. He opened the door. "*Chao co*," he said.

Andrea smiled slightly. "Goodbye."

Col. Ngai Quang stood in front of the large mirror in his dressing room and carefully knotted the tie of his best civilian suit.

He was preparing to go for another evening of gaming at Tsing Chai's mah jongg parlor. Ngai was in such a jocular mood that he hummed to himself. His world had gotten a bit unsettled when the Black Eagles had returned to Saigon and aligned their activities with the national police — particularly Colonel Tran and Sergeant Chin. This had cut Ngai off from them, making it impossible to supply Tsing with any more information on their operations.

But the wily Chinese had made contacts in Japan and now a small force of Nipponese gangsters and professional killers, all with plenty of experience in working at their profession in a crowded urban environment, had come in to lend a hand. The final destruction of Maj. Robert Falconi and his cohorts would take a lot of pressure off Ngai.

And make this world a much safer place for him too.

Ngai lived in a mansion surrounded by a high wall. His neighborhood, the richest in Saigon, was inhabited by indigenous brass hats with a few foreign VIPs thrown in. The place was a virtual armed camp with special army and police units patrolling this hallowed sanctuary twenty-four hours a day.

Ngai came from a wealthy merchant family. As the second son, rather than the eldest, he hadn't had too much pressure put on him to go into his father's business. Free to choose his own way, he opted for a military career.

Ngai had always loved uniforms and the pomp of parades. His favorite sight as a boy was when the French Foreign Legion, marching in their somber slow-step, would take part in Saigon military ceremonies. The martial grandeur moved him like nothing else. When he reached the right age, he begged his father to grant him permission to go into the army. Arrangements were made and he entered the military academy and graduated as a second lieutenant when he was twenty-one years old.

But he was extremely small and thin, even by Vietnamese standards, and the rigorous life in the combat army such as infantry and armor was more than he could stand. He eventually ended up with a staff assignment and settled into the intelligence section. He wasn't disappointed. Despite the lack of adventure, he still was able to wear a uniform with the epaulettes and fancy trimmings, which was more important to him than branch assignments. Anyway, no matter, he had to admit to himself, he wasn't all that fond of slogging through jungle and rice paddies anyway.

Besides, there wasn't much chance to enrich one's self through graft in the infantry.

Ngai could be independent in his choice of professions, but when it came to marriage his parents were very strict. He was forced into an arranged wedding with the daughter of one of his father's business associates. The girl was homely and dumpy with a quite bland personality. He endured his wife by ignoring her most of the time. The woman didn't express much disappointment in this herself. She wasn't exactly enamored of the skinny little man she'd been forced to marry.

Their life together wasn't all that bad, however. There

was his army pay, bribes, and generous allowances from both families. The couple enjoyed the better things of Vietnamese society: parties, jewelry, fancy American cars, good Japanese appliances, expensive clothing, etc. But there was one more thing that completed the contentment in the little officer's life.

Gambling!

Ngai was addicted to gambling with all the intensity the visitors to opium dens had for their drugs. He didn't care to wager on sporting events, cards, or dice—Ngai loved the clack of mah jongg tiles.

He made nightly forays into the Chinese section of Saigon where the best parlors were located—particularly one that became his favorite. It was owned by Tsing Chai.

Entire nights were passed in that particular parlor as Ngai delved in an orgy of wild bets that eventually cost him a small fortune. His wild and reckless wagering brought him to the attention of Red operatives—like Tsing Chai—who had been placed and financed into setting up gambling dens by their superior officers.

Their big aim was to find people exactly like Ngai. Individuals who held sensitive positions in the army or government, who had absolutely no common sense when it came to gaming. Ngai caught their attention within a relatively short time.

Unknown to him, he was drawn into an intense well-planned schedule. At first he won great amounts of money in Tsing's. This kept him coming back until going there was a deeply ingrained habit. It seemed he could do no wrong as each dawn found him walking away with his pockets crammed with hundreds of thousands of piasters.

Then his luck dimmed somewhat. This was to keep him from getting suspicious. He didn't suspect anything, but his spirits began to sink.

Then he started winning again.

But after a few months he started sliding—faster—faster

and faster—until the bottom fell out.

By then he was deeply in debt to Tsing Chai to the extent that the situation was impossible. He was so far behind that he faced absolute, total personal disgrace and ruin.

Tsing Chai was an extremely fat man. His wide, moon-like face was creased in what seemed a perpetual smile. Like all people who overindulged in food to the extent of being horribly obese, he was self-centered, selfish, and ruthless in a clandestine kind of way. Despite being well known and documented in Vietnamese police and crime circles, no one was aware he was a conscientious, hard-working agent of the Communists.

As such, he'd been keeping a very close eye on Ngai.

He approached the army officer just before dawn following a long night of playing mah jongg. Ngai was red-eyed and exhausted after losing the final piasters he'd borrowed only a few hours previously. His head was bowed in despair and he knew he was completely and totally ruined.

Tsing approached him with a kindly expression on that great expanse of a face. "My dear *Dai Tai* Ngai. I am so sorry to hear of your long run of bad luck."

Ngai looked at him with downcast features. "Nor am I overjoyed with the misfortune. It appears that I owe you much money. And, I am sorry to say, more than I can repay within a reasonable period of time."

Tsing Chai laid a kindly hand on his shoulder. "Let us go into my office and see what can be done about this most dreadful and unbearable situation." He motioned gently for Ngai to precede him. "I think there is a way you may be able to ease your indebtedness to my humble parlor."

Ngai, knowing full well he was about to sink into a moral cesspool, nevertheless allowed himself to be escorted back to the private rooms.

Tsing Chai even poured him a drink. "If you could get something for me, I would be most grateful."

"What is that, Master Tsing?" Ngai asked with misgivings.

"Nothing much. Only a roster of the recent graduates of the South Vietnamese Army Intelligence School."

Ngai was no idiot. He knew this was the start of a general bleeding. But he had no choice.

He complied and was caught in the classical trap.

The debt was halved and there was even an extension of credit. With more demands coming fast and furious, Ngai was soon supplying top secret documents and other information to Tsing Chai. Yet he kept on with his wild gambling, unable to stop himself.

Finally the colonel made a decision. His life was ruined, but not having the physical or moral courage to follow the officer's code of a self-inflicted bullet to the head, he decided to get what he could out of the situation. He kept up the mah jongg playing while becoming a Communist agent working hand-in-hand with Tsing.

Whatever Tsing demanded — Tsing was given.

But Ngai got along too. He received not only money — which he quickly gambled away — but was given other things as well.

All expensive presents from Tsing.

These weren't handed to him out of generosity on the Chinese agent's part, though. If Ngai had been allowed to accrue too many debts, and not seem to be spending money on nonessential luxuries, he would eventually attract the attention of both police and military intelligence. This would lead to an investigation that would compromise not only himself, but Tsing and his organization too.

But, by having a nice house, automobiles, and other expensive playthings, Ngai would appear to be leading the life of a respectable, patriotic army officer from the upper classes instead of throwing away huge amounts of money at the gaming tables.

His latest assignment from Tsing Chai (and coordinated through the efforts of Major Xong who reported directly to

137

Lieutenant Colonel Krashchenko of the KGB) was to keep close tabs on the newly organized unit, the Black Eagles. By pulling rank and diplomatic pressure, Ngai was able to force the CIA case officer Chuck Fagin to keep him fully briefed on Falconi and his men.

But with the new set-up involving the national police, this had fallen through. Ngai knew he was under a dark cloud, facing the possibility of assassination if his value to the Communists finally diminished.

Now, putting on his suit jacket, Ngai smiled to himself in the mirror. The arrival of the Japanese hit men who would terminate the unsuspecting Black Eagles once and for all, had cleared up the situation.

Things were back to normal.

Ngai could get back to spying on his country with the minimum of personal risk.

CHAPTER NINE

The small briefing area was just the right size for the assembled Black Eagles.

The seven of them, along with Sgt. Chin Han and a corporal of the national police, fit into the room quite comfortably. A couple of pitchers of iced coffee and tea sat at a table on one side of the room. Several sipped the cool liquids from paper cups wishing something a bit stronger and more alcoholic was available.

Maj. Robert Falconi stood in front of the assemblage looking like his old self. He was dressed in lightweight OD jungle fatigues, as were the rest of the men. It was obvious these hadn't been worn out in the field under combat conditions. Brand new, starched and pressed, Falconi's uniform looked sharp enough for him to receive an inspecting general. After weeks of wearing civvies, he seemed to like being back in the old grind. It hadn't hurt his mood a bit to note the other Black Eagles were back in uniform too. He even had a smile for the men.

"Good morning," he greeted them. "I suppose—as the old saying goes—you're wondering why I called this meeting."

Archie Dobbs raised his hand. "Is it to give us all promotions, Skipper?"

"Sorry."

Malpractice McCorckel had a hopeful expression on his face. "Are you going to tell us we've got six months R&R?"

"I can't even promise you six *days*," Falconi said. "But I'll make a special note of your suggestion. Six months sounds pretty good to me."

Calvin Culpepper lit a cigarette. "Whatever the reason you got for gettin' us altogether in uniform again is prob'ly exciting though, ain't it, Falcon?"

"If you consider ambushing a convoy exciting, then I suppose it is," Falconi said.

"Yeah," Lightfingers O'Quinn said seriously. Humorless and hardworking, he hadn't recognized the poor jokes of his buddies as attempts at levity. The marine took everything he heard verbatim. "I consider that a sort of fun way to pass the time."

"Then, my friend," Falconi said, "you're about to have a hell of a lot of fun. That is exactly what we're going to do. We'll be heading out into the boonies—though not too far—and play the role of bushwhackers."

"Hey! Hey!" Archie exclaimed. "We'll head 'em off at the pass, right, sheriff?"

"Exactly," Falconi said. "And the man with the word is here. I don't think you've all met him, but he's one of Sergeant Chin's number one guys. There's no doubt you've seen him from time to time." He motioned to the other policeman standing beside Chin. "Gentlemen, this is Corporal Hai."

Hai stood up and displayed a friendly smile. "I have met most of you during the previous raids. I hope to know you all soon." His English was excellent. Although he was obviously Chin's junior in rank, he was an older man. Short and muscular, he looked compact and strong in his uniform.

Balding slightly, his face was open and amicable. "I have worked for several years in an undercover capacity and have been able to develop some excellent sources of information," Hai said. "This has brought about some interesting intelligence regarding contraband being shipped into Saigon via ARVN trucks."

"Are we talking about narcotics?" Master Sergeant Gordon asked.

"Not this time," Hai answered. "Black market stuff—all stolen from the Americans. There's practically everything you can imagine involved—transistor radios, cigarettes, toilet articles, foodstuffs—in other words, items that were destined for the various PXs."

"How did the black marketeers get it all?" Lightfingers O'Quinn asked. As a supply man he was always interested in the transfer and issue of goods—even when it was stolen.

"I am sorry to report that the Chinese Communist gangster Tsing Chai is masterminding a plot in conjunction with various high-ranking officers of my country's army. They have formed an organization to spirit items from warehouses to hiding places out in the countryside. Then, when the time is right and arrangements properly made, they arrange to have the stuff trucked back into Saigon. Then the merchandise is sold on the black market by their agents."

"I suppose it's all brought into the city in trucks supplied to the South Vietnamese army by the United States, right?" Top asked.

"Right," Hai answered.

Archie Dobbs was not impressed. "So what's the big deal? We stop the vehicles, retake the goods and throw a bunch of crooks in jail."

"I'm afraid it won't be that easy," Hai cautioned him. "The people involved here have too much to lose in money and personal freedom. The transportation outfit the trucks belong to can best be described as a gang. Most are not even real soldiers. They've been brought in from Saigon—gener-

141

ally from the Cholon district — and put in uniforms. They return to their real status after each run."

"In other words," Malpractice said, "the sons of bitches are going to fight us."

"That's putting it mildly," Hai said. "You'll find them as deadly as the Viet Cong or Pathet Lao."

"We are now back to war again, huh?" the South Korean marine Chun Kim remarked with a delighted grin on his face. "Get to kick ass."

"It certainly appears so," Falconi said. He motioned to Hai. "Proceed with the briefing."

"Yes, sir." Hai walked to a wall map and pointed to a side road off Route 13 to the north between Saigon and Ben Cat. "This is the direction they follow to bring in the loot and merge it into the regular military traffic. We want to intercept them before they can lose themselves in other convoys — and they will make an attempt to break through to do exactly that."

Calvin, a demolitions man, shrugged. "Why not plant some mines and just blow up the lead vehicles? That should stop 'em."

"An excellent idea, Calvin," Falconi said. "It's one I put forward and had turned down. The brass doesn't want any of the trucks damaged any more than necessary. In fact, they plan on having those deuce-and-a-halfs returned to other units after this operation."

"I don't give a damn what they want," Archie Dobbs said sullenly. "Some of 'em are gonna have bullet holes in 'em, Skipper. And I'll bet we'll have to destroy at least the front truck, right?"

"That's better than having them all blown up," Falconi said. "And another thing — they want prisoners too."

"This is most important," Hai interjected. "We need them for interrogation so that we can penetrate deeper into their organization."

"Christ!" Malpractice moaned. "That makes the job

more dangerous for us. We'll be shooting high and they'll be pouring the lead right back into us."

"Nobody said the fucking job was going to be easy," Falconi said, intoning his old saying. He motioned to Hai. "Continue with the briefing, Corporal."

"Yes, sir." Hai turned back to the map to begin giving the finer details of the operations order.

Col. Ngai Quang carefully scrutinized the large report.

He sat at his desk, languidly smoking, as he pored through the thick document. This was the latest compilation of intelligence sent in from active units operating in the field. The words, written in terse military terminology, told of fire fights, ambushes, raids, and other combat. There were lists of friendly casualties (including a couple of American Special Forces advisors), and the always inflated body count of enemy dead. The ARVN commanders sent in exaggerated figures based on actual sightings as well as extremely generous estimates of the number of corpses and wounded dragged off by the enemy after the battle.

Ngai snorted a short laugh. If the figures were true, there wouldn't be a Communist left alive in all of Southeast Asia. Still, he reminded himself, such information made the Americans happy. He scribbled out a cover letter of approval and set it aside to be typed later.

A knock on the door interrupted his work.

"Yes?"

A sergeant stepped in carrying a uniform on a hanger. The paper covering over the apparel bore printing identifying it as coming from the Tan Son Nhut Air Base dry cleaning plant. "*Xin loi ong, Dai Ta* Ngai. This was just delivered for you."

"*Cam on ong, Trung-Si*," Ngai said. "Put it in the closet."

The sergeant quickly complied, then withdrew, leaving the colonel alone in the office. Ngai waited for a minute or so, then he stood up and quietly walked to the door. After making sure it was locked he went to the closet and took out the garments.

He paid no attention to the clothing. Instead he pulled the cardboard tubing off the hanger. A piece of thin tissue paper, tightly rolled up, was inside. Ngai opened it and read the message quickly. Then he put it in his ashtray and set it afire. After making sure it had all burned, he got his cap and the report he'd been reading and walked out into the main office where junior officers and sergeants sat working at their desks.

Ngai dropped off the report with his letter of approval. "Have that typed up. I shall be back to sign it later."

"Yes, sir, " the sergeant said.

"I have business downtown," Ngai said setting his cap on his head. "I shall return in two or three hours."

"Yes, sir."

After Ngai left headquarters, he made no attempt to conceal his route to Saigon's commercial area. The colonel traveled in a chauffeured military sedan and had the driver park in front of a well-known men's clothing store. He went inside and spent several long moments perusing a rack of white, tropical civilian suits.

A salesman approached him. "May I be of assistance, *Dai Ta*?"

"I'm thinking of purchasing something suitable for travel," Ngai said. "It will take me some time. You have a wide selection here." Then he paused and spoke slowly and deliberately. "A Vietnamese gentleman should always dress well to impress others."

The salesman recognized the code words. He replied properly. "Yes. We are all ambassadors when we go abroad."

"Your garments are of excellent quality."

"*Cam on ong*," the man said. "Please take your time. Our dressing rooms are in the back in case you find something to your liking."

"*Cam on ong*," Ngai said continuing to examine the merchandise.

Finally a thin man, appearing to be rather well-to-do, also came into the store. Although Ngai recognized him as Xong who normally drove the dry cleaning delivery truck, he made no attempt to speak to him. In a few moments, Xong took a suit from the rack and disappeared into the back.

Ngai did likewise.

He went to a dressing booth and stepped inside the curtain. Then he rapped three times on the back. It slid open, and Ngai stepped through to a larger room. He bowed to Xong. "I received your message."

"You did well to come right away," Xong said. "I cannot stay away from my truck too long."

"I admire your talents at disguise," Ngai said in making a professional judgment. "By stepping from your driver's uniform into a business suit, you have completely altered your appearance. Only someone who knew you personally could have recognized you."

"Never mind that," Xong snapped. "I have good news. We have another source of information on the Black Eagles."

"*Mung ong!*" Ngai exclaimed. "That is exactly what we have been needing."

"Your role in this latest development has been most disappointing," Xong said.

"There was nothing I could do," Ngai protested. "I told you that the American Fagin did not trust me."

"Still, Ngai, you did not display the proper spirit or determination in correcting the situation," Xong said coldly.

Ngai knew better than to argue. "I am sorry."

"The problem is solved, however," Xong continued. "There is now a source available to us in the national police. He can forward information to you through normal chan-

145

nels."

"But how can he do that without alerting his superiors?"

"That is not for you to worry about," Xong said.

Ngai's pride was stung despite his deep, gnawing, personal knowledge that he was a turncoat. "Who is the informant?"

"I won't tell *you* that, of course," Xong replied in unhidden contempt. "You are to obey orders without question."

"I was only worried about the possibility the man is under suspicion from his own people."

"He is completely trustworthy in their eyes," Xong explained. "His dispatches will be sent out with a top secret classification which means they receive no scrutiny on the lower levels of command."

"But what about the upper echelons?" Ngai asked.

Xong smiled. "He can slip them right under their noses. The beauty of it is, that if you are discovered with the information, you can show you did not request it. The intelligence, as you can say, simply showed up on your desk. You only assumed it was a change in policy, so did not question the source."

Ngai nodded. "Which means they cannot prove I am the cause of any compromise regarding Falconi and his men."

"Exactly!"

"This solves a lot of problems," Ngai said.

"We are now very, very close to throwing our net over Falconi and destroying his organization," Xong said. "We will proceed toward that end with cautious determination. We know now for sure that Tsing Chai is their target."

"Then when will they make their final move?" Ngai asked.

"We do not know," Xong answered. "That is why it is of the utmost importance that you transmit all information you receive in a speedy and accurate manner."

"Of course. Are there any changes in my orders or procedures?" Ngai asked.

"No. You will continue to pass on information as before through Tsing Chai," Xong said. He slid open the back of the dressing room. "Wait five minutes before you leave."

"Yes, Comrade," Ngai said. He checked his watch, then called out to the salesman. "May I try on some more suits?"

"Yes, sir," the man answered. "Please make yourself comfortable. I will fetch some selections for you."

"*Cam on ong*," Ngai said. He smiled to himself. The sooner the Black Eagle detachment was wiped out, the sooner he could get back to his normal life of gambling and safely passing on secrets.

And that would take place quickly, no doubt—along with Falconi's demise or disappearance.

Andrea Thuy Roget, alias Loc Andrea, stepped from the creaky elevator and walked down the heavily carpeted hall of the Palais Hotel's fourth floor.

This would be her eighth work assignment since joining Nguyen's stable of high-class whores. Each sexual sojourn seemed to increase the separation between her and Robert Falconi. In fact, Andrea had been surprised to find that having these liaisons was proving emotionally therapeutic for her. Even though she had yet to actually come into contact with the quarry of this particular operation, her old enthusiasm was returning. Each episode was like taking a step closer to the final confrontation which would bring about yet another victory over the Red despoilers of her country and her life.

Her broken heart was mending fast.

Andrea stopped in front of the correct door. This would be an American, she recalled Nguyen telling her, who was a minor bureaucrat in the State Department. It was supposed to be a rare trip out of Washington for him, so no doubt he was taking the opportunity to get away from a faded middle-aged wife, and dally with a beautiful Asian girl.

147

Andrea knocked.

The door opened to reveal a short, fat man. Bald and showing some age, he still had a friendly face—it was almost fatherly. "Please come in. You are from Nguyen?"

"Yes," Andrea answered. "*Ong* Nguyen send me." She made a particular effort to speak in a heavy accent, and purposely mangled her English. "You likee?"

"Sure," the man smiled. "I likee fine."

"I am called Andrea," she said walking farther into the room. She looked around. This was an expensive suite. The tab was being picked up by the American taxpayer, no doubt. The bedroom would be separate from the main chamber.

"I'm Eddie," the American said. "You want a drink, Andrea?"

"Oh, yes, very nice. Thank you, please."

Eddie went over to a small dry bar in the corner of the room. "A friend of mine told me about Nguyen," he said. "How's a scotch and soda?"

"Very nice. Yes, please."

Eddie mixed the drink. "He said the man was the source for the most beautiful women in Saigon. So, since this is my first trip to Vietnam, I thought—well, why not try a pretty Vietnamese girl."

"Oh yes. We very nice."

"So I've heard!" he said with enthusiasm. He handed her the drink, taking the opportunity to stare down her low-cut blouse and let his eyes drink in the gorgeous breasts. "Well, sit down and relax a bit. You're not in any hurry, are you?"

"This all night, right?"

"Sure. That's what I asked for. Okay by you?"

"Sure. I likee." She took a sip of the drink while he mixed another for himself.

Eddie sat down beside her. "Beautiful city Saigon."

"Oh, yes. Very nice."

He took a healthy gulp of his scotch. "I've never—y-

'know, been with an Oriental girl before."

"Oh! I show you a good time," Andrea said. She knew the chance that this visitor would prove a connection with the real organization they were after was very small. But at least he formed part of her cover. The more of the prostitute's life she led, the easier it would be for her to be accepted into that world and eventually end up with the Chinese Tsing Chai or one of his colleagues.

Anyway, this was easy.

There had been several occasions in past solo operations when Andrea had gone to bed with men who were Communist officers. She'd loathed and despised their touch, but forced herself to endure each episode knowing she'd eventually kill the Red son of a bitch.

Eddie was different—actually easy. Harmless and nice, he served a subtler, more gentle side of the dangerous life she had chosen to return to.

"Ah—tell me, Andrea," Eddie said. "What's your, well, your specialty."

Andrea recognized at once what he was getting at. Here was a man, long married, with a wife who was a sexual iceberg. No exotic playing with the little lady when it came to beddy-bye time. It was climb on, pump away, then climb off. The only pleasure he probably got was closing his eyes and pretending she was somebody else.

Andrea smiled at him. "I do anything, Eddie, and everything. You tell me what you likee, okay?"

"Oh, boy! Okay!"

Another ten minutes of small talk went by while they finished their drinks. The girl smiled to herself. Eddie would probably have gone crazy if he'd known he was about to have sex with a female ARVN lieutenant assigned to MACV-SOG who was part of an operation to move in on Communist agents.

"Well, shall we go into the bedroom?" Eddie asked.

Andrea smiled. "Sure. We go."

He led her across the expanse of the sitting room and opened the door for her. She stepped into the sleeping chamber and noted the huge, canopied bed. A large bathroom could be seen through another door.

The United States Department of State went first class.

Eddie stood there awkwardly for a few seconds, so Andrea took the initiative and began to slowly undress. She looked at him and smiled as she lethargically disrobed. Finally she was naked. She walked seductively to the bed and lay down on it.

By then any shyness he felt had dissipated. Eddie hurriedly yanked his clothes off and joined her on the bed. Without preliminaries, he got between her legs and plunged inside.

Andrea feigned passion and pleasure as she groaned and undulated her hips beneath him. Eddie's breathing was heavy and rapid, his eyes drinking in the beautiful woman he was possessing with such abandon.

Suddenly he stopped.

His voice was almost apologetic. "Andrea — could we try another position?"

She smiled. "Sure. What you want?"

"I've often wanted to do it from behind, y'know what I mean?"

"You mean like doggy?"

"Yeah," Eddie said grinning.

"We do." Andrea knew she had been right about the guy. His wife probably wouldn't do it with him except in the missionary position. She got on her hands and knees, lowering her face to the bed.

Eddie panted in excitement as he got himself behind her. He pushed forward missing the mark until Andrea reached under and grabbed his manhood.

"Wait. I put it in right place."

"Okay! Okay!"

"Now. You push, Eddie."

150

He did as she told him, sliding into her. Eddie thought he'd died and gone to heaven. His hands slid all over her body, caressing thighs, belly and breasts as they roamed over every part of Andrea he could reach.

He climaxed in spasms, jerking so hard he almost slipped out. But he got the job done. After a few moments he withdrew from her, then collapsed in happy fatigue to the bed.

Andrea turned around and lay down beside him. "You likee, Eddie?"

"Ooooh! Yeah. I likee a lot."

Andrea let him relax for a few moments. This, like all other times, took her farther from her love for the American major. She felt freer now than since that first time she'd made love with Falconi. She was back in her element. A woman who belonged to no man — only a cause.

"Say, Andrea?" Eddie said.

"Yes?"

"Do you, y'know, do like the French?"

Andrea noticed the unfortunate man who was sexually frustrated at home, had come to life again. She reached over and took him in her hand, manipulated him to even more hardness. She bent down, taking Eddie into her mouth.

"Ooooh, Lord!"

Now he was convinced he had indeed died and gone to heaven.

CHAPTER TEN

Many times, in Maj. Robert Falconi's dangerous profession, ambush was simply part of a day's work. Although the activity sounded relatively simple, i.e., hide somewhere and wait for somebody to come along, then blow the bastards away; being a successful bushwhacker was a complicated process in most instances.

There are actually three types of ambush: area, point, and hasty.

The hasty ambush is the simplest. It *has* to be since it is almost always virtually unplanned. This type of activity takes place when an unexpected opportunity or contact with an enemy force pops up. A quick reaction is thrown together. Naturally, a seasoned combat leader is good at this while it is riskier for rookies.

The other two types can be planned out at more leisure.

The point ambush is directed at a single area where the targets will be passing through. With enough time, the ambushers can situate themselves in the best areas of concealment, pick or clear good lanes of fire and, in other words, make sure not one enemy sonofabitch is going to be able to escape.

The area ambush is simply a combination of several of the aforementioned.

Maj. Robert Falconi organized a point ambush by dividing his unit into three groups. First was the rear security force. This would consist of Lightfingers O'Quinn and Malpractice McCorckel. Their job would be to close in the rear once the ambush went down. This would prevent any of the victims from being able to retreat back to safety.

The front security force, who would do about the same thing in the front, was Chun Kim and Calvin Culpepper. Naturally, their responsibility would be to see that none of the ambushees were able to get away by speeding through and out the front of the killing zone. Kim's effectiveness was strengthened somewhat by the addition of an M79 grenade launcher. This was one of his favorite weapons, and one he had used frequently on previous missions.

If the front vehicle looked as if it might be able to escape the initial bursts of fire, it would be disabled by a rocket grenade. Thus, it would block the narrow road. Since trucks in the rear would be forced to attempt to evade the trap by using reverse gear, it was thought the extra armament wasn't needed there. Skilled riflemen, like Malpractice and Lightfingers, could deal with that problem by artfully employing their M16s.

Besides, they only had one launcher.

The attack force, with the added strength of Sergeant Chin and Corporal Hai of the national police, would consist of those two Vietnamese along with Falconi, Top Gordon, Archie Dobbs and Chuck Fagin.

Those were five very mean guys who were above average in the practical application of fire and maneuver.

A quick reconnaissance of the area showed an excellent spot some five miles west of where the road junctioned with Route 13. With the advantage of having the time to carefully choose their firing positions, the Black Eagles and their two allies were able to situate themselves to the best advantage.

While this all seemed to the Black Eagles like the operation was wrapped up before it started, they each kept one undeniable fact in the back of their minds: People who get ambushed have a nasty habit of shooting back.

This wasn't going to be a piece of cake.

Malpractice lay in the thick grass that covered the knoll. He had a good view of the road. He held a worn-looking Prick-Six radio in his hand. The communication device, its olive-drab surface scratched and faded, had been on all four of the Black Eagles' previous missions.

Lightfingers O'Quinn, a couple of meters away, held up his hand to signal silence. He listened for a few seconds, then shook his head. "Nothin'. Thought I heard the whine of a GI motor."

Malpractice checked his watch. "The bastards are due any time now."

"Man, this is a roundabout way to do things, ain't it?" Lightfingers remarked.

"Yeah. It sure as hell ain't our usual style," Malpractice agreed. "You'd think it'd be easier just to charge that Chinaman's mah jongg parlor and police the sonofabitch up."

"I suppose Fagin knows what he's doing," Lightfingers said. "Tsing Chai might be poised to haul ass at the first opportunity. Us screwing around with other things should calm him down some."

"Yeah. Then we can catch the bastard and his whole organization with their pants down." Malpractice was quiet for several long moments. "What do you think o' Fagin?"

"Well — I'm changing' my mind," Lightfingers said. "I did think he was a chickenshit asshole for leavin' us stuck out in that B camp. But I guess he was doin' right."

Malpractice nodded his head. "Yeah. If he hadn't gotten suspicious o' that guy Colonel Ngai, we'd be rottin' in some

NVA prison camp somewhere."

"Or molding away in the ground," Lightfingers added.

"I think I'll buy Fagin a box o' his favorite cigars when we're done with this operation."

"Me too," Lightfingers echoed. "The guy's got balls, pal. You notice him on them other raids?"

"Sure did," Malpractice said. "Didn't flinch a bit."

Again the pair, manning the rear position, lapsed into silence. Suddenly Malpractice raised his head and listened. He lowered it. "Here they come!"

Lightfingers took a cautious glance, then ducked back down in the natural cover offered by the grass. "Right!"

Malpractice hit the transmit button. "Falcon, this is Tailgunner. Five rabbits, close up, comin' down the road."

"Roger, Tailgunner," came back Falconi's voice. There was a second of dead space before the Black Eagles commander spoke again. "Nosegunner, did you monitor that transmission? Over."

Up at the front of the attack position, Chun Kim spoke into his own radio. "Roger, Falcon. I ready. Out."

The Korean marine, with Calvin Culpepper just across the road from him, aimed his M79 grenade launcher in the direction the trucks would be approaching from.

Within ten minutes the unmistakable whine of American deuce-and-a-half engines could be heard gradually growing louder.

Kim settled down, ready for action. He slipped off the safety forward and peered down the narrow road. Suddenly the front of a truck appeared over a small rise. He waited for a few seconds more, then aimed carefully.

The launcher barked and kicked back against his shoulder.

The 40-millimeter grenade lobbed out of the tube and smacked the truck directly in the grill. The round went off sending pieces of metal flying out in all directions. A cloud of steam, hissing angrily, shot out of the ruined radiator.

The big vehicle stopped and the other one behind it, following too closely, slammed into its rear end.

Back in the middle of the attack force, Sergeant Chin hollered out in Vietnamese. "Everybody out of the trucks with your hands up!"

A voice, screaming in the same language, answered in what could only be an insult.

Chin swung the muzzle of his M16 in that direction and squeezed off a round. A man standing in the back of the second truck caught the bullet dead in the chest and pitched over the side to land with a dull plop on the road.

Then hell broke loose.

Back in the rear, the last truck in the convoy made an attempt to escape. The driver threw it into reverse and stomped on the accelerator.

Lightfingers leaped to a standing position for a quick aim through the open panel in the canvas stretched over the cab.

Then he fired.

The bullet smacked into the back of the driver's head throwing him forward on the steering wheel. The truck, still chugging along, continued to back up in a slow turn. It rolled up an incline at an angle. Finally it tipped a bit, the men in the back leaping out frantically, then the vehicle rolled over, spilling its cargo across the expanse of road.

The surviving passengers made an impromptu charge toward Lightfingers and Malpractice. There were six of them.

"Oh, shit!" the medic yelled.

The two Black Eagles fired frantically at the attackers. The first two pitched face down to the ground. A third went down, but used one of his dead buddies as cover. His own weapon spat death toward them.

"My kingdom for a grenade!" Lightfingers exclaimed ducking to the earth.

Malpractice rolled into the deeper grass, then got to his hands and knees to crawl rapidly and in a near panic forward. When he figured he had gone far enough, he stood up. The guy, who now had Lightfingers pinned down, was a bit to his left. He fired.

The gangster spun around and sat down abruptly on the ground facing Malpractice.

Lightfingers took the opportunity to put a shot of his own in him. The man jerked hard from the impact of the round, then slumped over.

But the third and fourth were close to Malpractice. They turned their combined attention on him, forcing him to quickly withdraw back to heavier cover.

Then they whirled their weapons on Lightfingers.

The marine fired in haste, but he was good. Two more baddies rolled to terra firma, their black marketeering days ended.

Malpractice linked up with Lightfingers and their fusillades knocked down numbers five and six.

The rear was secure.

In the meantime, things were hot and heavy in the middle of the ambush. Master Sergeant Gordon, on the side opposite Falconi, Dobbs and Fagin, was sharing his problems with Chin and Hai. Although their positioning in the operation was such that they offered no danger to their comrades across the road, they had to be careful in moving around or they would most certainly send some unintentional rounds winging at the others. A bullet didn't distinguish between friend and foe, it simply slammed into whatever — or who-ever — was unlucky enough to be in the path of its trajectory.

When three of the bad guys made a break for the jungle off to his side of the road, Top didn't dare fire. He got mad and decided he'd be damned if the sonsofbitches were going to get away. He went after them.

The master sergeant was a big man, but he moved with great agility and silence through the heavy vegetation. Plenty of patrol work in the Korean War and missions with the Black Eagles had sharpened his hunting skills razor sharp.

He slung his M16 as he moved through the trees, pulling his Colt auto from its shoulder holster. He estimated the escapees' route and angled off to make his interception. Having longer legs than the Vietnamese, he moved a lot faster.

He stopped and listened momentarily when he got the chance. The distant rustling in the brush gave undeniable evidence that he was closing in on the three fugitives.

Finally he heard the loudest disturbance off to his left rear. He stopped—listened some more—then moved that way a few yards. When he reached the most advantageous position, he squatted down.

Sixty seconds later, an Oriental wearing a set of fatigues way too large for him, stepped into a small clearing in front of Top. The Black Eagle, his .45 poised, stepped out.

"Stop! Hands up!"

The man held an M16. He didn't hesitate in cutting loose on full automatic at the master sergeant.

Twigs, leaves and bark flew crazily around Top's head for the brief millisecond it took him to react. His pistol barked.

The slug impacted with the other's forehead, punching into the skull. Then, mushrooming nicely, it exploded the cranium outward, carrying the victim backward through ten feet of empty air before allowing him to drop to the spongy earth in an undignified heap of dead humanity.

Top scampered away from the noise with the knowledge that the remaining duo would do the same. Again he practiced that most important skill of combat in a dense area. He became absolutely still while tuning his ears for any hint of unnatural sound that was alien to that particular environment.

He was rewarded.

A slithering of feet sounded some ten meters away. A real display of total ineptness in the jungle. Top knew the guy had to be a civilian criminal from an urban environment. That would be one of the assholes that Corporal Hai said would be dressed as a soldier.

Top found him traveling in a disoriented circle. The Black Eagle ducked quickly behind the thick trunk of a tree. As he did so, he slid his pistol into its holster and quickly, but silently, drew his knife. Then he waited.

The man drew off once, but, being lost and uncertain, it wasn't long before he was back in the original area, completely disoriented. Finally he walked past Top's tree. The master sergeant leaped out and slashed the sharp blade of his weapon across the gangster's neck. The man gurgled and grabbed at the wound. Top moved in for the final stroke.

The third escapee suddenly appeared a few feet away. He elevated the barrel of his weapon for a quick shot. Once more Top found himself the object of a black marketeer's fusillade. But this time his own firearms were too far out of reach.

He whipped his knife hand toward the criminal, sending the weapon zipping across the short open space between them. The blade bit deep into the man's throat. There was no shock power, as with a bullet, so the victim didn't stumble back. Instead he grasped at the obscene object buried in his throat and tried to pull it out.

Top nonchalantly swung his M16 off his shoulder. After aiming carefully at the bobbing smuggler, he squeezed off a round and ended the poor bastard's misery.

With the ambush now deteriorating somewhat because of the panic-stricken scurrying of the targets, Falconi and Dobbs formed up as a two-man hunter-killer team.

A group of black marketeers, although unable to fight their way through the Black Eagles' trap, had pulled together into a strong formation off the road. From their vantage point, they were able to hold off any serious attack. If they could last until dark, their escape would be a certain thing.

"There's too many of us trying to get to 'em," Falconi said. He had noted Fagin, Chin and Hai attempting to maneuver into position for a kill. Top Gordon, coming out of the woods, joined them. Within a few moments all four were pinned down.

"We could get behind the bastards or flank 'em," Archie suggested.

"Yeah," Falconi agreed. "As long as the other guys keep their attention."

Archie winked at his commander. "Time's wastin', Skipper."

"Let's go!"

The two pulled back from the main action, then cut off for the deeper woods. Falconi, respecting Archie's orientation abilities in the jungle, followed along. The detachment scout moved twenty-five meters into the dense vegetation, then made an abrupt turn. Although unable to pick out the target area's shooting because of the sound of other firing, he made a rapid guestimate. Then stopped.

"I figure they're straight that way, Skipper," he said pointing.

"And I figure you're right," Falconi said. "Let's get 'em, Archie."

The two moved with speedy stealth through the clinging plant life of the rain forest. Archie's uncanny ability to keep his bearings in the swirling green foliage enabled them to travel in a straight line. Finally he signaled a halt.

"Listen, Skipper."

Falconi tuned his ears to the sound of the fighting. Within seconds he was able to pick out a distinct part of the shooting a few meters ahead of them. He nodded. "That's where we want to go."

"I suggest discretion," Archie said. "Them's fancy words for crawlin'."

The two flopped belly down and wormed their way forward. It took a very uncomfortable quarter of an hour before they arrived at a point where they could see the people they had to attack.

"Five of 'em," Falconi said in a hoarse whisper.

"Yeah," Archie answered. "They got our guys pinned down."

"Unless front security or rear security comes in, the situation is gonna get out of hand."

"You're not forgettin' us, are you, Skipper?"

"Nope," Falconi said. "And it seems we're the men of the hour."

"Orders, Skipper?"

"Yeah. The same one Custer gave his guys—don't take any prisoners."

"Custer's shit was weak, Skipper," Archie reminded him.

"Let's hope ours isn't," Falcon said. "Charge!"

The two leaped to their feet, their M16s on full auto, and raced toward the five bad guys. Yelling loudly enough to attract their own men's attention—in the wild hope of getting them to either raise their fire or cease it—Falconi and Archie swept forward throwing out a curtain of bullets.

The black marketeers, startled at this unexpected attack from that quarter, turned to face these new adversaries. It was a bad idea for three of them. They paid for the impetuous response with their lives, the duo's bullets crashing into them, hitting them so hard that their bodies bounced off each other before finally tumbling back to the ground in a twitching pile.

The survivors displayed more intelligence. They threw down their weapons and raised their hands.

"Let's go!" Archie barked. "Stand up and keep them mitts o' yours way high."

As the prisoners complied, Fagin, Top, Chin and Hai left their own area and joined them. Fagin, unaccustomed to the fatigue uniform he wore, looked a bit awkward in his brand new, stiff equipment. But his grin was easy and happy.

"I didn't know if we were going to be able to hang on to these guys or not," he said.

"We sized the situation up and galloped to the rescue,"

Falconi said. He watched the two Vietnamese policemen search the captives in a not too gentle fashion. "It'll be up to the security details to wrap this baby up."

Even as he spoke, Kim and Calvin were slowly moving in from the front. They covered each other as they searched the lead truck. Both the driver and his passenger in the front were dead. Shards of shrapnel and truck metal had been driven into them from the rocket grenade the Korean marine had fired to open the attack.

The second vehicle had no cadavers in it, but there were several scattered around it. These unfortunates had gone down under the enfilading fire of the attack force only moments after their friends in the front had given up the ghost. The bodies, bloodied from the fatal wounds, lay sprawled in grotesque immobility on, under and around the truck.

Back in the rear, Malpractice and Lightfingers, holding their M16s ready, slowly checked out the rear deuce-and-halfs. All had flat tires and were punched full of bullet holes. Gasoline leaked out of one punctured tank, but luckily hadn't caught on fire.

"Too bad about these vehicles," Lightfingers, the supplyman, said.

"Yeah," Malpractice said. "We were supposed to avoid ruining them if possible."

"There's going to be a lot of paperwork involved in writing these babies off," Lightfingers said patting the side of one of the olive-drab trucks. "I'm sure as hell glad they weren't assigned to us."

"Yeah. The American taxpayer sure got a screwin' today," Malpractice said. "Not only did he pay for these trucks that were given away, but he also donated the stolen items in the back."

Lightfingers spat. "This war is dirty in more ways than one, ain't it?"

"Amen, buddy," Malpractice said. "Let's get on up and join the rest o' the guys."

Master Sergeant Gordon took a quick headcount and was pleased to note that the Black Eagles had taken no casualties. Not even a slight wound.

Falconi was not only happy about that, but tickled about the success of the thing too. Maybe it would discourage any more of the ARVN brass from trying to make a personal profit on American sacrifices for their country. If it hadn't been for the two South Vietnamese policemen with them, he would have been downright bitter. But they'd risked their lives too. He walked over to Corporal Hai and offered his hand.

"Congratulations. Your informants gave you the right word, didn't they?"

Hai grinned. "It always pays to keep a few rascals on the payroll."

When Malpractice and Lightfingers joined the main group, the latter went from truck to truck checking out the cargo. He came back shaking his head. "The stuff is all shot up. Not hardly any of it's salvageable, Skipper."

"We didn't expect it to be, Lightfingers," Falconi said. "Just remember that if we can't use it, neither can the black market."

Archie Dobbs laughed. "There were some boxes holding cheap perfume in that third truck. All shot to hell. It smells like a New Orleans whorehouse over there."

Calvin Culpepper wiped a large hand across his sweating brow. "Speaking of whorehouses—" He let the statement hang.

"Don't worry, guys," Falconi said. He reached over and patted Fagin on the shoulder. "Our fearless case officer has informed me that we get a night off tomorrow."

"Hoorah!" Archie shouted. "I'm gonna get laid!"

"I just wanna get drunk," Calvin said.

"I'm gonna get laid," Archie insisted.

"A big steak dinner for me," Malpractice announced.

"I'm gonna get laid," Archie reiterated.

Falconi grinned. "Good thing this outfit doesn't have a chaplain. The poor bastard'd turn in his cross and *he'd* get laid."

"Not before me, he wouldn't!" Archie said.

Tsing Chai stood in his communications room located just off his office. He watched intently as his senior communications man ran a net check from the Soviet R-108 radio.

This type of commo equipment was designed for tactical field use with only a limited range. But to the north, located in a pottery factory, was a Russian R-401 radio relay system. This set-up allowed the smaller, clandestine stations of agents like Tsing to communicate to North Vietnam through their facilities.

The operator turned to his chief. "Communications established, comrade. Any messages?"

"None at this moment," Tsing answered. "Simply make the usual coded check-in. And hurry. I don't like being on the air anymore than is absolutely necessary."

"Yes, comrade."

"Sometimes I wish Comrade Xong would use other radios when he wishes to contact Colonel Krashchenko in Hanoi," Tsing complained.

"He has faith in us, comrade."

"Perhaps," Tsing mused. "At any rate, shut down as quickly as possible." He turned and waddled out of the room to his office.

Tsing Chai's life was doubly tasked through his real job as a Communist agent, and having to act as a minor gambling czar for a cover. Despite the financial backing of the Communist government up north, he still had the usual headaches.

There was a staff to deal with and be paid, public relations of a sort, bribes that had to be laid out to corrupt

South Vietnamese officials, correspondence, spying activities, sabotage, and countless other activities that left him little time to rest. Tsing consoled himself by indulging in his favorite pastime — eating.

Now, as he settled down at his desk, he removed the cloth covering of the tray waiting for him there. The Chinese was delighted to see that this evening's meal would consist of squid, cooked with salted bamboo shoots, leeks and celery. Boiled rice and tea completed the meal. The amount he planned to consume would have done credit to Kaminatake the ex-*sumotori*.

He had just dipped his chopsticks into the squid for the first delicious bite when a knock on the door interrupted him. He sighed audibly.

"Yes?"

The door opened and Kahn, the chief security man, stepped in. "That little *bo-cau* of a delivery truck driver is here," Kahn said. "I tried to send him on his way with a cuff to the back of the head, but he says you insisted that he deliver your clothes to you personally."

Tsing gulped at the thought that Kahn might have struck Major Xong even out of ignorance. "Yes! Yes! That is correct! Please send him in."

"Yes, Master Tsing." Kahn turned and motioned to someone out in the hall. "Let's go, you rabbit fart, and don't take up too much of the master's time."

Xong scurried in, a look of mortification and fear on his face. "*Toi tiek! Toi tiek! Xin loi ong! Cam on ong!*"

Kahn closed the door leaving the two alone.

"I am most sorry, Comrade Major," Tsing blurted. "But, Kahn doesn't —"

"Never mind that. He's doing just as he is expected to do," Xong said.

"May I have some food brought for you?"

"Of course not, you idiot! Wouldn't that be stupid? I'm sure your corps of bodyguards would be most curious about your showing such courtesy to a delivery truck driver," Xong said.

"Of course, Comrade. Forgive my impetuous stupidity. But, please, sit down."

Xong carelessly dropped Tsing's dry cleaning to the floor, and took a seat. "I've come to see how things are going and to give you some most important news."

"Yes, Comrade."

"But first I would like to know how our Japanese friends are getting along."

"Fine, Comrade," Tsing answered. "They are all here now — six total. Our visitors are patiently biding their time until they are needed."

"Well, that will be very soon," Xong said. He lit a cigarette and exhaled smoke toward the desk. "Did your black market shipment come in?"

"No, Comrade," Tsing replied. "We don't know what happened to it."

"It was ambushed by the capitalist dog Falconi and his men," Xong said.

Tsing gritted his teeth. "That is terrible!"

"Oh, no! That is wonderful!"

Tsing was puzzled. "I don't understand, Comrade."

"The information they received that enabled them to intercept the shipment was provided through my efforts," Xong said smiling.

"But, why?"

"In order to implant confidence in my man who is a member of the national police," Xong said.

Tsing was astounded. "Could such a thing be possible, Comrade? Of course, you don't mean Colonel Tran's staff."

"I certainly do," Xong said. "It is something I have been working on for the previous two years. Now that it is done, I can think of no better reason to put my spy to work."

"Then we will know exactly what the Black Eagles are going to do before they do it," Tsing said. "Like when they were in the field operating against our comrades."

"Yes. That will be done through Colonel Ngai as usual," Xong explained. "The situation is arranged so that even if it is discovered that he has the information, it will appear to have come to him through proper channels."

"*Mung ong*, Comrade!" Tsing cried. "That is such wonderful news my heart can hardly bear it. But if the Black Eagles captured any of the men in the ambush, they might talk."

"I made sure that brand new people, completely unaware of our real organization, were the only ones in the convoy," Xong said. "And I have another happy bit of intelligence to pass on to you. By using my infiltrator we will be able to draw the Black Eagles into a trap. An ambush even more deadly than the one they sprang on the trucks this afternoon."

"That sounds like it will be the destruction of Falconi and his men that we have been trying to accomplish for the better part of a year," Tsing said.

"It is exactly that," Xong said. "But you must remember that Comrade Colonel Krashchenko of the KGB wants Falconi taken alive."

"It will be done," Tsing reported.

"I will give you my plan now," Xong said. "Our Japanese friends will play a big role in it."

Tsing smiled widely. "They are ready for action now, Comrade," he said settling down to receive his orders for the operation.

CHAPTER ELEVEN

All seven Black Eagles strolled along Saigon's Truman Key. The street, lined with night clubs, bars and whorehouses, was a bedlam of noisy activity and frenzied fun-seeking. The throngs of people who sauntered up and down the avenue were boisterous and vociferous as hucksters, whores, peddlers, and even beggars fought for their attention.

Now, once more back in civilian clothing, the Black Eagles walked lightly, seeming almost carefree, as they took in the sights of the city.

"Sure you guys don't want to go over to the Wildcat Bar?" Archie Dobbs asked.

"If it's all the same to you I'd like to do my drinking where American civilians hang out," Lightfingers O'Quinn said.

"Too bad," Archie said. He winked at Top Gordon. "You'd like the Wildcat. There's a coupla girls there named Julie and Linda that are real crazy about Special Forces master sergeants."

"I'll go with the others," Top said. "Thanks for the info though. I'll keep it in mind for future forays out into the night life. but I guess I'm in the mood to see how our civilians around here have fun. It might even make me feel like I'm home again."

"Hell, I'm gonna go with the flow too," Archie said. "I ain't that crazy about the Wildcat."

Robert Falconi, his hands nonchalantly stuck into his pockets, ambled along in the midst of his men. "Where'd you hear about this place we're going?" he asked Lightfingers.

"I been there before," the marine answered. "With Manuel Rivera."

The mention of Rivera's name caused a momentary cloud of gloom to pass over the group. He had been one of the original members of the Black Eagles. He died on their second operation, shot down in the mission directed against the prison camp. His death had been a particularly gruesome one during an aerial attack by Soviet MiG-17 aircraft piloted by North Vietnamese pilots.

The Black Eagles, pinned down between a river and a high bluff, were taking a hell of a pounding at that particular time. During a napalm attack, Rivera had been engulfed in flames. Screaming his agony, he had leaped to his feet and run wildly until NVA infantry showed unintentional mercy by shooting him down.

His charred body had to be left unattended in enemy territory.

Archie Dobbs shuddered involuntarily with the memory of Rivera's demise. "Poor ol' Manuel."

Malpractice McCorckel, the detachment medic, sensed the bad mood everyone was sinking into. "What's the name o' the place?" he asked in an attempt to swing things back to a lighter vein.

"The Hard Hat," Lightfingers answered. "I think the customers started calling it that and the owner decided to make it the official name."

"Sounds like a hangout for American construction workers," Falconi said.

"Right, Skipper," Lightfingers told him.

"Did you two have a good time there?" Malpractice asked in an attempt to continue to lighten things up.

"We got into one helluva brawl," Lightfingers said. He displayed an uncustomary grin. "What a night!"

"Hey," Archie said. "What about women in the place?"

"You'll find what you're looking for," Lightfingers told him.

"Hey, no shit? You mean the place is full o' beautiful movie stars?"

"I mean the whores in there are good enough for you," Lightfingers said falling back into his usual caustic self.

"Must be some o' that two hundred *dong* pussy then," Malpractice remarked with a laugh.

Archie displayed a theatrical scowl. "Fuck you very much."

Chun Kim and Calvin Culpepper grinned at each other as they listened to the exchange between their detachment mates. The Korean was always quiet and Calvin only spoke when he had something to say. These personal habits, along with getting assigned to perform special jobs together on the missions, caused them to become taciturn but close friends.

When they reached the bar, the group took enough time to take in the exterior. Not particularly fancy except for a neon sign, it seemed to fit in well with the other similar establishments on the street.

Lightfingers led the way in. He stopped in surprise. What had once been a rather drab, but reasonably priced hangout, had been through some big changes.

Remodeled and fancier, the interior boasted a long bar complete with a formica top. Much longer and grander than the one Lightfingers remembered, he could see the back of the building had been enlarged to accommodate the new addition.

The tables were of similar construction, with chairs made

of good quality material. The people seated at them, or casually straddling the stools at the bar, were obviously construction workers. Husky, boisterous and a bit shaggy by military standards, they were gathered in small groups exchanging bawdy jokes and comments among themselves and the whores who circulated in their midst.

A shiny, new juke box wailed a Country-Western song.

The women were also of a different breed. Archie Dobbs' first comment on sighting them was, "This sure as hell ain't two hundred *dong* pussy, guys."

"It sure ain't," Malpractice said with a delighted grin.

Falconi laughed. "It's a good thing you guys were able to save some money out there in that B Camp. It looks like you're going to need it."

Calvin Culpepper, his ebony face broken into a wide grin, shouldered his way forward through his friends. "I can't think of a better way to invest my fun money, fellahs."

Falconi and Top Gordon, as the ranking men, led the group forward as the Black Eagles unconsciously alluded to their leadership positions. They went to a couple of corner tables and shoved them together. Then the seven comrades-in-arms settled down to an evening of diversion.

The first girl who approached them was a waitress. "Okay, guys, how you doin'?" she asked.

"Great," Top answered. "What's on the beer menu here?"

"I don't got no 'merican beer," she said. "I got better. I got San Miguel."

"Jeez! That's good stuff," Archie said.

"You betcha," the girl said with a wide grin. "We numbah one in the Hard Hat, GI."

"What makes you think I'm a GI?" Archie asked.

"Easy to tell," the girl said. "Okay. Seven San Miguel, for seven GI, okay?"

"Okay!" Malpractice sang out.

"I always figgered that San Miguel is the best beer in the Orient," Archie said.

The group happily looked forward to the first delicious taste of the cold brew. Their mood plunged somewhat when they found that they'd been charged two hundred piasters a bottle.

"What the hell's this?" Lightfingers demanded. "The last time I was in here the beer was a lot cheaper."

"But it no San Miguel," the girl said. "Ever'body who come to Hard Hat want San Miguel. Cost more."

"Aw, Christ!" Archie complained. He had volunteered to pay for the first round. "I guess them construction guys can afford to drink better'n us poor army folks."

"We high-class here," the waitress said taking Archie's money.

She turned and walked away, passing the three available whores who now undulated up to the table. The lead one, a flashy slim type with a bee-hive hairdo, situated herself between Falconi and Top. She leaned forward to give the tableful of men a good view of her breasts. She wiggled a bit. "Hey, GI, you likee?"

Archie Dobbs licked his lips. "Yeah!"

"No falsie, hey!" the girl said jiggling again. "Ever'body want good time? You got me an' my two friend. My name Rose. That Lilly. That Daisy."

The other two crowded in with grins and a tantalizing swing of their hips.

"Rose, Lilly and Daisy," Falconi mused. "The Flowers of Vietnam, right?"

Rose laughed. "Oh, yes. Cons'ruction workers give us names. They like flower." She kissed Top on the crown of his balding head, then turned her attention back to the other Black Eagles. "C'mon, guys, fucky-fucky, sucky-sucky for t'ousand *dong*."

Calvin winced at the price. "Man, these civilian construction workers really did fuck things up for honest soljers, didn't they?"

"Hell, these broads are good looking," Lightfingers pro-

tested. He was beginning to feel embarrassed about bringing his friends into such a high-priced establishment.
"That's gotta be worth somethin', right?"

But Archie wasn't too charitable. "Who gives a damn
about looks? Stand 'em on their heads and they all look
alike anyhow."

Calvin, who felt a bit sorry for Lightfingers, slapped his
friend's shoulder. "Hey! I like this place. I'm glad we came
here!"

The girl named Lilly left her spot and forced herself onto
the husky black man's lap. She winked and playfully poked
his chest. "Hey! You got big peter, hey? Black man's got long
snake." She laughed.

"Not me, mama," Calvin said. "I got short-changed in
that department."

"Oh! Too bad for you," the girl said with a giggle.

"I make up for it though," Calvin said as he grabbed one
of her breasts. "Mother Nature gimme a pile-drivin' ass."

Finally Archie could stand it no longer. "C'mon baby," he
said. He got to his feet and reached over taking Rose by the
hand and pulling her from between Falconi and Top Gordon. "Where we goin'? A hotel?"

"Oh, no, honey," Rose said going with him. "We got nice
rooms in back. No extra charge."

"For a thousand *dong* there'd damn well better not be,"
Archie said as the two disappeared through a door by the
juke box.

Malpractice McCorckel, another who could not contain
himself, took Daisy and quickly followed. Calvin, with
Lilly still on his lap, stood up and carried her after the departing medic.

The flurry of activity by the horny Black Eagles attracted
other women to the table. Within a scant three minutes,
Chun Kim and Lightfingers had also made hasty exits in the
direction of the delights available to them in the back of the
establishment.

174

Maj. Robert Falconi and MSgt. Top Gordon, both older and wiser men, politely declined the preliminary offers of commercial sex in order to enjoy their beer.

Top took a healthy swig of the San Miguel. He looked over at his commander. "So how's it going, Skipper?"

Falconi was a little confused by the question. They had been in long daily contact since Operation Asian Blitzkrieg. Top should most certainly know how things were with him. He shrugged. "Okay, I guess. Why do you ask?"

"Just taking the team sergeant's prerogative to inquire into the CO's private life," Top said.

Then Falconi knew what he meant. "You're talking about the situation with Andrea, aren't you?"

"Yep."

Falconi sighed. "I gotta admit something, Top. The thought of her being bedded down by other men sort of hurts."

"But evidently not enough for you to put a stop to it," Top said.

"I don't know—" Falconi was hesitant.

"You heart's all twisted up into knots, Skipper," Top said. "You're gonna have to untwist it, and get back to normal."

"Hell! I know that!" Falconi said.

"You haven't been laid since we got back," Top said bluntly.

"Neither have you. I noticed you didn't go off with any of these chippies."

"*I* have a reason," Top countered. "I'm keeping an eye on my commanding officer."

Falconi sighed and set his beer down. "Very well, Team Sergeant. There's obviously some business you want to conduct in the line of duty—right?"

"Right," Top said. "I want to set you straight before you turn into a useless sack of shit."

"So, have at it."

"Okay, sir," Top said turning into the serious noncommissioned officer. "There's a turmoil building in your head. You're torn between two paths to follow. One, the more emotional, is to make Andrea your woman—and yours alone—to satisfy any jealous feelings you have about her and other men. The second, of course, is getting your ass back to normal and leading the Black Eagles on their missions."

"I presume you have some advice for me then," Falconi said. "Which way should I go?"

"The second way, Skipper," Top said. "You'd regret any other decision."

"And my—pardon the expression—fits of jealous rage and grief?"

"Forget it! You're not in love, Falcon. Those emotions will fade away, don't worry."

"That's exactly what Fagin told me."

"He was right," Top said. "Get the woman out of your system."

"I'm trying, Top," Falcon said sincerely.

"Right now some other guy is sliding his greasy dick into her," Top said heartlessly. "She's lying there with her legs spread, her vagina open and full of his penis. He's going to pump away until he comes in her. He'll squirt that thick, white stuff up into her body—just like you used to."

The mental picture the master sergeant formed for him seemed to hit Falconi right between the eyes. But he bore up under it. "Okay. Okay. I've accepted the reality. Now what do I do?"

"Get laid," Top said standing up. "I sure as hell am." He scooted his chair back and stood up. Top walked over to the bar and grabbed the first available girl standing there. Then he took her into the back.

By then Archie and Malpractice had come back. They ordered another round of beer and sat in silence, savoring the pleasure of the previous half hour. Falconi watched them, envying their carefree fuck-'em-and-forget-'em attitudes.

There was nothing worse in the entire world than caring for a woman, the Falcon decided. It was worse than a bullet in the guts.

Well, his mind mused, damned near.

Another twenty minutes passed and the entire detachment was once again seated around the table enjoying their beer. Their talk was instinctively subdued and private, as it generally was with fighting men involved in clandestine operations.

By now the group had increased the enjoyment of the San Miguel with shots of Canadian Club whiskey. Top Gordon, having served in the 82nd Airborne Division, developed a taste for that particular brand of liquor in that unit's non-commissioned officers clubs. It was one of those inexplicable facts of military life that occur now and then. A large outfit of thousands of men will get into the habit of going for one type of drink or food to the extent that a minor tradition is born. Pay call in the 82nd was invariably followed by a stop to the club for a "CC" straight-up, on-the-rocks, CC-and-Seven — no matter. Canadian Club was *the* drink in Master Sergeant Gordon's day.

Falconi had a large capacity for liquor under normal circumstances. But Top's carefully worded probe and revelation of his deep feelings caused the alcohol to boil through his system.

A construction worker, his arm around one of the girls, walked up toward the juke box. He nodded to the table of Black Eagles. "How you fellers doin'?" he drawled in a Texas accent.

"Pretty good," Archie Dobbs answered.

"We'd be doing better if you people hadn't fucked this place up," Lightfingers said.

The civilian sensed the animosity. "What the hell you talkin' 'bout?"

"I was in here a year ago and the Hard Hat was great," Lightfingers explained sullenly. "Good beer at good

177

prices — same for the pussy."

"Get the hell outta here if'n you don't like it, shithead," the Texan snarled.

Falconi stood up and hit the man so hard his head cracked the plastic covering of the juke box.

Unconscious, the civilian slid to the floor, while the machine, activated by the impact, put a record on. It was an old country standard: *I Don't Hurt Anymore.*

This was a signal for the other construction workers in the room to charge the corner table. Whores screamed, glasses flew and furniture splintered as the two groups collided.

Top Gordon, the Black Eagles involuntary point man, met the vanguard of the attack with a vicious grin and a straight jab into the face of the lead man. The guy's head popped back, so Top punctuated his disapproval of his actions with a bolo punch to the midsection. The master sergeant pushed the sagging civilian aside and went over him to meet the next man head on.

Archie Dobbs, snapping out of his lethargy brought on by the sex he'd just enjoyed, made a quick leap to the table and dove over the front rank of Black Eagles to land on top of the other workers. He dragged four down to the floor. Leaping back upright, he kicked skulls and jaws in a savage attack that, unfortunately, was only of a three-second duration.

It would have lasted longer, but a large, hammy fist collided with the right side of Archie's jaw. He stumbled sideways and was hit again — this time in front. Staggering backward, he bumped into Chun Kim who pushed him back into the fray. Unfortunately, Archie's senses were scrambled by then. A construction guy grabbed his collar and slugged him repeatedly until the Black Eagle's scout sank to the floor.

Kim, furious over Archie's predicament, rushed forward and emitted a loud karate yell. He leaped into the air and

178

executed a flying wheel kick that knocked one civilian into two of his buddies. Then the Korean slammed the next opponent with the heel of his hand in a *chong-kwon* blow and spun to drive his elbow into another. Other workers nearby rushed forward. They surrounded the feisty South Korean marine, but drew off from his various feints and attacks.

Lightfingers and Malpractice executed their fighting in a more conventional manner. Fists and feet did their job as the two stood toe-to-toe and slugged it out with ambitious attackers. Both showed the effects of their efforts through bloody noses, while Lightfingers, with a nasty gash over his left eye that allowed blood to flow into it, could see out of only one eye.

Falconi, all his previous emotional turmoil fueling his anger, took on one man by smashing him in the face with a forearm. The next guy was peppered with alternating left and right jabs until the Falcon took him out with a whistling uppercut. The construction man's eyes crossed and his feet came off the floor before he fell back on top of his other unfortunate buddies.

A big man, his meaty shoulders hunched for action, moved forward deliberately toward Falconi. He feinted with his right, causing the Black Eagle commander to pull back in the opposite direction. A hammerlike fist slammed into Falconi's shoulder. He dropped a bit, then threw a short right, with the knuckle extended, into the guy's solar plexus. He followed this up with a left cross, then kneed the bastard in the balls.

An enraged scream of pain announced the success of the effort.

With the man bent over, Falconi hit him with the knife edge of his hand between the shoulder blades forcing him the rest of the way to the floor.

Whistles blew when the MPs and civilian police charged through the bar door. The bartender, who had run out frantically to fetch them, pointed in the direction of the Black

Eagles.

"They start it! They start it!" he cried with an indignant ring of accusation in his voice.

Falconi calmed his men when they started to charge the law. "Easy, guys. Easy."

When the cops and MPs saw there would be no resistance, they relaxed. This wasn't all that unusual. Since all the brawlers were Americans, the local police held back. The ranking military policeman, a sergeant, looked at the men on the floor. He could see they were all civilian with one exception. He pointed to Archie Dobbs who was crawling slowly in a circle.

"Is that one o' your guys?" he asked.

"Yeah," Falconi said.

"You military?" the MP asked.

"That's us, buddy," Top Gordon replied.

"Fuckin' civilian assholes making twenty bucks an hour 'cause they're in fuckin' Vietnam," the sergeant said. He made no attempt to conceal his contempt for the construction men. "Who's the rankin' guy here?"

"Me," Falconi answered.

"Okay, bud. I don't want your goddamn name, your goddamn rank or goddamn nothin'," the MP said. "Just haul ass with your guys, okay?"

"Okay!" Falconi turned to the Black Eagles. "Move out."

"Right, Skipper," McCorckel said. He bent down and grabbed Archie, hauling him to his feet.

The group went outside to the sidewalk. "Now where we goin'?" Calvin Culpepper asked.

Archie, hanging onto Malpractice, looked around with his head bobbing. "Le's go Wildcat Bar—girl there'n love wi' me—I know she does—le's go Wildcat Bar—"

"Well, guys," Falconi said with a grin. "Archie's always been the best point man in the U.S. Army. We've followed him through the boonies. I see no reason not to follow him now. The Wildcat Bar it is."

The group, laughing and hollering, with Archie slowly regaining his senses, pushed their way through the crowded streets.

Falconi and Top Gordon trailed the group. "How you feeling, Skipper?"

Falconi grinned. "That fight helped put things right. There's only one other thing left to do."

"What's that, Falcon?"

"I'm gonna try some of that two hundred *dong* pussy that Archie thinks is so great."

Gordon, delighted, laughed loudly. "Welcome back to soldiering, Skipper. I've missed you."

Andrea Thuy Roget, in her role as Loc Andrea, returned to the apartment house she used in the assignment. The *concierge*, in the small lobby of the building, greeted her politely. Although a typical and traditional Vietnamese male, he showed a marked respect and courtesy toward the prostitutes who lived in the set of flats he managed. They not only paid the inflated rents on time, but both them and some of their customers gave him generous tips for running errands.

Andrea went up the narrow stairs knowing the man would be following her with his eyes, trying to see as far up her skirt as possible. She lived on the third floor. It was ironic that this foray into operations had provided her with the opportunity to live in more luxurious surroundings than her army pay allowed. Even the hallways, with their carpets and potted plants, were more elegant than the drab, drafty ones in her apartment house in the *Quartier des Colons*.

She reached her door and noted the small piece of nearly invisible transparent tape stuck just above the knob. That was a signal that Chuck Fagin was inside waiting for her. Usually, when returning, she entered her apartment with a great deal of care—and her small Beretta pistol held at the ready.

She entered and closed the door. "It's all right, Chuck," she called out softly.

"Hi." The CIA case officer appeared from the bedroom. "How's it going?"

"Nothing too unusual in where I've been lately," Andrea said. She was a cold professional now. Before, after not having been on ops for a while, she might have felt a bit awkward standing there in front of Fagin after having had intercourse with several men. The American had become like a brother to her. But each sexual foray into the night, each different man she serviced, had driven her farther and farther away from conventional feelings — and romantic ones too.

"You look tired," Fagin said.

"It's been a busy night," she said. "I'll be right with you." She went into the bathroom and closed the door. Andrea looked at herself in the mirror. Her makeup was slightly mussed, but not badly. She'd had another session with the American Eddie who had developed such a passion for dog-fashion intercourse. He'd shoved her face down in the pillow with his frantic shoving.

Fagin's voice came from outside the door. "Want me to fix you a drink?"

"Oh, God, yes!" Andrea said. "A scotch and water, please. And make it strong."

"Yes, ma'am." His footsteps faded away.

Andrea removed her clothes, noting a small bit of sperm that had leaked from her vagina and coursed slowly down her thigh. She grabbed a piece of toilet paper from the roll and dabbed at it. Next she douched repeatedly before stepping into the shower.

Five minutes later, clean and refreshed, while clothed in a faded but comfortable housecoat, she joined Fagin in the living room. She grabbed the drink and took a deep swallow.

Fagin, sitting in an easy chair, watched her. "Anything to report?"

"Nothing," Andrea said. "I've yet to come into contact with anyone who even remotely has a thing to do with the Black Eagles."

"Damn! Damn!" Fagin said. "How many trips have you made to the Cholon district?"

"Eight," Andrea said. "All with Chinese or Vietnamese businessmen. I've been to a couple of officers clubs and about every good hotel in the city. But I've not been with anyone yet who means a thing to us in our missions."

"If we don't close in pretty quick—"

The phone rang, interrupting Fagin. Andrea crossed the room and picked up the instrument. "*A-lo . . . chao ong, Ong Nguyen, Ong manh khong . . . Co, toi noi tieng Nhat . . . cam on ong, Ong Nguyen . . . chao ong.*" She hung up and turned to face Fagin. "That was Nguyen, the whore-master."

"Another job for you, huh?"

"Yes. He asked me if I spoke any Japanese. When I told him I did, he instructed me to go to Tsing Chai's mah jongg parlor in Cholon tomorrow night—and present myself to Master Tsing personally."

Fagin dropped his drink.

The two sentries at the gate leading into the headquarters of the National Police stepped forward as the delivery van came to a stop.

"*Chao ong,*" the driver, Xong, said politely.

The senior guard did not exhibit any of the social graces. "You know the procedure."

"Of course," Xong said. He got out and went around the back, opening the doors. Only a few items of clothing hung on the racks. "I always deliver to National Police Headquarters last, so that the truck will be empty and make the search easier for you."

The subordinate sentry made no expression of gratitude for the gesture as he climbed into the back. As usual he pounded the sides and floor in search for any hidden compartments. The paint showed scuffs and dents from his previous efforts. He quickly, but thoroughly checked the clothing, then climbed out.

The other sentry, unsmiling and bored, made a silent indication that Xong could drive through the gates. The driver got back behind the wheel. *"Cam on ong. Chao ong."*

He slipped the vehicle into gear and eased forward slowly, going up the drive at no more than ten miles an hour. Speeding trucks inside the gates were not given tickets — they were immediately and completely shot to pieces by the security forces stationed in there for just that purpose.

Xong parked and, following another rule, left all doors wide open so that the interior of his van could be easily examined from a distance. Then he trotted up the steps and entered the building.

There were more security checks to go through. The policeman charged with such duties knew him well, but they took no chances. He was shaken down and searched at each guard post. It was almost an hour before he was able to knock on an office door with his last garment to drop off.

The voice inside sounded curtly. *"Mai ong vao."*

Xong stepped in and bowed. *"Chao ong, Ha-Si Hai."*

Corporal Hai, who had spent a good part of the day with his immediate senior Sergeant Chin in planning out future operations with the Black Eagles, nodded. "Dry cleaning, hey? It is important for the police to look their best."

That was a phrase to Xong which meant the office was clear. He hung the garments up on a coatstand situated in a corner of the room. "It is time," he said.

"Then all arrangements have been made?"

"Yes. You have the Black Eagles there. Afterward you will receive the balance of the money due you," Xong said.

"I want my safety guaranteed," Hai said.

"How can that be done?" Xong said. "The only guarantee I can give you is that if you stay out of the line of fire, you will be spared death or injury. How you do it is up to you."

Hai nodded. It was a hairy situation, but that was the kind of a deal he really liked. The element of risk was almost as enjoyable to him as a woman. And this one would make him rich.

"We will be situated," Xong said going to the door. "Simply tell us when."

"It will be within forty-eight hours," Hai said. "*That* is guaranteed."

"Remember your bonus if we take Falconi alive," Xong reminded him.

"What about the other Black Eagles?"

"They must all die," Xong said. He nodded a curt unsmiling goodbye to the policeman, then opened the door and stepped out into the hall.

Corporal Hai leaned back in his chair and set his feet up on this desk. The long years of undercover work and exposure to danger had gone mostly unrewarded during his lengthy career in the National Police. The kid Chin, thanks to having an older brother serving, even outranked him.

Hai smiled to himself as he remembered an old Vietnamese proverb:

He who awaits his indemnities with patience, earns more than those who garner their rewards through instant gratitude.

CHAPTER TWELVE

If it hadn't been for the calm expressions on their weary faces, the Black Eagles would have appeared to be a group of men who had just been chastised for some breach of discipline.

They filed into MACV-SOG's Headquarters Number Four briefing room in silence with only a muffled comment between them now and then as they took seats in the chairs scattered around the chamber.

Maj. Robert Falconi occupied a front chair. The only evidence that he'd done any drinking the night before were his slightly bloodshot eyes. He'd gotten drunk in his own inimitable style. Consuming huge quantities of liquor and beer, he had displayed not the slightest lack of control of his physical actions despite the fact he'd been monumentally intoxicated. The lusty major, held back from satisfying his sexual appetite because of his involvement with Andrea Thuy Roget, had cut loose with a vengeance. No less then five of the girls at the Wildcat Bar had made lengthy trips to a nearby hotel with him. Falconi had, in his own words, been "laid, re-laid, and par-laid."

Another man able to consume huge quantities of alcohol

without any apparent ill effects was MSgt. Top Gordon. Rather than mix his drinks like his commander, Top had stuck to beer. The veteran NCO had poured gallons of the brew into his tough, muscular body between numerous *combats d'amour* with lithe young prostitutes who flocked to the horny group's tables like bees to honey.

The intrepid duo of MSgt. Chun Kim and SFC Calvin Culpepper, on the other hand, were not in a particularly admirable state of health. Plainly hung-over, they sat together as if somehow each other's company would offer some comfort or relief from the pounding in their heads. They, too, had turned their rutting instincts loose in numerous trips from the bar in the company of the sexual talent available in the Wildcat.

Also in bad shape, but not the least bit repentant, was Lightfingers O'Quinn. He leaned forward with his elbows on his knees, his face buried in his hands. If he'd been asked, Lightfingers would have sworn in all candor and veracity that even the follicles of hair on his head ached in independent spasms of agony to add to his overall condition of acute discomfort. He consoled himself with the thought that at least his pecker seemed satisfied with the way things had gone the previous night.

Archie Dobbs, who had taken a couple of real hard smacks to the jaw during the brawl in the Hard Hat, was in the worst shape. His desire to numb the pain of the battering he'd endured had driven him to drink even more than his usual habit of overindulgence of alcohol. This resulted in the worst morning-after in his twenty-five years of living. Archie was in such bad shape that he figured he'd be dead by noon — with any luck at all.

The one Black Eagle who was clear headed and in fine fettle, was the medic. SFC Malcomb "Malpractice" McCorckel was always a practitioner of preventive medicine. Malpractice had imbibed sparingly and with dignity. His consumption of beer had been limited to only six bottles the entire night as he watched his comrades drink themselves into near stupors. The only recreation he allowed himself was a secret attempt to keep up with Falconi in laying the Wildcat Bar's whores. But, after the fourth, he'd given that up and sat back to nurse his final beer of the evening until the party ended with the appearance of the rising sun over Truman Key's reveling crowds.

Then he and the other Black Eagles had crowded into a cab for a boisterous ride to the front gate of Long Binh. There they'd breakfasted heartily in the air force transient barracks. Lightfingers O'Quinn had a good contact there in the person of a generous USAF mess sergeant. They piled stacks of pancakes, eggs, hashbrowns and other food into their alcohol-abused stomachs. If it hadn't been for this period of gorging, their morning-after would have been even worse.

Then it was back to the gate for another cab for the ride across Saigon to Peterson Field—to the briefing they now awaited with something less than enthusiasm.

Malpractice stood up and looked around at his buddies. Ever the medic, he had taken note of their poor physical condition. "I hope last night was a good lesson for you dumb bastards. I like beer as much as the next guy, but it's stupid to drink the goddamned stuff 'til it comes out your ears. As far as you silly asses who mixed hard liquor with it—well, you got just what you deserved."

A low groan sounded from the group.

"And another thing," Malpractice continued. "I hope you used rubbers when you fucked them whores. It may surprise a coupla you dandies who think you're so good lookin', but them broads ain't madly in love with you. They screw other guys too. I don't give a damn how clean the whore is either. All it takes is the joker ahead of you to clap her up."

Somebody moaned aloud. "Aw, shut up, for Chrissake!"

"Just remember what I said," Malpractice remarked before sitting down again.

The various reveries and clouds of headaches were broken by the sudden opening of the door. Chuck Fagin, robust as always, strode into the room with the two national policemen, Sergeant Chin and Corporal Hai, following him.

"Good morning, buckos!" Fagin boomed. "And how are we this morning?"

Silence.

"C'mon! C'mon! Where's that ol' spirit?" Fagin asked with a big grin. He looked around from face to face, finally stopping at Archie. "Well, Sergeant Dobbs, what have you to say for yourself? How was last night? Want to fill me in?"

Archie raised his red-clouded eyes and gave the CIA case officer a dull glare. Then he raised his clenched fist and sprang out the middle finger.

Fagin laughed. "Ah, yes. It seems a bit of steam was blown off last night, hey? That's good, it really is. Because you should all be in the mood to jump right back into the swing of things." He treated them to another grin. "But first — a couple of administrative announcements."

As Fagin settled into a drone regarding various official bits of information that had to be dispensed to all American military personnel in Vietnam, Corporal Hai made himself comfortable in a chair in the back of the room. He looked around the crowd, his eyes settling on Sgt. Chin Han for a moment.

Hai hated Chin with every ounce of his being.

The sergeant had come up rapidly through the ranks thanks to his older brother Chin Duc. No doubt the younger sibling was capable and courageous, but his promotions held other men — like Hai — back. After nearly twelve years service, Hai was still a *ha-si*, a corporal.

Hai had worked hard in his job. He'd gone into undercover work after several boring years of security duty and street patrol. Imaginative and ambitious, he'd worked twelve to eighteen hours a day in his assignments. The result of this had been the painstaking organization of a net of informants which could supply him with intelligence on practically any illicit activity in Saigon.

But Hai, naive and unaware of interbureau politics, had stupidly shared his investigative work with others. These more savvy, ambitious types had taken credit for his hard work and gained promotion and plush assignments while he had still plodded along as a street cop, solving case after case with superiors garnering the rewards of his skillful devotion to duty.

That had included Chin's older brother. Hai smiled to himself as he recalled how the elder Chin had been found on a garbage dump in the Cholon. Murdered and tortured after fucking up an undercover assignment in penetrating Tsing Chai's organization.

But vengeance would soon be taken on Chin Han too. Hai's contact and arrangements with the Communist agent Xong would pay off doubly. Chin would be disgraced and/or killed, and the Black Eagles would also be wiped out. Hai had hated the French when they'd occupied his country, and he looked on the Americans in the same way. All foreigners were interlopers who should stay the hell at home.

The fact that the Communists were paying him a great deal of money to act as a double agent also gave Hai some comforting thoughts. Idyllic days in Switzerland awaited him at the end of his road of betrayal.

His thoughts were interrupted when Fagin called out his name. "Now Corporal Hai has developed some unusual intelligence that has resulted in the next mission. He'll conduct the briefing. Corporal Hai?"

Hai stood up. He smiled as he walked to the front of the room. He turned and bowed. "Good morning, Black Eagles."

Still hung-over, they merely nodded politely to him as they waited for him to begin the briefing.

"Just as Mister Fagin says, I've come across some most interesting information," Hai said. "This involves a couple of young GIs who are taking care of a stash of hashish that has been smuggled out of Turkey and into this country. There's quite a large amount involved."

Falconi raised his hand. "If it's a big bunch, why only a couple of guards?"

"My informant tells me it is to avoid attracting too much attention to the area," Hai answered. "It would appear that our activities have begun to worry large segments of Saigon's underworld. They seem to think that if usual security precautions are established in their home areas, we will be attracted to it."

"And they're right," Malpractice chimed in cheerfully.

"At any rate, this isn't too far from where you gentlemen were last night," Hai said. He winked at them. "That was you on Truman Key, was it not?"

Archie nodded painfully. "Yeah . . . oh, yeah." His voice was almost a whisper.

"They tell me the girls there are still marveling over your endurance and manly strength," Hai said.

Top Gordon, sexually satiated, grinned lazily.

Hai went on. "And the local merchants who supply San Miguel beer have been forced to send an emergency order to the Philippines to make up for a most drastic and unexpected shortage in their supplies of that particular brew."

Calvin Culpepper groaned.

"To go on," Hai continued. "Our target is a small warehouse. The merchandise is hidden under a false floor, but we are not concerned with that. Our first order of business will be to eliminate the two guards. They have been instructed not to resist any raid, but to inform their superiors of any intrusion so that a larger force can be quickly dispatched to the area."

"How will they do that?" Lightfingers, who really didn't give a damn, asked.

"An alarm exactly like the ones used in banks back in your country," Hai explained. "The guards will step on it to activate a buzzer several blocks away."

"Rather elaborate," Falconi remarked doubtfully.

Hai shrugged. "My informant assures me this is the ar-rangement."

Falconi, now almost completely out of his hang-over, be-came more interested. "Then surprise is our primary con-cern. We'll have to hit the place completely unexpectedly, and keep the alarm from being sounded."

"Right," Fagin agreed, joining in the briefing. "Then *we'll* step on it and arrange a reception committee for the bad guys who show up. Instead of catching us, it'll be our trap for them."

Falconi nodded. "Okay, sounds great. But their warning system doesn't seem kosher to me. It's pretty elaborate for a temporary storage dump."

"Hey, don't worry about it," Fagin said. "Hai's got the best net of informants in Saigon. Whatever he tells us is the way it is."

Falconi was insistent. "Why the hell would they go to all the trouble and expense to install electronics in a place like that?"

"I don't know," Fagin said. "Maybe they use it several times a year or something."

Hai, his mind enjoying the game, smiled. "Shall I go into the execution phase of the raid?"

"Please," Fagin said.

The Black Eagles, despite their aching heads and stom-achs, sat up straighter in their chairs to find out exactly how the operation was going down.

Kaminatake was in love.

As a large Oriental man, he'd always found himself in-volved with diminutive women. There had been times when even prostitutes had expressed surprise and apprehension at his size when they first saw him. The ex-*sumotori* would never forget the consternation when, as a young apprentice, Uchida had taken him and some other novices to a bordello for an evening of relaxation and diversion. Kaminatake, very young and inexperienced, had been a bit nervous and had taken to the *sake* in a big way. This was during the socializing period normally observed before going off to pillow one of the ladies of the night.

Very large, and very drunk, he'd gone to a love-room with one of the brothel inmates. This was his first sexual experience and the woman had skillfully taken him through it. The only problem had occurred at the end, when his enormous bellyful of rice wine went straight to his head. He'd collapsed on top of the unfortunate woman.

Kaminatake had come to his senses from the yelling and pounding on his shoulders. It had taken other large apprentices, all their strength to pull him off the futon. The *baishunfu*, unconscious and bleeding profusely through the nose, had to be taken to the hospital.

Later the wrestling stable received the bill from the hospital. Her injuries had included three broken ribs, a ruptured spleen and dislocated shoulder. Uchida had diplomatically advised Kaminatake that, during sex, he should let the woman mount him — certainly not the other way around.

The experience had made him edgy and nearly impotent at times. Only after long periods of prolonged celibacy was he physically driven to have sex. And, even then, he had to be a bit drunk to get the job done. The last time he'd really rampantly taken a woman had been during his drunken binge in Tokyo when he'd ended up in jail.

Kaminatake's arrival in Vietnam did little to still his sexual frustrations. The women available in Saigon were even small than the Japanese whores. Thin, tiny and so delicate he felt as if he could break one in two like a stalk of brittle bamboo, he'd found his forays into sexual intercourse even less satisfactory than in Japan.

Then this new woman appeared. She'd been made available through Master Tsing Chai's connections with Saigon's pillow world.

Her name was Loc Andrea. Not only was she rather tall and robust, but she spoke Japanese! Beautiful and slender, there was an aura of the athlete about her as if she did exercises with the same dedication the sumo wrestlers did.

Now, clad in a Japanese kimono like Andrea, Kaminatake held up the small cup of warm *sake*. He bowed toward the woman and smiled. "*Kenko*, Andrea-san."

She returned the toast. "*Kofuku*, Kaminatake-san." She was also dressed in the Japanese style, though her kimono was not traditional and her hair was not done up in *geisha* style.

The couple was comfortably situated in a room on the second floor of Tsing Chai's mah jongg parlor. Though there wasn't much furniture there, only a table, sleeping *futon* and a cabinet in the corner, it was an attractive apartment. The floor was covered with intricately woven bamboo mats. The walls, of inlaid teakwood, added a warm lustre to the atmosphere.

Kaminatake took a sip and returned the cup to the table. They had eaten a half-hour previously. The meal, while not Japanese, had been markedly Oriental. Rice with marinated pork, a fish *canh* and stir-fried leeks, turnips and carrots made up the main meal. The dessert had been *jujube*, a sweet fruit with candylike qualities.

Andrea, who enjoyed the meal, had been amazed at the amount of food the huge man consumed. She had made a polite remark about the size of his supper. "I see a strong man has a strong appetite."

Kaminatake smiled at her. "I was once a professional athlete," he explained. "A sumo wrestler. Are you familiar with the sport?"

"I have only seen pictures," Andrea said. "But, as large as

you are, the wrestlers seemed to be of an even greater size."

"I was much more rotund several months ago," Kamina-take said. "Wait. I will show you." He got nimbly to his feet and padded over to a small cabinet in the corner of the room. He returned with a photograph. It showed him, wearing the traditional sumo *mawashi* loincloth.

Andrea examined the picture. She noted his huge belly and his tree-trunk legs. "Oh! You were truly formidable!" she exclaimed with the proper feminine admiration.

Kaminatake was modest, but he was so smitten by the beautiful woman that he wanted to brag. "I advanced fast through *sumodo*, and won many matches. In my last tournament I was undefeated." He stopped suddenly. Kamina-take did not want Andrea to learn of his disgrace. The big man couldn't bring himself to inform her of his downfall. He let the subject drop.

"Then you were a *toshi*—a champion?"

Kaminatake smiled sadly. "Some things are not meant to be," he said. If Andrea-san had been in his life, he was sure he would have behaved himself and gone on up the sumo ranks to the coveted *yokozuna*—the grand master champion.

Andrea wasn't sure what sort of misfortune had fallen the man, but she knew better than to pry. She decided to brighten the mood. "More *sake*, Kaminatake-san?"

"*Hai! Arigato*, Andrea-san."

The next half-hour passed with only a little conversation. Kaminatake swilled the wine as fast as Andrea poured it into the small china cup. By the time she had called out for more bottles he was good and drunk—and horny.

The ex-*sumotori* reached over and shoved his hand into Andrea's kimono. She smiled as he fondled her breast. "What is you want, Kaminatake-san?"

He leered at her. "*Sei*."

She fell into the classical Oriental woman role. With her eyes cast downward, Andrea waited for his next move.

It wasn't long in coming. Kaminatake stood up and grabbed her hand. She got to her feet and allowed him to lead her over to the *futon*. Then he stood, slightly swaying, waiting. Like most Japanese men, when he had let his desires be known, he ceased his aggressiveness and let the woman take the initiative.

Obediently, she undid his *obi* allowing the front of his garment to open. Though he'd lost a lot of weight, he still had a belly. Below it, his manhood stood out in anticipation.

After deftly manipulating his phallus to help him increase his firmness, Andrea slipped from her own clothing and daintily lay down on the sleeping mat.

Kaminatake dropped to his knees and, displaying amazing dexterity, moved himself into position. He plunged into her, thrusting so hard that his massive buttocks quivered with the effort. When he reached the final moment, he reached under her, holding the woman up as he ground out the climax.

Andrea gritted her teeth against the pain. When he'd finished and dropped her back to the *futon*, she let out an inaudible sigh of relief.

Kaminatake got to his feet and closed his kimono before going back to the table for more *sake*. Andrea, after dressing, joined him.

"You are a good *onna*," he said.

"*Arigato*."

"Will you come back to see me again?"

"Of course. My employer will send me if you ask for me by name."

"*Odoroku!* I will have Tsing-san do that," Kaminatake said. He held out his cup for a refill.

"I am honored that you are so kind to an unworthy Vietnamese woman like myself," Andrea said pouring again.

"You are a beauty," Kaminatake said. He slurped the drink. "I like your country. But it is very hot here."

"*Hai*," Andrea agreed. "If you are here for very long you will get used to it."

"My visit is only short," Kaminatake said. The sex and wine were combining to put him in a boastful mood. "When my business is finished here I must return to Japan."

Andrea feigned innocence. "Are you a gambler?"

He snorted a laugh. "No. I am still a *sumotori* at heart. I am a fighter."

"Are you going to fight someone here?" Andrea inquired. "In a wrestling match?"

He laughed again. "My colleagues and I are here to fight some Americans — " He looked around as if to make sure no one was listening. " — soldiers. Real tough fellows."

"Oh, my! When will this happen?" Andrea asked pouring more wine.

"We are clever," Kaminatake told her. "Tomorrow we have set up a trap for them. They will walk into it and — " He pointed his finger at her and made a noise like a gunshot.

"Are these Americans fierce? Will they not hurt you?" Andrea asked showing pseudo-concern.

"Certainly, they are fierce, but I am not afraid," Kaminatake said. "They call themselves *Kuroi Washi*."

"Black Eagles? They must be very good fighters. Are you sure you can defeat them?"

"Of course," Kaminatake said. "They are being fooled into thinking there is no real danger. They will be taken to a warehouse they think is lightly guarded. But my Japanese friends and I will be there. Ready and waiting."

Andrea made sure he took another two good drinks before she spoke again. "When did you say you will fight this battle, Kaminatake-san?"

"Tomorrow."

Andrea smiled and made a few admiring remarks about his ferocity and bravery. While speaking, she reached inside the sleeves of her kimono and slyly withdrew a small vial of chlorpromazine. This drug, used to safely sedate the violently insane, was part of Andrea's arsenal.

The next time she poured his drink, she deftly slipped the concoction into the cup.

Kaminatake drank deeply.

It took a total of five drinks before the drug took effect on the big man. Even then he only gave in to its influence gradually as he slowly nodded off before collapsing backward to the floor.

Andrea quickly dressed in her street clothes, cramming the Japanese costume she'd brought along into her large handbag. Then, after one more glance at Kaminatake, she slipped out the door and into the hallway. Moving quickly, she went to the stairs leading to the first floor and descended. The first thing she had to do, once out of the gambling parlor, would be to get to a phone and warn Fagin of the ambush that he and the others were walking into.

Andrea reached the ground floor and hurried to the door. She would have to struggle through the crowd of gambling patrons to reach the street. Most of the men in the crowd recognized her as a prostitute. Several took advantage of her closeness to reach out to caress her firm, shapely buttocks and thighs through the thin dress she wore. Angry as hell, Andrea had to ignore the outrages in her haste to get out of the building.

She was halfway across the room when a voice sounded loudly and shrilly from one of the tables.

"*Trung Uy* Thuy! Lieutenant Thuy!"

Andrea swung instinctively toward the man who had called out her name.

Standing there with his hands full of mah jongg tiles was a very surprised and excited Col. Ngai Quang.

CHAPTER THIRTEEN

Truman Key was in a kind of limbo as the Black Eagles, with their two national police comrades, moved into position for the raid.

It was dawn.

That was a quiet transitional time on the avenue when the period of night-time reveling had come to an end, and the street people of the day had yet to make their appearance. Only a few barely conscious tipplers—mostly GIs who were going to be late in making reveille at their units—staggered around. The majority of these tardy drunkards (who would soon be facing punishment under Article 15 of the Uniform Code of Military Justice—at the very least) were completely unaware of their surroundings. They barely comprehended what direction they were moving in, their confusion increased by the cloudy swirls in their minds that echoed the effects of the previous few hours' heavy and incessant drinking.

Down an alley, out of sight of the fading remnants of revelers, the raiders' vehicles were parked, and under guard of their drivers.

Falconi, his .45 drawn and ready, eased up to the door of

the building that was the target of the operation. Sgt. Chin Han was directly opposite him on the other side of the entrance to the mission area. This thing was going to be a piece of cake. In fact they had estimated the operation to be so easy that Fagin had stayed behind to tend to some administrative details. With both him and Andrea away from the office, the paperwork had begun to pile up.

The Black Eagles' commander looked across the street where MSgt. Top Gordon had a view of everyone in the assault formation. Top waved the okay sign.

Falconi looked at Chin and winked. "Shall we?"

"Let's," Chin said.

Falconi leaped in front of the door and kicked it open with a thunderous front kick. Then, with Chin behind him, the major charged through the opening. He stopped in his tracks as the others of the raiding party piled in to join the duo.

The building, a large warehouse, was empty. The entire storage area was absolutely bare. The sides of the walls were made of offices with dirty windows. They appeared to have been added after the original construction.

"Shit!" Falconi cursed. The word echoed hollowly through the expanse of the edifice.

Chin turned. "*Ha-Si* Hai!"

Corporal Hai came forward. "Yes, *Trung-Si* Chin?"

The sergeant indicated the bareness of the place. "It would appear your informants were mistaken."

The other Black Eagles moved in around their chief and the two policemen.

Hai shook his head. "This is most unusual. I've never known my sources to be wrong before."

Chin reholstered his weapon as did everyone else. His face was a mask of anger. "You will make a full, written report and submit it before the end of the duty day."

Hai seemed very apologetic. "Yes, *Trung Si*." He moved closer to Falconi. "Perhaps the criminals inadvertently moved out for some reason or other. I am very sorry, and most mortified. The only thing I can say is — "

Suddenly he grabbed Falconi and threw him heavily to the floor. For one brief instant, everyone looked at the two in astonishment.

Then the shit hit the fan.

Andrea gently rubbed her sore wrists.

Kahn, Tsing's chief bodyguard, who had handled her so roughly, looked down where she sat at Tsing Chai's desk. So did Tsing Chai and Colonel Ngai.

"I do not understand this discourteous treatment," Andrea said angrily.

"It has been prompted by our most acute curiosity," Tsing said. "We are wondering why a lieutenant in the army would be working as a common prostitute."

"Mmph!" Andrea said. She sat up straight and gently patted her hairdo. "Do I look like a street whore?"

"You do have a most pleasing beauty," Tsing said.

"Of course," Andrea said. "That is why I work for *Ong* Nguyen's organization."

Ngai sneered openly at her. "Come, come, my dear *Trung Uy* Thuy. Do you really expect us to believe that? One can hardly imagine a key person on the staff of a Central Intelligence Agency case officer working as a call girl without it being an official assignment."

"I need extra money," Andrea said.

"I know the neighborhood where you live! That also includes the rather austere lifestyle you follow. Are you telling us that you have suddenly and inexplicably developed a costly taste for luxuries?" Ngai snapped. "You are forgetting that I am a high-ranking intelligence officer!"

"Of course I am not," Andrea said.

"Then you will not be surprised that I know your exact address in the *Quartier des Colons*." He laughed at her.

"I've even been in your apartment, Lieutenant."

"Does anyone have a cigarette?" Andrea asked.

"Being able to smoke is about to become the least of your worries," Tsing said coldly. "We have a few questions to put to you, Miss Thuy. It would save you a lot of physical discomfort if you answer truthfully and quickly. Do you fully comprehend what I am saying to you?"

"Of course," Andrea said, appearing cool. "I've nothing to hide. Even if Colonel Ngai reports me and I am dismissed from the army, I shall have a nice life doing my evening work."

Ngai screamed in anger, "*You stinking slut!* You are not fooling anybody! Do you think we will stupidly accept the fact that as an assignee at MACV SOG headquarters you calmly and unknowingly sell your body around Saigon?"

"Believe what you wish," Andrea said.

Ngai was so angry that spittle formed at the corner of his lips. "It would take MACV SOG barely forty-eight hours to take action against you if they did not know you worked as a call girl. There is absolutely no doubt in my mind that you are operating in an undercover capacity."

Tsing, fat and jolly looking, smiled at her. "How soon are Falcon and the Black Eagles going to make their move on my organization?"

"Never," Andrea said. "They are only raiding narcotics targets which involve American military personnel. Anyway, what interest would they have in you, Master Tsing?"

Tsing hit her hard on the mouth.

Andrea winced, but made no outcry. She put her hand up to her lips and mopped at the blood trickling down her chin. "What's the matter with you, Master Tsing? You must ask yourself about why a group like the Black Eagles would be interested in a gambling house?"

"Because they—like you—know that what I have here is more than a simple mah jongg parlor," Tsing said.

"What did that oaf of a Japanese tell you up there last

night?" Ngai demanded shrilly. His nervousness and fear were evident from the beads of perspiration on his brow.

"He said he had once been a sumo wrestler," Andrea said.

"I am sure he told you more than that," Tsing said.

"That is all he said," Andrea insisted.

"We will soon see, my dear," Tsing said. "Every room in this establishment is bugged. As soon as my commo man fetches the tape we shall hear your entire evening with our illustrious Kaminatake-san."

"I do not see why I am not permitted to smoke," Andrea said maintaining her role as a good-girl-gone-bad. She glared at Tsing Chai. "You may be assured that I shall inform *Ong* Nguyen of your discourtesy and mistreatment of me. I am one of his best ladies."

"I am most certain that you are, my dear," Tsing said.

The door opened and the commo man, who had been required to dig the recorder out of a hidden panel upstairs, stepped in with the device.

"Now we shall find out the truth," Ngai said.

"Indeed," Tsing agreed. He nodded to the commo man. "Let us hear the tape."

The fusillade of shots exploded from the windows of the offices around the open bay area. Everyone dropped to the ground — with the exception of Lightfingers O'Quinn.

He staggered backward, a large crimson stain growing on his chest. He dragged his automatic from the shoulder holster. Another round hit him in the arm, shaking him so hard he nearly collapsed. Lightfingers fired once, then was hit again. He dropped to both knees, and tried to shoot once more.

The next bullet took off the top of his head and he slumped backward to the floor.

"Echelon left!" Top Gordon shouted. As the group set up an informal and impromptu fire-and-maneuver movement, the master sergeant noted Hai's unusual handling of Falconi. The police corporal was holding the American major down as he tried to get to his feet. Despite being exposed, there was no unfriendly fire going directly at them.

Top Gordon was the type of man who could smell a rat in a pile of horse shit.

He rushed over and slammed the handle of his pistol down between Hai's shoulder blades with every ounce of strength his muscular body could muster. The policeman grunted loudly, then collapsed.

Falconi rolled free and jumped to his feet pumping bullets toward the source of fire.

"To those offices on the left!" Top said. He made an attempt to drag Hai along, but found it too difficult.

Chun Kim, Malpractice McCorckel and Calvin Culpepper laid down a rapid base of fire. Falconi, Top, Archie Dobbs and Chin Han dashed off. After going a few meters, they also put out a curtain of .45 slugs. The other three joined them, then the procedure was repeated until they reached the safety of one of the offices.

Hai, now recovering, was in a confused state. He struggled up on his knees. Two rounds smashed into the policeman's chest, one exiting from the left side of his neck. The other tore out his back, bringing a large chunk of spine with it. Hai toppled over and twitched through his death throes.

Falconi, breathing hard, looked out at the area they'd just vacated. Lightfingers and Hai were both sprawled only a short distance apart.

Malpractice squinted his eyes as he looked across the warehouse at Lightfingers. His voice was subdued. "Oh, damn. He's had it."

"Can you tell from here?" Archie asked.

Malpractice nodded. "Yeah."

"Jesus," Calvin said. "Ol' Lightfingers."

Suddenly a fresh volley of fire came from another direction, splintering the walls behind them and sending pieces of glass flying around the small room.

"This is a situation that's easy to assess," Top Gordon said.

"Yeah," Falconi agreed. "We're heavily outnumbered, outgunned, outflanked and — "

"Out o' luck," Archie Dobbs added.

Kaminatake, with Kaji nearby, held the Nambu pistol and raised his head high enough to peer out one of the windows. The two occupied one of the small offices. Four more Japanese were situated in others. All had a good view of the area in which the Black Eagles had withdrawn, but Kaji was not happy.

"*Chikusho jigoku ni ochiro!*" he swore. "We should have mowed them all down with the first volley."

Kaminatake agreed, but he knew the problem. "They did not come in far enough."

Kaji gritted his teeth in anger. "That idiot police corporal who was supposed to betray them, moved too soon."

"He paid for his impetuosity," Kaminatake said. He had been ordered to give Hai special attention during the ambush. If the Vietnamese policeman became a target of opportunity by becoming separated from the Americans, the ex-sumo was to shoot him without hesitation.

"You did your job well," Kaji said.

"It is still too difficult to hit targets at that distance," Kaminatake said.

Kaji hefted his pistol and looked at it. "We should have had rifles — or submachine guns."

"What do we do, Kaji-san?" Kaminatake asked. He recognized the other's superiority in such a situation. He deferred to him in a polite way.

"What do we do?" Kaji replied with a question. Then he answered it himself. "We attack. After all, as *samurai* there is no other honorable course to follow."

"We will fight by the code of *Bushido*," Kaminatake said to echo his companion's attitude.

"As Sons of the Rising Sun we have no other course to follow," Kaji said.

"Is this like in the Great War against the Americans when our men would not surrender?" Kaminatake inquired.

"Exactly," Kaji replied, "We, like they, have three choices — victory, death or escape." He yelled over to the other men. *"Shitakumasu kogeki!"* Then he leaped up and rushed out of the office toward the area where the Black Eagles were holed up. He kicked off two shots from his pistol and screamed, *"Banzai!"*

Kaminatake's voice sounded slightly muffled over the tape recorder.

"Of course," the words came, "they are being fooled into thinking there is no real danger. They will be taken to a warehouse they think is lightly guarded. But my Japanese friends and I will be there. Ready and waiting."

The conversation between Andrea and the big sumo continued until there was the sound of the big man collapsing. A few minutes later the door could be heard opening and closing.

"That would be you leaving, my beauty," Tsing Chai said to Andrea. "Tell me, dear lady, what did you give the brute to make him fall over in such a manner?"

"I gave him nothing," Andrea insisted.

Ngai slapped her face with a stinging blow. "Stop that incessant lying, you whore!"

"Whatever drug you administered was not quite enough for that size an individual," Tsing said. "He came around after only fifteen minutes."

"Just about the time we brought you here," Ngai said.

"He didn't even have a headache," Tsing added with his evil cherubic smile. "In fact, there was not a second's delay in the departure of our formidable Japanese friends for the ambush of your comrades-in-arms."

"I have no comrades-in-arms," Andrea said. "I work in an office. Colonel Ngai knows that."

Ngai glared at her. "I also know the extent of your intelligence background and your relationship with the Black Eagles, Lieutenant Thuy. We also know you have been on a mission with them into North Vietnam. There is no point in lying to us."

"Of course not," Tsing emphasized. "You are in a most enviable position. Not only can you help advance the socialist cause in your country, but we can arrange safe transport for you to the north where other comrades in the Peasant and Worker's Paradise await to greet you with open arms."

Andrea knew all was lost. She remembered the indignities and torments she had been forced to bear under Communism in the past. She looked up at Tsing.

Again he smiled. "What do you think of that, Comrade Thuy?"

Andrea spat in his face.

"Here they come!"

Archie Dobbs' voice sounded almost shrill in his excitement when he saw the six assailants leap from the offices on the opposite wall and charge toward them.

Robert Falconi raised his pistol and sent the first shot through the window directly in front of him. The second bullet bowled the lead attacker over. The man, his Nambu clattering to the concrete floor, was dead before he joined the weapon there.

Two additional .45 rounds exploded outward. These, from Top Gordon's weapon, zipped through thin air. But their whistling passage caused the other men charging the Black Eagles to instinctively duck. This broke their stride.

A fusillade erupted from Falconi's men. Three more of

209

the attackers were hit. Screaming in an awful combination of rage and pain, these Japanese *karatekas*, adapting the fighting spirit of their art to gunplay, continued lurching forward despite the bloody wounds they suffered.

The final volley knocked them from their feet as if an invisible, giant broom handle had been slammed against them.

"Two of 'em in the back are gettin' away!" Calvin Culpepper yelled in rage. He made a dash for the door, but Falconi rushed him and tackled the angry black man, throwing him to the floor.

Calvin was pissed off. "Damn, Skipper! Let's go after them motherfuckers! They killed Lightfingers."

"Hold it," Falconi said holding him down. "That may mean a trap over there. They might have sacrificed some ne'er-do-wells just to draw us out of here."

Calvin calmed down. "Yeah. You're right."

Falconi looked at his other men. "There may be two — or two dozen over there — but we can't stay here. Pop fresh magazines into your weapons and get ready to move out — slow and easy!"

Andrea, on the floor, put her hand to her swollen jaw. She laboriously pulled herself to the chair and again sat down.

"You haven't the proper respect for the people's just cause," Tsing Chai said. He still smiled at her despite the fact he'd just knocked her down. "We must change your attitude, Comrade Thuy."

Andrea was so enraged that she quivered with the emotion. "My attitude was formed as a very young girl," she said through clenched teeth. "The benevolence and kindness of the Viet Minh and Pathet Lao have made me what I am."

Tsing continued to smile. "All that you require is reeducation, my beauty. Believe me, you will find the experience heady and wonderful as skilled comrades melt away your old prejudices and hatreds to replace them with a fervent love for Marxism."

"Bah!" Ngai hissed in fearful hatred. "Kill her! Shoot her! Like you did the last devil who infiltrated here. Let her friends in the Black Eagles find her on a garbage pile in the Cholon."

"I am most afraid that is exactly what will happen," Tsing said. He put out a pudgy hand and gently ran it down her bruised cheek. "Such a shame to turn feminine beauty like this into bloated, fly-covered fleshy putridness!"

Kaminatake, following closely on Kaji's heels, sprinted down the alley to their car. The chauffeur, one of Tsing's minor security men, looked at them in alarm as they approached. "What happened?" he asked. He looked past the two at the empty alley behind them. "Where are your friends? Are they not coming with you?"

"Everything went awry," Kaji said. "We had to open the ambush too soon. All our men are dead. We must get out of here quickly. As soon as those *Kuroi Washi* dogs find out there are none of us left in there, they will be out here shooting."

The driver needed no further encouragement. He leaped into his seat as the Japanese duo dove into the back. He gunned the motor and slipped the vehicle into gear. Then with tires squealing, the automobile raced out into the street to make a desperate run to the mah jongg parlor.

"What is to happen, Kaji-san?" Kaminatake asked.

"Before this day is out there will be many dead men," Kaji said. "A big fight is in the offing. It cannot be denied."

Kaminatake's *sumotori* spirit boiled to the surface. He grinned and gripped the Nambu pistol. "If I am to die, then I will take a great number of those Black Eagles with me."

Kaji had calmed down a bit. "I think Master Tsing has things better organized than that."

CHAPTER FOURTEEN

SSgt. Liam "Lightfingers" O'Quinn, United States Marine Corps, was dead.

There was no sense in mourning about it or even giving the matter much thought, as far as Maj. Robert Falconi's logic went. But, no matter how cold and detached he tried to be, his heart did mourn the tough supply man, and he knew he would be thinking a lot about the marine.

The MP escort whom Falconi followed through the corridors of SOG Headquarters stopped and opened the door. Then he beckoned the major to enter. Once inside the office, the Black Eagles commander was surprised to note that Andrea wasn't at her desk.

"Fagin?" he called out.

"Yeah. C'mon in." The CIA case officer's voice was muffled behind the second door in the room.

Falconi stepped into the office. "Where's Andrea? Still out on ops?"

"She's officially missing," Fagin said. He paused. "Unofficially—because we want to keep this quiet even between our own intelligence bureaus—she's somewhere in the interior of that mah jongg parlor. A prisoner, no doubt."

"Man!" Falconi sat down. "I was just about to climb all over your ass for not giving us the okay for a follow-up yesterday."

"I expected you to," Fagin said. "Now you know why I wouldn't let your guys close in on Tsing Chai yet. I didn't want to jeopardize Andrea."

"I have to admit something to you, Fagin. The Black Eagles are learning to respect the hell out of your intuitions and orders," Falconi said. "You kept us out in that Godforsaken B camp because you had a hunch that we were being compromised through Colonel Ngai. You turned out to be right."

"Even a dumb bastard like me can figure out a few things after twenty-three years in this dirty business," Fagin said modestly.

"And you were right in aborting any after-action following the ambush in the warehouse."

"Okay! Okay! I'm brilliant," Fagin said. "I can live with that." He paused. "Too bad about Lightfingers O'Quinn. He was a hell of a guy."

"Yeah," Falconi remarked. He didn't like to dwell on his dead men. It was too painful. He got off the subject fast. "I'm a little embarrassed about holding back when there were only two other baddies in there."

"Never confuse prudence with stupidity or cowardice," Fagin told him.

"It's still embarrassing."

"Never mind. Let's get down to business," Fagin continued. "I have some news for you."

"Fire away."

"All the people you guys offed in that warehouse were Japanese," Fagin said. "A fingerprint check through our Toyko office showed these guys to be employed by a Mister Matsuno."

"A Communist agent?"

"Nope. The guy's an opportunist," Fagin explained. "He

doesn't belong to any Japanese criminal gang or organization. Matsuno is strictly a free-lancer who involves himself in all sorts of enterprises — legal or illegal — with profit being his sole motive."

"Then what the hell was he doing sending his boys to deal with Tsing Chai?" Falconi asked.

"They've done business in the past in which narcotics were involved. Tsing was into dope for the detrimental effect it would have on Americans in Vietnam. Matsuno was interested in the potential profit. Evidently he owed a couple of favors or something," Fagin said. "The Japanese police will find out about that."

"So what's going down?" Falconi asked.

"We're going to hit Tsing Chai and wrap up his little organization," Fagin said.

"Right away?"

"Nope. Tomorrow night," Fagin said.

"But if they've got Andrea —"

"If she's going to talk, she will have already done it," Fagin advised. "And if she didn't —"

Falconi nodded. "Yeah. They've snuffed her already."

"I want to hold off because the Chinese bastard is figuring on us to charge right over there without delay. If we do what he expects, he'll be sure of himself. But if he has a few hours to sit and mull things over, he'll be less certain of what the hell's going on."

"Psychological warfare is good up to a point," Falconi cautioned.

"Are you questioning my judgment?" Fagin asked. "A couple of minutes ago you were going on about what a smart sonofabitch I was."

Falconi grinned. "Okay."

"Your new men have come in," Fagin informed him. "They're down in 'A' billets. I think you ought to go down and meet them."

"Will they be going along on the next raid?"

215

Fagin got up and walked around the desk. "You're damned right. We'll need every gun we can muster. I don't want to use any more goddamned Vietnamese on this operation."

"Not even Chin?"

"Not even Chin."

The two went out into the hall where the MP waited for them.

Fagin patted Falconi's shoulder. "I've got a couple of things to tend to. I'll see you later."

"Right."

The MP, already knowing where the major wanted to go, turned silently and strode down the hall to the staircase. They went past the first floor to the living quarters set up in the basement.

The escort left him at the entrance.

"Tin-*Hut!*" a voice bawled as they stepped into the room.

"At ease," Falconi said. He glanced over the seven men standing there. A stack of 201 personnel files was on a field table by the door. Without another word, Falconi slid into a chair and pulled out the first folder.

"Swift Elk, Ray," he called out.

A tall, dark sergeant first class stepped forward. "Here, sir."

SFC Ray Swift Elk was a full-blooded Sioux Indian from South Dakota. Lean and muscular at a bit under six feet in height, his copper-colored skin, prominent nose and high cheekbones gave him the appearance of the classic prairie warrior. With twelve years of service, he was an intelligence sergeant.

Falconi noted his MOS. "Our last intel NCO was an Indian too. Jack Galchaser. He was damned good at the job."

"I'll carry on where he left off, sir," Swift Elk said.

"I won't worry about that," Falconi remarked. He pulled the next file. "SSgt. Charlie Tripper."

"Here, sir."

216

Tripper, with nearly eighteen years in the army, was rotund. His face, a bit blotched and ruddy, showed evidence of its owner's habits of imbibing hard liquor. He was a supply sergeant, who was known to carry enough surplus to equip units three and four times the size of his own. Yet the sharpest inspector generals had never been able to discover as much as an extra paper clip during the many hours they'd spent poring over his property books and searching the nooks and crannies of his equipment bins.

"Nice to see you, Sergeant Tripper," Falconi said. "I see by your records that you've been busted recently. Care to give me the details?"

"It was personal, sir," Tripper said.

"We'll go into that later." Falconi got the next folder. "PO2C Durwood Martin."

"Aye, aye, sir. That's me." Martin was a short, husky man with hair as black as Swift Elk's. But his skin was as fair as a teenage maiden's. It didn't match his murderous face. "I'm called Sparks, sir. I'm a communications man from the navy SEALs."

"We've had guys from your unit in the Black Eagles before," Falconi said. "They were all good men. One of 'em was our radio man like you're going to be. His name was Sparks too."

"Navy tradition, sir."

"Then it's a damned good tradition," Falconi said. He perused the next documents. PO3C Blue Richards."

"Here, sir. I'm a demolitions man from the SEALs," he said in a marked southern accent.

"You'll be working under our senior demo sergeant, Calvin Culpepper," Falconi said. "Where are you from, Richards?"

"Alabama, sir."

Falconi took a closer look at his forms. "According to this, your name, indeed, is Blue. Where'd you get a tag like that?"

"My daddy named me after his favorite huntin' dawg."

Falconi suppressed a laugh. "Sounds like a real honor."

"It is if you take into consideration how much my daddy thought o' that ol' dawg, sir."

"Sgt. George Whitaker."

"Sir!" A tall man, wearing an Australian digger hat, stepped forward. He literally crashed to the position of attention and delivered one of the sharpest salutes that Falconi had ever seen. "Sergeant Whitaker, George! Australian Army SAS! Heavy weapons specialist! Reporting for duty as ordered, sir!"

"Glad to have you aboard—as Sparks and Blue would say—you're our second SAS man."

"Yes, sir! I'm taking SSgt. Tom Newcomb's place."

"Good," Falconi said. "Stand at ease, Sergeant Whitaker. Lighten up."

"Sir!" The big man slammed himself into a position similar to the American army's parade rest.

Falconi took another file. "Sgt. Toby Barker, United States Marine Corps, infantry light weaponsman."

"Here, sir."

Falconi noted a husky, clean-cut youngster who looked like he should be playing football for Notre Dame. "Are you a jock, Sergeant Barker?"

"Hell, no, sir. I'm a fighter and a lover."

"Great. Everybody in the detachment is good at fighting, but there's a couple of clumsy bastards that could use a few lessons in relationships with the opposite sex."

"Be glad to lend a hand, sir," Barker said.

"The last man, who I'm sure is not least, is from the army. His name is—"

"SSgt. Dennis Maywood," the soldier said announcing himself. He stepped forward through the crowd. A diminutive man who must have only barely passed the army's minimum height and weight requirements, Maywood had a deep, resounding voice completely out of character with his physical appearance. "Skinny Maywood, I'm called, sir. A light weapons leader outta camps, so when a chance came along for some *real* action, I jumped at it."

Falconi was incredulous. "You were bored in the A camps?"

"Yeah," Maywood said. "Sometimes a day or two would go by without any action. Besides, I heard my ol' pal Archie Dobbs was in the Black Eagles."

"Yeah, he is," Falconi acknowledged.

"By the way, when do we start kicking some ass?" Maywood asked.

Falconi liked the little guy's feistiness. And his 201 file showed he was no bullshitter. He was on his second tour (not counting one in Laos in the late 1950s), had been wounded twice and wore the silver star with an oak leaf cluster.

"Sergeant Maywood," Falconi said. "You'll be pleased to hear that you'll be up to your neck in trouble by tomorrow night."

"Aw, shit! I gotta wait 'til *tomorrow*?"

CHAPTER FIFTEEN

The gambling parlor seemed muffled and musty to Kahn as he walked through the room. The lights were out, and the tables were covered with heavy cotton cloths. There was usually plenty of noise with the exclamations of the players and the loud clacking of their tiles. The silence seemed extraordinarily heavy and oppressive.

Kahn, Tsing Chai's senior bodyguard, was in a mood as dark as the parlor. Everything seemed to be going to hell. He'd felt uneasy about the Japanese reinforcements since their arrival. Taciturn and snobbish, they'd stayed together with a subtle display of contempt toward him and his men.

Kahn grinned as he recalled the return of their boss Kaji and the big bastard Kaminatake from the ambush attempt against the Black Eagles. The two had been plainly shaken by the incident. Evidently they hadn't expected the American Falconi and his men to be the first rate fighters they were.

Tsing had ordered the building prepared for an immediate assault. Customers were summarily expelled from the premises and all doors and windows locked according to the security measures already planned out in the event of such an emergency. The final communications were broadcast north through the relay station, then the radio operator began dismantling the equipment and burning all documents and code books. Armed to the teeth, Kahn and his men — with the two Japanese—had braced themselves for the storming of their citadel.

But twenty-four hours had dragged by with nothing happening.

Perhaps the girl they held prisoner had told the truth. There was no reason for the Black Eagles to suspect Tsing Chai of anything. The turncoat policeman Corporal Hai might have made it all up in order to get some money out of the gambling master. His reports were never substantiated. Their principal source of information, Col. Ngai Quang, had been unable to get any real intelligence on the Black Eagles since their return to Saigon. It had been reasoned that Ngai's failure was due to suspicion being cast on him by the Americans. But perhaps it had been the natural jealousy between Vietnamese army intelligence and their police that had caused the breakdown in communications and information swapping.

Whatever the cause, Kahn was growing weary of the entire situation.

He decided it was time to check the street for any unusual activity. He went to the front door and opened the spy hole. Kahn peered out carefully for several long moments. The traffic seemed normal, with people ambling up and down the narrow thoroughfare. He pulled his keys from his pocket and unlocked the heavy portal, and stepped out into the entrance way.

The .45 slugs bashed his chest so hard that he was flung a dozen feet back into the parlor.

Top Gordon, in the alley on the other side of the building with Chun Kim and Calvin Culpepper, heard the shots. He tapped Calvin's shoulders. "Now!"

Calvin, kneeling in front of the master sergeant, held an electronic detonator in his hands. Always an observer of safety precautions under any set of circumstances, he whispered loud enough for his friends in the alley to hear. "Fire in the hole! Fire in the hole!"

Calvin cranked the handle, sending a charge down the wire to the caps planted in the plastic C4 explosive. A large report burst with a roar and the rear door of Tsing Chai's establishment flew inward.

"Go!" Top yelled. He charged forward with Kim and Calvin right behind him. Farther down the alley, the two SEALs, Sparks Martin and Blue Richards, leaped from their cover and rushed after them.

The door had done more than structural damage when it was blown inward. The battered body of an unlucky security man who'd been standing behind it was lying against the wall. Bloody and torn, he stared at the intruders with unseeing dead eyes as they charged into the interior of Tsing's domain.

Andrea Thuy had not heard the shots that had felled Kahn, but the explosion in the rear had penetrated to the room where she was.

The woman was in poor physical shape. Lying on the floor naked, with her hands tied behind her back, she had endured numerous rapes and beatings. Both her eyes were swollen nearly shut. Her once sensuous mouth was swollen from Tsing's repeated slaps and her body was covered with bruises and cigarette burns.

Andrea struggled to a sitting position. She peered around the room as best she could. The door opened and she could barely make out the hem of Tsing Chai's silken kimono.

"Your friends have come for you, my beauty," he said. He reached down and grabbed her shoulders, hauling her to a standing position. "But they are too late."

Barely able to maintain her balance, Andrea looked in the Chinese's face. She could see the hatred there, but she didn't flinch from his fury. "I would — advise you to — surrender — and make — a deal — " She had to take a couple of deep breaths before she could continue. " — there is always — a chance for you — to defect — give intelligence — "

Tsing snarled and grabbed one of her breasts, giving the nipple a cruel twist. "I shall never betray the revolution!" he hissed. "And you shall pay the supreme price for going against the people."

Andrea raised her eyes and found herself looking into the business end of a Russian Tokarev automatic pistol.

"Prepare to die, you reactionary bitch!" Tsing said.

Falconi leaped over Kahn's body and charged into the gambling parlor. Archie Dobbs, Malpractice McCorckel and Skinny Maywood were on his heels.

Two of Tsing's men appeared in a side door. The lead bodyguard managed to get off one shot before a volley of .45 slugs tore into him and his companion. Both bounced off the wall and careened in a bloody twosome on top of a mah jongg table. The piece of furniture gave way under their weight and crashed to the floor.

"Watch it, Skipper!" Archie yelled.

Three more of the security men charged in through another entrance. The concussion in the room was deafening as seven weapons exploded into action. Ricochets whined, and wall panels splintered under the impact of numerous slugs.

Falconi and the other four Black Eagles were able to utilize the cover offered by the gambling equipment. It was to Tsing's men's credit that they made an attempt to advance, but courage without common sense sometimes causes disaster.

A total of a dozen rounds zapped into them from four angles. Each took multiple hits making skulls crack apart and hunks of torn flesh splatter the wall behind them.

With the big room now cleared, Falconi led his team through the curtained entranceway that offered access to the interior of the building.

Archie, panting heavily, kept close to his leader. "Wonder what else we'll find in here."

Behind him, Skinny Maywood was in such a hurry that he pushed Archie. "Don't worry about it! Let's go!"

Archie started to say something back to him when he felt the blow of the bullet that hit him. It flung Archie back against the smaller man.

Skinny Maywood struggled out from under his friend. With all the shooting going on, he only had time to take a cursory glance at Archie. Then he continued after Falconi.

Malpractice, bringing up the rear, saw Archie go down. "Oh, God!" he exclaimed in a voice close to sobbing. "Not another one of the old guys." He ran over to the wounded Black Eagle and knelt down beside him. "Archie! Archie!"

There was no answer from the detachment's scout. His eyes, wide-open and glazed over, stared blankly upward.

Kaminatake, his Nambu still in his shoulder holster, had hurried down the hall at the first sounds of battle.

The ex-*sumotori* wasn't looking for a fight. There was only one thing on his mind at that time. He saw that the door to the room he sought was open. He rushed through it and stopped.

"Tsing-san!" he shouted.

Tsing Chai, his pistol pointed at Andrea Thuy's head, turned to see who had called out to him. He quickly put his eyes back on the helpless prisoner. "What do you want?" he demanded angrily of the Japanese.

"What are you going to do?" Kaminatake asked.

"It should be obvious even to you!"

Kaminatake charged forward into the fat, soft Chinese and sent him careening across the room. Tsing, his eyes wild with desperate anger, had managed to hang on to the Tokarev. He raised it — but not fast enough.

The Japanese slammed into him again. This time the weapon flew from Tsing's hand. Kaminatake then threw his opponent to the floor in a classic *oshi-taoshi* technique. Tsing's spine cracked so suddenly that it sounded like a plank of wood hit by an ax.

Andrea, disoriented but determined, edged toward the pistol lying on the floor a few meters away.

Top Gordon dropped to a low kneeling position as he made a quick aim at the man standing at the top of the stairs. The guy was a trifle quicker, but not too accurate. Plaster blasted out from the wall by the master sergeant's head.

Top went a bit lower and squeezed the trigger.

The bullet went in under the man's jaw and continued through the top of the cranium. The bodyguard's eyeballs flew from their sockets from the force of the inward pressure of the slug's expansion. Blood and brain matter oozed down his cheeks from the hollowed eye sockets. He stood in complete stillness for one second, then pitched forward down the steps.

Top stepped on him, as did Kim, Calvin, Sparks and Blue as they continued their assault up the stairs.

"You sonofabitch!" Malpractice cursed. "Don't you go into shock on me."

Archie Dobbs, his eyes rolling crazily, tried to look at the medic. His face, white as chalk, had a particularly dumb expression on it. "I got shot — I got shot —"

Malpractice tore open the sleeve of Archie's shirt. "I know you got shot, you dumb bastard." He could see that a portion of the deltoid muscle had been blown away. People reacted in different ways to wounds. Archie had received a heavy blow when the round hit him. Then he'd hit the floor hard, his head bouncing off the boards there. Disoriented and bleeding heavily, he was a sure-fire candidate for deep shock. The kind that killed people.

The fighting had died down considerably by then. Their particular fire team had accomplished its mission of securing the downstairs. Top Gordon and his men in the rear were cutting loose with occasional shots, but the surprise of the assault had paid off in spades. Caught flat-footed, Tsing's fortress crumbled rapidly.

Now the only thing that concerned Malpractice was saving his buddy's life. He worked frantically while Archie slipped deeper and deeper away from him.

Kaminatake caught sight of Andrea out of the corner of his eye. He took a couple of quick steps and kicked Tsing's weapon out of her reach. Then he gently picked the young woman up.

"We are going to get out of here," he said.

The big Japanese carried her down the hall. He had no real plan. He knew what direction the attack was coming from, so he instinctively moved away from it. He entered the last office in the corridor.

Col. Ngai Quang, cowering there, looked up in alarm as Kaminatake entered with the woman in his arms. The Vietnamese, his voice shrill with panic, clapped his hands together. "Good! Good! We can bargain for our freedom with her."

"You talk as if the battle is lost," Kaminatake said with a frown.

"Of course it is lost, you oaf!" Ngai cried. "We are completely surrounded in the midst of a hostile city. How do you expect us to fight through? But it will be possible to exchange the woman—"

Kaminatake kicked hard, catching Ngai in the crotch. The turncoat screamed in shocked agony. He rolled on the floor clutching his mashed testicles until Kaminatake approached him.

The sumo took one more contemptuous look at the cowardly weasel, then performed a *shiko* stamp movement that cracked Ngai's skull like it had been a ripe watermelon in the hot sun. A liquid slime of brains and blood splashed across the carpet.

"Kaminatake-san!"

The sumo turned and saw Kaji standing in the door. "*Hai?!*"

"It is time to die like *samurai*," Kaji said. "But first we must kill the woman."

Kaminatake carried Andrea over to a chair and gently sat her in it. He pulled his Nambu from its holster. "I love this *onna*," he said. "*Dozo*, Kaji-san. Let me do the deed."

"*Hai*," Kaji agreed. "It is proper that way."

Kaminatake, his eyes misting with tears, aimed the pistol straight into Andrea's face.

Fagin stood by the ambulance as Archie Dobbs was put inside. He watched the medics slip the stretcher into the stowage loops. Then the door was closed and the vehicle took off with siren whining.

Fagin turned to Malpractice. "What's the verdict?"

Malpractice grinned. "The dipshit's gonna be okay. He scared the hell out of me though. For awhile it was nip and tuck in that hallway. He damned near bought it, but I guess he's too dumb to know when he's hurt bad."

"Think he'll go Stateside?"

"If he wants to," Malpractice said. "The wound really

wasn't that serious. In fact, I don't think he'll be impaired at all. He lost more flesh than muscle, but he sure bled like a gutted goat."

"He's a good man," Fagin said.

"Yeah," Malpractice agreed.

Fagin glanced around. "Where's Falconi?"

"Inside," Malpractice answered. "The place is secured with maybe one or two bad guys left. We still haven't found Andrea. There's a chance they're holding her in a far corner of the building."

"Christ!" Fagin exclaimed. "That'd be a situation more dangerous than the initial assault."

"Prob'ly," Malpractice agreed. "One thing's for sure. The dyin' ain't over yet."

Once again Andrea Thuy looked into the bore of a pistol pointed at her head. She took a deep breath and closed her eyes. To die like this would be to give her life for a cause she believed in with all her heart. That, at least, would console her soul during its journey through the black void of death.

The pistol report filled the room.

Kaji, his forehead splintered by the bullet, fell backward.

Kaminatake, in a cold rage, fired into the body until the final case was ejected leaving the cocking lever standing out from the pistol receiver.

He turned to Andrea. "They have always lied to me about those stupid philosophies," he said. "*Bushido, Sumodo* — all of it. I was a good wrestler. For years I received no pay, working hard at perfecting my skills. In the end I was cast aside despite all the sacrifices I made. Now I have decided to be selfish and live for myself and what I want from life. And the most important thing to me now is you."

Andrea, exhausted and at the end of her emotional rope, could only plead weakly. "Please — "

Kaminatake walked toward her. "I want you to be my

229

onna—my woman."

"Hold it!"

Robert Falconi stood framed in the doorway, his feet straddling Kaji's body. He held his pistol ready to fire.

Kaminatake glanced in Andrea's direction. "Who is he?"

Andrea spoke in Japanese. "He is the chief of the *Kuroi Washi*."

"Put your hands up," Falconi commanded in a firm voice.

"*Nippon-go deki-masu ka?*" Kaminatake asked.

"What did he say?" Falconi inquired of Andrea.

"He said—"

Kaminatake was so fast it seemed as if he flew. He charged into Falconi knocking the American out of the door and across the hall into another room. His pistol spun off to parts unknown.

Falconi got to his feet in time to meet another assault. This one sent him spinning through the entire expanse of the room. He narrowly avoided a nasty collision with the far wall. The major's basic theory of war was that a good offense was better than a bad defense.

The Falcon attacked.

He slammed the heel of his hand into Kaminatake's jaw, drove a knuckle into the Japanese's solar plexus, and delivered a sharp pivot kick into his thigh.

Kaminatake grunted, then picked up the American and threw him back into the hall.

Falconi's mind reeled. He made another attempt to bring Kaminatake down with a blow to the collarbone with the knife edge of his hand. Normally this would have caused a fracture.

Kaminatake didn't even blink. He picked up the American in a *yori-kiri* sumo hold and flung him down the hall to the head of the stairs.

The leader of the Black Eagles bounced hard twice off the floor and once off the wall. Each collision with the building brought stinging bruises and scrapes to Falconi's punished body.

Kaminatake took a deep breath, then performed a deliberate *shiko* exercise, his feet hitting the floor so hard that the walls vibrated. "Now for my thundering *tachiai*!"

Stunned and groping, Falconi barely managed to get to his feet when he caught the blurry sight of his huge opponent rushing toward him. Falconi timed his movement—then ducked.

Kaminatake sailed over the major into the high, empty space above the stairs. He continued his ascent in a graceful arc that ended when he hit the floor by the bottom step. He landed on top of his head. Even his massive, muscular neck could not stand up under the sudden impact of his large body.

The vertebrae wrenched violently, snapping the spinal cord.

By the time Falconi had recovered sufficiently to be able to go down and examine the former wrestler, Kaminatake was dead. Blood flowed from his eyes, nose and ears.

His final bout had been a defeat.

Fagin, sitting on one of the mah jongg tables, looked up as Top Gordon led Falconi and Andrea into the large gambling hall. Andrea, obviously in bad shape, walked unsteadily with Falconi's arm around her. She was dressed in one of Tsing Chai's fine silk kimonos.

Falconi turned Andrea over to Malpractice. "Get her to one of the field hospitals at Tan Son Nhut."

"Right, Skipper," Malpractice said. "There's an air force ambulance outside right now." He gently took Andrea out of the building.

Falconi nodded to Fagin. "We found both Tsai and Ngai up there. Both are dead."

"Good," Fagin said. "Looks like Operation Saigon Showdown is wrapped up."

"Yeah. I'll be glad to get back out in the field," Falconi said as they walked outside. "The fighting seems cleaner in the boonies somehow."

"You're right about that," Fagin said. "We just got a call in from Long Binh about Archie. He's going to be okay. Should be back to duty within a week."

"Great!" Falconi exclaimed in sincere happiness. "Well, as soon as I wash up I think I'll take the boys out for a few more of those San Miguel beers."

"Mind if I come along?" Fagin asked.

"We'd love to have you, pal," Falconi replied grinning. "Let's get out of here."

"Right."

As they walked across the street where their vehicles waited, a dry cleaning delivery truck slowly rolled by in front of the former mah jongg parlor. The driver, Xong, glanced at the happenings around the area, then pressed gently on the accelerator and drove from the scene.

He had many reorganization tasks ahead of him.

EPILOGUE

In the city of Hanoi, North Vietnam there was a young boy who was totally dedicated to Communism.

Ever since the French withdrawal in 1954 he had been exposed to Red propaganda, education and indoctrination until, by the age of nineteen, he was a veritable fanatic in the cause of Marxism and the world domination of socialism.

When the war in the south broke out, this young man wanted more than anything to be able to serve in the struggle against the Army of the Republic of Vietnam and its American allies. That was all he thought of day or night. Finally, unable to contain himself any longer, he left his school and volunteered to go to the south and aid his Viet Cong comrades.

The party commissar complimented him on his drive and patriotic attitude. He informed the youth of the Ho Chi Minh Trail. This crude, but vital link between the north and the Communist forces in the south was the only effective supply route that served the Viet Cong revolutionaries and the North Vietnamese soldiers. The boy's job, the official informed him, would be to take items down to his comrades who needed them desperately.

Starry-eyed and determined, the young man was given a pack. In it were placed two 82-millimeter rounds. With wishes of good luck ringing in his ears, the stalwart young Communist headed south.

At first the going was rather easy. The trail was wide with plenty of rest stops and facilities to eat along the way. At each place he, and others toting stuff south, were greeted as heroes. After a night's rest and a good meal in the morning, he would resume his trek toward the war.

But, as time and distance passed, things got worse. The trail grew cruder until it was nearly impassable at certain points. The monsoon rains came, creating muddy conditions. The boy, still lugging those two mortar shells, trudged forward determinedly through the muck and goop. Each step became agony as he pushed onward.

Then there were no more rest stops. He was forced to walk for twelve, sixteen, sometimes eighteen hours a day. His food ran out and he became sick. Feverish bouts of malaria and beri-beri added to his physical torture. Yet he would not be discouraged as he let his burden remind him of the importance of his mission.

Finally the trail got so narrow that it was barely discernible. Heavy plant life and thorns clung at his clothing and ripped it to shreds. His sandals, brand new at the start of his journey, had long since worn away. His feet were cut and bleeding. Infectious sores covered his body and his sickness grew worse.

Finally he reached a point where there was no trail at all. He limped and staggered in the correct direction through sheer instinct.

Then, at last, he reached the end of his journey.

There was a mortar sitting there at the very end of the Ho Chi Minh trail. A gunner got up from where he was sitting and walked to the boy. He took one of the shells and dropped it down the mortar tube.

Whoomp!

He took the second round and did the same thing with it.

Whoomp!

Then he looked at the boy and said, "Okay. Now go back and get two more."

That was a favorite anecdote in the various service clubs of the American units in South Vietnam.

Falconi and the Black Eagles had laughed when they first heard it. But they wouldn't have shown such humor if they'd been aware of a certain amount of menacing veracity to the joke.

It was this same fanatical devotion of Communist zealots that would be encountered by the Black Eagles on their next mission.

NEW ADVENTURES FROM ZEBRA

DEPTH FORCE (1355, $2.95)
by Irving A. Greenfield

Built in secrecy and manned by a phantom crew, the *Shark* is America's unique high technology submarine whose mission is to stop the Russians from dominating the seas. If in danger of capture the *Shark* must self-destruct — meaning there's only victory or death!

DEPTH FORCE #2: DEATH DIVE (1472, $2.50)
by Irving A. Greenfield

The *Shark*, racing toward an incalculable fortune in gold from an ancient wreck, has a bloody confrontation with a Soviet killer sub. Just when victory seems assured, a traitor threatens the survival of every man aboard — and endangers national security!

THE WARLORD (1189, $3.50)
by Jason Frost

The world's gone mad with disruption. Isolated from help, the survivors face a state in which law is a memory and violence is the rule. Only one man is fit to lead the people, a man raised among the Indians and trained by the Marines. He is Erik Ravensmith, THE WARLORD — a deadly adversary and a hero of our times.

THE WARLORD #2: THE CUTTHROAT (1308, $2.50)
by Jason Frost

Though death sails the Sea of Los Angeles, there is only one man who will fight to save what is left of California's ravaged paradise. His name is THE WARLORD — and he won't stop until the job is done!

THE WARLORD #3: BADLAND (1437, $2.50)
by Jason Frost

His son has been kidnapped by his worst enemy and THE WAR-LORD must fight a pack of killers to free him. Getting close enough to grab the boy will be nearly impossible — but then so is living in this tortured world!

Available wherever paperbacks are sold, or order direct from the Publisher. Send cover price plus 50¢ per copy for mailing and handling to Zebra Books, 475 Park Avenue South, New York, N.Y. 10016. DO NOT SEND CASH.

TRIVIA MANIA
by Xavier Einstein

TRIVIA MANIA has arrived! With enough questions to answer every trivia buff's dreams, TRIVIA MANIA covers it all—from the delightfully obscure to the <u>seemingly obvious</u>. Tickle your fancy, and test your memory!

MOVIES	(1449, $2.50)
TELEVISION	(1450, $2.50)
LITERATURE	(1451, $2.50)
HISTORY AND GEOGRAPHY	(1452, $2.50)
SCIENCE AND NATURE	(1453, $2.50)
SPORTS	(1454, $2.50)
TELEVISION (Vol. II)	(1517, $2.50)
MOVIES (Vol. II)	(1518, $2.50)
COMMERCIALS & ADS	(1519, $2.50)
PEOPLE	(1520, $2.50)
MUSIC	(1521, $2.50)
COMICS & CARTOONS	(1522, $2.50)

DYNAMIC NEW LEADERS IN MEN'S ADVENTURE!

THE SAIGON COMMANDOS SERIES
by Jonathan Cain